JAMES NORCLIFFE is an award-winning poet and writer, and the author of several children's fantasy books celebrated for their unexpected plot twists and magical wit, including the internationally acclaimed Loblolly Boy series. Born on New Zealand's West Coast and raised in Christchurch, James has worked in New Zealand, China and Brunei Darussalam on the island of Borneo. He now lives in Church Bay, Canterbury.

For more information: jamesnorcliffe.com

The Frog Prince

James Norcliffe

VINTAGE

VINTAGE

UK | USA | Canada | Ireland | Australia
India | New Zealand | South Africa | China

Vintage is an imprint of the Penguin Random House
group of companies, whose addresses can be found at
global.penguinrandomhouse.com.

Penguin
Random House
New Zealand

First published by Penguin Random House New Zealand, 2022

10 9 8 7 6 5 4 3 2 1

Design by Carla Sy © Penguin Random House New Zealand
Cover photograph from iStock by Yvonne Stewart Henderson
Author photograph by Sharon Bennett
Page 6 from *The Frog Prince* illustrated by Walter Crane,
published in 1874 by George Routledge and Sons
Prepress by Image Centre Group
Printed and bound in Australia by Griffin Press, an Accredited
ISO AS/NZS 14001 Environmental Management Systems Printer

A catalogue record for this book is available from the
National Library of New Zealand.

ISBN 978-0-14-377549-2
eISBN 978-0-14-377550-8

penguin.co.nz

Randell Cottage
Writers Trust

MIX
Paper from
responsible sources
FSC® C009448

creative nz
ARTS COUNCIL OF NEW ZEALAND TOI AOTEAROA

For Cheryl Pow & Bart van Stratum
with gratitude and affection

Iron Heinrich

there was a tenderness
in the lily pond
as the princess
leaned over her reflection
over ripples of white silk
and suggestion

a tenderness as her soft
warm lips and soft warm
breath came ever closer
to the cold clamminess
of the frog's green forehead
his spawn-scented mouth

her heart was not in it
she could not see ever after

Iron Heinrich saw it
that's why he clanked
and clanked
and clanked
with laughter

David's Story

It was strange climbing the hill again above the town. It was as if he were climbing into and out of the past simultaneously. The gravelled pathways, littered with twigs and leaves after the recent storm, twined and intersected among the shadows of branches. His path was steep yet wide enough for a vehicle. It was a grey day, not yet autumn, and the way was dark. Although Kessenich below was only a few hundred metres away and the hum of its white noise just discernible, the old trees surrounding him might have been there forever: primeval, vaguely threatening.

He was still fit enough, despite his convalescence, and it took him only a few minutes to reach the broader path at the top of the escarpment. At this point his sense of timelessness faded and the here and now returned as an elderly couple approached him. They were wearing matching red parkas and walking a pair of matching poodles in matching tartan jackets. His minimal German allowed for a nod and a *Guten tag*, which the couple ignored, although the woman did glance at him curiously.

He saw in the distance the monument he had hoped to find, and he remembered — all but relived — his surprise the first time he came across it. Cara had been with him. Just over a year ago.

Kaiser Wilhelm. Not Kaiser Bill, as he had first assumed, somewhat puzzled at why the face of World War I should be commemorated, given the ignominy of defeat — he of the flamboyant moustache and spiked helmet. But no, this was Kaiser Bill's grandfather, Wilhelm I.

It was not surprising that there should be a monument to the first modern German emperor, the Prussian who united Germany in the second half of the nineteenth century. What *was* surprising was that it should have been built here — among these dark trees facing a junction of dark paths so far away from people. It should have graced a city square, an ornament among the elegant townhouses of the civilised and cultured. Also surprising was its form: an asymmetrical stack of cylinders in brown stone rising for four or five metres to a peak like some nightmarish pipe organ. Below this was a bas-relief portrait in green bronze of the emperor, mounted on a white marble portico with two columns, an arch and a pediment featuring a Prussian eagle. It was a bizarre mixture of discipline and confusion.

Cara had examined the portrait and turned to him, smiling.

'*You* should grow a beard.'

'An emperor's beard?'

'Don't get delusions of grandeur!'

'Why is it here?'

'The beard?'

'No,' he laughed, 'the monument.'

Cara seemed momentarily puzzled. 'Oh?'

David explained what he meant. 'I mean it's hardly the centre of the universe, is it? Hidden away in a forest like the witch's house in "Hansel and —"'

'Context changes,' she said. 'All the trees may not have been here at that time. Picture it. He'd be high on a hill overlooking the Rhine. They probably thought he'd enjoy the view.'

'But *he's* not here,' said David. 'This is just a monument, not a tomb. He's probably hundreds of miles away.'

'Wherever he is, it's a pretty awful monument.'

He glanced at her. 'Context changes, okay. But these trees and paths, if he could see them there would be nothing to tell him that anything has changed in — what is it? — a hundred and twenty years.'

'Oh, but it wouldn't take much to show him. A short walk to a gap in the trees and a look at the Rhine with those huge barges and ships.'

She broke off to take a photo of the monument on her phone, then moved to the steps to bend down before the portrait and take another.

'Can't see the wood for the trees?' he asked.

'Well, the river for the trees.'

'He wouldn't even need to see the river. All he'd need to see is you in that T and jeans snapping him with an iPhone.'

'I guess,' she said, turning back to him. 'Here's an idea, why don't you?'

'Don't I what?'

'Grow a beard.'

'I might,' he said. 'I just might if you really want me to.'

She considered this. 'Why not? But not an emperor's beard; that's not your style.'

'Perhaps a Charles Darwin beard?'

'What's that like?'

'Full and unkempt.'

'That's your style.'

'Apparently Darwin had facial eczema. Shaving brought it on. Cut-throat razors and coarse soap. After about fifty years of putting up with it, one day he said fuck it, and never shaved again.'

'I bet he didn't.'

'No, it's true,' he protested.

'I mean said fuck it. He probably said rats or botheration or something equally Victorian. And isn't it sheep that get facial eczema?'

'Darwin, too.'

'Sheep don't shave.'

He was about to offer a witty rejoinder but Cara had lost interest in the monument and was moving further down the pathway. It had been the liveliest she had been since they left Arras and he had been obscurely grateful. She had seemed increasingly distracted of late, as if he had somehow become a passenger, not a fellow traveller, on her journey.

He loved her. Cara Bernstein. French teacher. Colleague at Huntingdon.

What else? American. What else? At that point, if he were honest, not a lot. It didn't really matter. What mattered was the fact of her: her reality.

David had fooled himself once before that he was in love — a delusion that had led to a short-lived marriage and a rapid divorce. He was convinced his love was genuine this time, just as he now knew his first had been illusory: a play relationship in which he had wallowed in a starring role.

He knew he had no starring role this time. Cara was elusive and often hidden, but this only increased her fascination. She was a mess of contradictions, of course: open but private, light-hearted but serious, enchanting but infuriating. He hadn't long been at the school and was still new to northern France when they had struck up a conversation in the staffroom. Her smile had been so warm he had felt obscurely honoured. When she offered to show him around the countryside he couldn't believe his luck. She was as good as her word and a first-class guide. Her French was as excellent as his was clumsy. They visited villages and small towns and World War I sites, and lunched at small estaminets or country cafés when they hadn't packed a hamper.

Their friendship quickly deepened and it seemed inevitable they would become lovers, although, to David's disappointment, their lovemaking had been always on Cara's terms: playful rather than with the intensity and reciprocal passion David yearned for.

David now found himself on a pathway he remembered: the one that led to the graveyard.

The monument was easy; the graveyard was difficult.

When he had first seen it he had been enchanted. He assumed Cara had been enchanted, too. It was otherworldly. Literally, because it was the world of the dead, but also because of the beauty, the stillness, the great trees holding up their arms to shelter this final city of the burghers, the worthies and the dignitaries, a last city of marble and basalt and sculpture. There were seraphim and cherubim, angels and madonnas, carefully crafted paths and steps, stone trumpets sounding the eternal last hurrah and hosanna.

However, Cara's distraction had returned. It was as if she had turned down a dimmer switch. He found himself without light.

It was, he should have realised, entirely the wrong time to pull out the small box he had been cradling in his pocket since the start of their walk. The background was perfect — the trees, the marble, the beauty — but Cara's mood was not. Perhaps some crazy impulse had persuaded him that the gesture might somehow lift her.

'What's this?'

'Open it.'

He'd seen the ring in a shop in Arras. A simple thing, quite unadorned: a single sapphire set in a silver band. It was, he imagined, exactly the kind of unfussy, plainspoken ring that would appeal to Cara.

She opened the black velvet box, quickly took in its contents and glanced up at David.

'Is this what I think it is?'

She was smiling.

David nodded. He could not quite read her smile.

She sighed and shook her head. 'I do wish you hadn't.'

David was beginning to find the smile disconcerting. He tried to test it.

'What are you saying? *I do wish you hadn't* or *Oh, David, you shouldn't have?*'

The smile faded and she said, 'I'm saying I do wish you hadn't. I like you a lot, David — you know that. More than most people I've known.'

'So, what's the problem?'

'There's no problem.' The smile returned. 'You're a lovely guy. We have fun. But you are a bit of a sentimental bear. You must know that.'

David felt stung but was determined not to show it. 'A teddy bear?'

This time she laughed. 'If you will . . . And people don't marry their teddy bears.'

'People have done worse!'

'I guess they have. But—'

'Why not?'

'You are a sweet man, probably nicer than anybody else at Huntingdon and, as I said, we have fun.'

'We've had more than fun!'

Cara's voice took on an edge of rebuke.

'David, a few pleasant nights does not mean we have to spend a life together. I'm sorry.'

There was no answer to that.

There was nowhere else to go.

'I guess . . .' he said reluctantly.

She gave him a small look of relief as he took the box from her and replaced it in his pocket.

'I'm sorry, David,' she said, 'I've been a little mean. It's a very nice offer and I do thank you for it. Honestly. But you know . . .' She took his hand and squeezed it.

He gave her a tight little smile he hoped was sufficiently hurt but not too tragic. He was confused and upset, and he was gloomily grateful when, a short time later, they separated to follow their own discoveries.

Only later when he checked his watch and realised they needed to be getting back did he discover that the hillside pathways among the crypts and tombs were a maze. He retraced his steps and found other steps he had never traced, but there was no sign of her.

Cara had vanished.

He shouted her name but there was no answer. He checked his watch again and redoubled his speed. Up paths and down paths, but no Cara.

He took out his phone and called her. Voicemail. He left a brief message.

He sat down on a step and tried to think calmly, rationally. Cara could be playful at times — quite often, really — but this wasn't a game. In a game she would have allowed herself to be discovered eventually, back against a tree or hidden in an alcove.

Something must have called her away. A call of nature? There were no public facilities on the walk. But there were trees everywhere and the place was practically deserted.

He called her again, and sent a text. No response.

If she'd been some other woman, he might have presumed she had been annoyed by his awkward proposal. But Cara wasn't some other woman. That was the reason he loved her. He wanted to marry her, for Christ's sake.

In any event, she hadn't been at all perturbed by his proposal. Bemused, perhaps, but she had been gentle with him, matter of fact. Typically Cara. There was no suggestion she felt the need to rush off and find the smelling salts.

It was becoming dark. Bewildered, and out of options, David returned to the little hotel in Kessenich only to be told Cara had checked out.

She had left no message for him.

He pressed the desk clerk until he could no longer bear the man's insufferable politeness and faint, knowing smile.

Whether to call Cara's bluff or to wring out another complete change he was never really sure, but, afterwards, he did let his beard grow, and eventually it developed into a Charles Darwin beard, full and unkempt.

Perhaps that was why the woman with the poodles had looked at him so curiously.

Cara's
Manuscript

— KASSEL, 1810 —

'Fräuleins?'

The two young women entered the gloomy sitting room and glanced about curiously. Mathilde smiled and extended her hand for the man to take. However, he did not take it, instead patting his sides distractedly.

'Heller,' said Mathilde. 'I am Fräulein Heller, and this is my younger sister Helga. We have brought a story for you. Our grandmother . . .'

The man glanced at them in turn, but quickly, and nodded.

Is he shy? Mathilde wondered. He was much younger than she had expected, but he still appeared very much the scholar she had been told about.

'I know,' he said, 'such stockings, but I must. The position, you understand. And these clothes.' Again, he gestured down his sides with distaste.

Mathilde did not see anything especially disconcerting about his dress.

'Position?' she asked. She felt it unusual that a man should draw attention to his clothes, and so disparagingly.

He explained that his position in King Jérôme's library demanded the costume; that was the price he must pay for the salary.

'My brother Wilhelm, too,' he added.

'Your brother?'

'He has a position at the library too. I must apologise for him. He should have been here to meet you. I have no idea what is delaying him.'

The sisters were unsure how to respond. Mathilde smiled again, a little more nervously. The man was clearly not prepared to proceed with their business in the absence of his brother, and did not seem to have sufficient small-talk to put them at ease. He ushered them to a small sofa but remained standing himself, glancing from time to time at the clock on the mantelpiece.

'Your search for old tales,' Helga said, to help fill the silence, 'has something to do with your position at the library?'

He glanced at her. 'Oh no, Fräulein Heller, not at all. This is very much a private project that my brother and I . . . Well, not private, really — you see, Herr Brentano . . . Excuse me.'

He abruptly left the room, leaving the door open. They heard his footsteps retreating down the hallway and his voice calling 'Wilhelm! Wilhelm!'

Taking advantage of his absence, Mathilde opened her leather bag and took out some sheets of paper. She glanced at Helga, giving her a small smile before reading silently for some time, as if rehearsing lines. When she heard the sound of returning footsteps, rather than putting the papers back in her bag, she held them in front of her.

The man came back through the door accompanied by another dressed in much the same way.

'What is it, Jacob?' the man said, before realising they had company.

The man who had first greeted them turned and, acknowledging the other, said, 'Fräuleins, my brother Wilhelm. Fräulein Heller and . . . ?'

'Helga,' said Helga.

' . . . and Fräulein Helga Heller have brought us a story.'

Wilhelm glanced briefly at the women and bowed his head formally. 'Fräuleins,' he said. 'Welcome.'

As the front door closed behind her, Mathilde gripped Helga's arm so firmly, Helga glanced at her sister curiously. Mathilde looked quite flustered.

'What is it, Mathilde?'

Mathilde shook her head, face reddening.

Suddenly Helga guessed. 'Is it Wilhelm?'

Helga considered Wilhelm the more attractive of the brothers — more open, less distracted. He smiled more and seemed more solicitous of them. She felt a small pang of jealousy that Mathilde should have felt the same.

To her relief, Mathilde shook her head.

'Jacob?'

All Mathilde could do was nod. Helga smiled. 'Let's go home,' she said. Arm in arm the sisters made their way down the steps and onto the street.

He stayed with her. All the way home he was with her, more real, more present than the gracious buildings lining Königstrasse. She allowed herself to be guided by Helga as if she had momentarily lost her ability to see.

Was it his gravity, the seriousness and the attentiveness with which he had listened to her? For he had attended to the story she read out with a deep earnestness she found rather flattering. He had not studied her; his eyes remained fixed on some other, more distant place, but he was concentrating intently.

Earlier, once Wilhelm had joined them, Jacob had retreated, had allowed Wilhelm to talk for them both. Thereafter he had scarcely said a word. There was no need, of course. Wilhelm had spoken so easily, and in such a friendly manner, Jacob's retreat might have gone almost unnoticed. It was as though he had stepped out of the light.

But Mathilde noticed. She listened to Wilhelm's words, but it was to Jacob she kept glancing for reaction, for confirmation.

He was slender and, she imagined, gentle.

His gravity was part of it, but only part. There was something else.

It was his seeming vulnerability.

That was it.

Grave. Quiet. Vulnerable. But aware.

A deer in a clearing.

Attentive, alert, ready if needs be to run into the forest.

Oma must know other stories she could bring to him, to lay before him like benedictions. Mathilde's head was all at once full of half-remembered stories, of Oma's soft voice as she drifted into sleep underneath her feathery counterpane. Stories of goose girls. Snow queens. Dwarfs. Dark forests, the branches of black trees dangling like fingers. Bright axes flashing in the winter light.

'What do you think, brother?'
    'Promising, I feel,' said Wilhelm.
'There was nothing especially new there, neither in the plot—'
'Nor the telling,' Wilhelm completed his brother's sentence.
'However—'
'There could be others.'
'I'm sure there will be others,' said Jacob. 'Their grandmother is local?'
'They didn't say.'
'I imagine she is, and if she has lived here many years—'
'Exactly.'
'Even if there is nothing we have not heard before, there may be additions, extra detail—'
'Different emphases,' added Wilhelm. 'Such things could be valuable. Even in the tale she told there were subtle things. I would like to have a closer look at these, even though we have that longer version from Fräulein Wild. However, I note that Fräulein Heller did not leave her transcript.'

Jacob gave a self-deprecating smile. 'How foolish of me not to have secured it. The difficulty was their leaving in such a hurry.'

'The one who read — Mathilde? She did seem a little discomposed towards the end of the visit. Increasingly so, I thought.'

'She could hardly have been over-awed. I suspect she is well born, and she was wearing far better clothes than we can afford for Lotte.'

Wilhelm smiled. 'I had no idea, brother, that you had all at once become an expert on women's clothing!'

'You know what I mean.'

'I'm not sure I do,' said Wilhelm, 'but I do know one thing.'

'And what is that?'

'It won't be the last we see of the Fräuleins Heller, mark my words.'

David's Story

— ARRAS —

David Cunningham walked down the carpeted corridor and paused by the door labelled *Headmaster*. Gilt lettering, no-nonsense sans serif. None of that weak-kneed modern kowtowing to non-sexist language here. *Principal* stood no show at the Huntingdon International School: the Huntingdon International School had principles.

David knocked and listened for the response. He presumed Agnès, Michael's secretary, would have alerted the headmaster, but all the same there was a protracted pause before he heard the headmaster's voice.

'Come in!'

David opened the door and gave a half wave to the figure behind the desk.

'David. Good to have you back! Come in, come in. Sit down.'

Michael had stood up and he waited until David sank into a leather easy chair before seating himself again. He could have left his desk and joined David in an accompanying chair. This was his usual practice. Apparently, though, for some reason this interview warranted a measure of formality. The long pause that followed the opening pleasantries was also designed, David guessed, to give the headmaster an advantage.

'I got your email,' said Michael eventually, 'but I'm not sure I fully understand what happened.'

'I don't really understand what happened either,' said David. 'In fact, I'm completely flummoxed.'

He looked across the room and out the window where a line of poplars marked the end of the playing fields. He wished Michael had responded to his email, not because there was much more to add, but he would have been able to better express his confusion in a written reply.

'So what exactly did happen?' asked Michael.

'Just as I described in my email,' said David. 'We were visiting Bonn. We had planned to take a cruise down the Rhine but we had a couple of days to kill before that, so we set off to explore some hills across from the hotel. Big dark trees, the odd view of the river. Then we found this old graveyard. Nineteenth century and older. It was fascinating and we spent a considerable time there.'

Michael nodded at him. 'Go on.'

'It was crisscrossed with pathways and terraces and trees all about. Somehow as we wandered around we became separated. There came a point when I realised I hadn't seen Cara for ages and it was time to be getting back. So I hurried about the graveyard calling her name but there was no sign of her. I kept searching, only then realising just how big the place was. I guessed she might have had the same problem and perhaps thought I'd gone back without her.'

'Crossed wires?'

'It was the only thing that made sense.'

'Unlikely,' said Michael drily.

'I know, I know, but you don't think entirely straight when the mysterious comes along.'

'Did you ask anybody else whether they'd seen her?'

'The whole place was deserted. We hardly saw another living soul.'

'Just hundreds of dead ones.'

'Right.'

'Did you try to call her? Text her?'

'I tried phoning and got her voicemail. I've left several messages since, and sent numerous texts. I've emailed, too. Nothing.'

'So, all very strange,' said Michael. 'What next? Did you suspect foul play?'

'I didn't know what to suspect. It did cross my mind, of course. I kept searching and calling her name for ages and then eventually assumed she must for some reason have gone back to the hotel without me. As you know, Cara can be a little unpredictable.'

'Part of her charm,' said Michael, who didn't know that.

'And then the weirdest part of all, when I returned to the hotel and asked whether she'd turned up, the clerk told me she'd checked out.'

Michael Bastion had spent years cultivating the image of headmaster. Now in his early fifties, he had so far been very lucky: his dark hair was silvering at the sides, the lines on his face had become sculpted into academic creases, albeit crinkling good humouredly around his understanding hazel eyes. His voice had deepened into a velvet authority. He dressed impeccably: a reefer jacket and university tie for informal occasions and a merchant-banker pinstripe suit for formal. He was wearing his charcoal pinstripe at the present time. David, always conscious of his own relative scruffiness in Michael's presence, considered the man a pompous poseur and a bit of a wanker. However, David loved his job teaching English to the senior group and was cautious about jeopardising it.

Michael sat silently, considering David's story while absently shooting his cuffs, revealing silver links with black onyx hearts.

He had rarely experienced a ripple in his placid existence. He was the only son of a solicitor (father) and academic (mother), growing up in an English village not far from Cambridge. There was a minor public school followed by an almost distinguished career at a Cambridge college, where he had quite early and easily fallen in love with a girl from his college possessed both of a rower's shoulders and a powerful sex drive. Miranda happened to be the daughter of an expatriate headmaster, Oliver Huntingdon, who had established a small, exclusive international school in a chateau near Arras in northern France, a region best known for its rolling countryside pockmarked by the remains of World War I battlefields.

Shortly after their marriage Michael and Miranda were offered positions at the school, and the years that followed saw the birth of their two daughters and their inevitable promotion to senior positions — Michael to deputy headmaster, just prior to his father-in-law's retirement, and then to headmaster immediately following it. In the ten years since, he had steadfastly held to the founder's guiding educational philosophy: let there be no ripples.

And here was a ripple, or at least a potential ripple.

He glanced again at the young man sitting before him. He had considered David Cunningham an asset to the school. Enthusiastic, enterprising, a very good teacher by all accounts and, most importantly, popular with the students and their parents.

There were drawbacks. The school did have minimum dress requirements and David did not quite respect their spirit. Rather than a suit, he wore one of two or three jackets of disreputable tweed usually set off by a mismatched tie, sometimes regrettably frivolous. He also had a tendency towards similarly frivolous socks, and his leather shoes, while unobjectionable, always gave the impression of being a reluctant substitute for trainers or, worse, sandals. Michael considered that a headmaster was never off duty and liked to think his staff felt the same way. Clearly, David did not. At this very moment that on-duty off-duty world he inhabited was abundantly evident. It was obvious the man hadn't shaved for three or four days. Designer stubble? This was a phenomenon Michael disliked intensely.

David was a New Zealander and in this there were advantages and disadvantages as far as Michael was concerned. His academic qualifications were beyond reproach, but certainly not Oxbridge. He had attended a university somewhat deceptively called the University of Canterbury. For all that, he was cheerful and invariably polite and cooperative. If he had subversive opinions about the school and its administration he kept them to himself in staff meetings and the staffroom. Moreover, he had never forced himself into Michael's sanctum with any complaint about a colleague or some personal grievance, something that might have disturbed the equilibrium of the headmaster's routine by compelling some delicate and embarrassing footwork.

Until now.

Michael, of course, had not been unaware of the developing relationship between David and Cara Bernstein. He had observed it himself, and Miranda had mentioned it more than once in passing. He disliked the fact of budding romances within the staff; they were invariably distracting to everybody and often divisive. They were potentially ripple-producing. There was little to be done about such situations, though. Even as a headmaster he could not issue a Cnut-like injunction, human nature being what it unfortunately was. All he could do was monitor the situation and hope for the best. In this particular instance the relationship between the English teacher and the French teacher had so far been conducted with reasonable discretion and caution. Nothing had disturbed the water.

Until now.

'I suppose . . . ' said David.

'You suppose?'

'She hasn't been in touch with you?'

Michael shook his head. 'Not a whisper.'

There was another silence.

'I'm bound to say, David, that this whole situation is worrying. I am concerned about what might have happened to Cara, of course, but then I'm mindful that she apparently checked out of the hotel herself and so probably was not abducted or the victim of some mishap or emergency.' Michael paused. 'However, there are other concerns. For one thing, term starts in a week and we do need some indication of whether she intends to return to work. I mean, we can't just assume she'll turn up.'

David nodded miserably. 'I realise that,' he said.

The ripples spread and Michael gave David an appraising glance. 'To that end,' he said, 'I really must be assured that you have told me the whole story.'

'What do you—'

'I mean, did you two have an argument of some sort? Was there some difference, some tiff that might have prompted her to storm off?'

David shook his head vehemently. 'No, I told you, nothing like that. And she didn't storm off. We'd been in a good space — cheerful. Cara had been okay all morning, teasing at times, perhaps — you know how she can be. That's what makes the whole thing so weird.'

'Think,' said Michael, considering this. 'Was it perhaps something you said? Something she might be festering over?'

David shook his head again. Earlier, he had resolved not to mention his clumsy proposal. It was a private matter and he had convinced himself that, given Cara's gentle reaction, it had not caused her disappearance. 'Nothing like that. The last thing I remember before we wandered around the graveyard was a bit of banter when we came across this ugly monument to Kaiser Wilhelm. Cara suggested I should grow a beard.'

'And you refused? Perhaps that tipped her over?'

'I didn't refuse,' said David. '*Au contraire* . . . I agreed to grow one. Actually, I've started already.' He rubbed at his stubbly chin. 'It's as itchy as sin.'

Michael sighed. 'Small mercies,' he said. 'At least she didn't request a facial tattoo.'

David allowed himself a fleeting smile.

'So, a mystery,' continued Michael, 'and, not to put too fine a point on it, a blasted nuisance. Look, let me know immediately if you should hear from her. I will, of course, let you know as soon as she gets in touch with the school.'

The headmaster stood up.

The interview was over.

Cara's
Manuscript

Mathilde knocked lightly before opening the door to the parlour. It was that time in the early afternoon when her grandmother usually napped, and Mathilde did not want to wake her, even though she was eager to report on their visit to the scholarly young brothers. She need not have worried. Her grandmother was quite awake, sitting in her chair, bright eyes concentrating on the knot pattern she was creating with a small ivory tatting shuttle. As always, she was wearing her black widow's gown and white cap.

'Oma?'

The old lady laid her handwork on her lap and looked up, smiling.

'Mathilde. You saw the brothers?'

'We did, Oma, we did.'

'They received you?'

'Like true gentlemen.'

'And the story? They were pleased to have the story?'

'I believe so, Oma.'

Mathilde frowned a little, remembering how the brothers had listened to the story. Jacob, the one who had made her heart pulse, had sat before her, eyes closed, leaning his brow into his fingers, focusing on her every word as if trying to memorise the tale even as she told it. The other, Wilhelm, had stood smiling slightly, open-eyed, listening attentively but not with especial focus. Neither brother had interrupted, neither had asked a question or sought clarification afterwards. In fact their somewhat non-committal response had perplexed her so much that she had quickly folded her paper when she finished reading and packed it away in preparation to taking her leave.

The brothers had been courteous in their thanks, but what they had actually thought of her offering she had no idea.

'You think so?'

'They did not say so in so many words, but they were kind enough to listen.'

'Hmm,' said her grandmother.

'They must hear a great many stories, Oma. I am only one of many who have brought them tales.'

The idea troubled her. Other young women reading to the brothers — other young women undoubtedly more attractive, more personable, more confident than she.

'Hmm,' her grandmother said again. 'Perhaps they did not care for the story.'

'I'm sure they did, Oma,' protested Mathilde. 'It's just—'

'Just what, child?'

Mathilde puzzled at the problem. 'It could be that they have already heard the tale. It is a folk tale, after all, and they have been gathering stories for some time. There must be many stories they hear repeatedly.'

'I suppose so,' said her grandmother.

'So I'd like to take them more,' said Mathilde. 'There must be others. You have told me many other tales and there must be some you have not yet told me.'

The old lady smiled. 'To be sure,' she said. 'To be sure. Although some are tales too dark even for a dark night, tales too dark to be told to impressionable girls on the edge of sleep at bedtime!'

'Tell me those stories, Oma,' said Mathilde, her eyes shining, 'and I shall write them down and take them to the brothers.'

'There is almost always a forest,' said Mathilde's grandmother, 'and it is dark, and the trees are tall and the trunks close together. There are pathways through the forest, but they are narrow and ill-defined and they frequently fork. It is hard to know which fork you should take, or why.

'There are wild animals, too, although you rarely see them. Instead you hear their scurry, their gallop, their snuffling and shuffling, their moaning, barking and howling. None of which tells you their size. They could be small and insignificant, but then again they could be large, with powerful shoulders, huge padding paws, claws, needle teeth and slavering chops. It is one of the paradoxes of the forest that the more frightening the beast, the more silently it stalks. The pigeon makes a clatter in the air; the owl makes no sound in flight.

'Those humans who live in the forest must band together and learn the ways of the undergrowth; must arm themselves with crossbows, staves and sharp, shiny axes. Those less than human find caves or hollow trees in which to dwell, or rely on enchantment or magic.

'Often in the forest you will come across a small cabin in a clearing. There will be a stone-flagged pathway, a porch with an old besom leaning against the wall, a pebbled window with the flicker of candlelight behind it, a heavy door with an iron ring for a handle. To knock or not knock at the door is a difficult decision, but it is one we must make.

'The forest spawns danger and evil. It is a place where fugitives seek refuge, for pursuit rarely follows. Pursuit itself is terrified of the forest. And this is the irony of the forest: it is where safety lies in peril and peril lies in safety.'

'Where is it, this forest?' asked Mathilde, awed by her grandmother's revelations.

'It is where all the tales begin and end,' said her grandmother.

'And where is that?' asked Mathilde.

'It is where we live,' said her grandmother. 'It is where we all live.'

David's
Story

Michael put down his newspaper and glanced at Miranda, who was finishing the last of her toast and marmalade.

'Darling, you're a woman . . .' he began.

'This is something you've just discovered after twenty years of marriage?'

'No, but you have a woman's perspective.'

'That, too?'

Michael smiled at his own clumsiness and took a draught of coffee.

'What's this all about?' asked Miranda.

Michael swallowed his coffee, placed his mug down carefully and said, 'I had David Cunningham in my office yesterday afternoon.'

'Ah,' said Miranda, 'the case of the vanishing Cara Bernstein.'

'Exactly,' said Michael. 'It's such a damnable nuisance. He still hasn't heard from her and so far she hasn't been in touch with the school either. I have no way of knowing whether she intends to come back to work on Monday.'

'But why would she need to get in touch with the school?' asked Miranda reasonably. 'She's on leave, on holiday, for god's sake. She hasn't resigned. Surely she doesn't need to contact the school in the middle of her break to say, *No worries, everybody, I've not resigned*?'

Michael nodded unhappily. 'I suppose that's right,' he said. 'It's just—'

'Just what? Are you miffed she hasn't sent you a postcard? *Having a lovely time in Cologne. Wish you were here.*'

'Now you're being silly.'

'No, *you're* being silly. It's not a problem until it becomes a problem.'

'*My* problem,' said Michael, 'is that I suspect it *will* become a problem. The way David described it, the whole thing is very strange.'

'That's just David's side of the story. I expect it's nothing more than a lovers' tiff.'

'He says not so.'

'Well, he would, wouldn't he?'

'I believe him.'

'So what exactly did he say?'

Michael outlined David's account as completely as he could recall it. Miranda, meanwhile, refilled her cup from the Moka pot and paused over Michael's cup. He shook his head.

'So?' she said in response to his interrogative gaze.

'So what's your take on what might have happened? I mean from a woman's perspective.'

Miranda laughed. 'It's so sweet that you believe there is such a thing. Where do you want me to start? I mean, the possibilities are endless.'

'Beyond foul play.'

'I'm not even considering foul play. That's such a . . . No, simply in human terms.'

'Okay,' said Michael, 'hit me with a few.'

'For starters,' she began, 'I'm not nearly so inclined to believe Mr Cunningham as you seem to be. *Cherchez l'homme*, as I believe it's said. If we throw doubt on his version, all sorts of possibilities emerge. I would think an argument most likely — probably a loud, shouty argument, with his infuriating her so much she says *I'm out of here.* Or there may not have even been an argument: it could have been just something he said, and doesn't even realise he said, but for Cara it was the last straw, the tipping point in a series of resentments.'

'But he says she was happy!'

'Precisely. He *says* she was happy. He may have even believed that. Men can be pretty obtuse when women hide their true feelings.'

Michael did not respond.

'And why didn't he do more to find her?' continued Miranda. 'Did he contact the police and report her missing? Was there a proper search of the graveyard? There could have been — what do they call it? — forensic evidence.'

'But she checked out of the hotel. She didn't go missing in the graveyard.'

'How do you know that? David said she checked out.'

'Good god!' said Michael. 'Are you suggesting—'

'I'm suggesting nothing,' said Miranda. 'Nothing at all. We're ruling out foul play, remember? It's just that if she didn't check out, or even if she did, David seems not to have done an awful lot to find out what happened to her. He apparently checked out of the hotel himself and drove back here. Was that a guilty conscience, do you think?'

'These things you're suggesting are only possibilities if you accept that David is lying — or at least dissembling,' said Michael. 'He has tried calling, texting and emailing her several times. As it happens,' he added stubbornly, 'I believe him.'

'Your privilege,' said Miranda, shrugging. 'I didn't hear the story from the horse's mouth. That may be a disadvantage. But it might be an advantage as well.'

'Okay, for argument's sake,' persisted Michael, 'let's assume that David *is* telling the truth. Where does your feminine point of view take you if that is the case?'

'Oh, all sorts of places,' said Miranda. 'You want to hear them?'

'Of course.'

'Okay. Clearly something must have happened . . . Let's put it like this. All of a sudden, like a train, Cara jumped the tracks. Now a train doesn't jump the tracks out of the blue. Something precipitates it: a landslide, sabotage, something on the track, some mechanical fault . . . all sorts of reasons.'

'I get that,' said Michael, 'but it's a metaphor that doesn't take us very far.'

'I think it does. What might cause a woman to suddenly jump the tracks?'

Michael shrugged. 'Tell me.'

'Well, two broad sets of possibilities: outside and inside.'

'You've lost me.'

'Okay, outside: she came across somebody on that hillside or in that graveyard, perhaps a figure from her past, a former lover, and all at once their suppressed feelings were reignited. She flees with him — or perhaps her, we should add — and she can't face the complications and pain of having to explain the whole thing to David so she just leaves.'

'But David said they didn't see anybody, either in the graveyard or in the forest.'

'Possibly *he* saw nobody, but that doesn't mean that Cara saw nobody.'

'But,' protested Michael, 'this is stretching coincidence too far. This is real life, not a Hardy novel.'

'Why should it have been a coincidence? Why could the meeting not have been prearranged? People have phones! And it may not have been a former lover: it may have been a family member with an important message, it may have been somebody . . . someone more shady, perhaps with a hold on her, a blackmailer, a—'

'Svengali?'

'Why not? In fact, if it comes to that,' continued Miranda, 'it may not have been a physical presence. Perhaps there was a message on her phone, or a call. Or something in the graveyard, a name, a place on an inscription or something might have prompted a memory, a memory so strong it demanded action.'

'And inside?'

'What I've just described is inside — a memory provoked by something in the graveyard. Another inside possibility is a realisation.'

'What kind of realisation?'

'What do you call it? An epiphany. Picture it: she and David are getting closer and closer together. It's a process of discovery, a love affair. They're sleeping together probably, planning to sail down the Rhine together. Getting in deeper and deeper. Perhaps she remembered the Lorelei story and sensed destruction. Perhaps she just suddenly wanted out, could find no way of rationally explaining this to David, so just cut and run.'

'Simple as that?'

'I've no idea — I'm only guessing. But I remember now Cara asked me once about another old story, "The Frog Prince". She was very interested in it as she thought it rather weird.'

Miranda told Michael she had checked out the story and agreed with Cara: it was a strange story. She recounted it to him.

'So how does this fit with Cara and David?'

'I imagine she'd been kissing David. One does when one is in love. Perhaps her sudden realisation was that she had been kissing a frog and that no matter how often she kissed him he was never going to turn into a prince. He was going to remain a frog forever.'

'Could it be as simple as that?'

'It makes sense and you know it's not an uncommon experience.' Miranda rose from the table. 'Anyway, there are jobs waiting, things to do. Will you clear up?'

Michael nodded. David as frog. David in his shapeless tweed jacket with leather patches on the elbows, for god's sake. His unfortunate ties and baggy corduroy trousers. Who wore those anymore? A frog, certainly. But clearly Cara hadn't seen him like that, not at the beginning at least. However, it did make sense, as Miranda said, and it happened all the time. Falling in love was so often sudden and irrational; falling out of love could be just as sudden, just as irrational.

Michael was not especially given to sympathy, but he felt a pang for his senior English teacher. And then, with another pang, he recalled the pointed tone of Miranda's final comments and it occurred to him that it may not have been only Cara Bernstein and David Cunningham she had been alluding to. She could have been referring to things closer to home. He sighed. Miranda did have her good points, but subtlety wasn't one of them.

*C*ontext changes.

Cara's words echoed. For days David had been revisiting the final couple of hours they had spent on the hillside at Venusberg, trying to recall every word. What had seemed at the time a throwaway line he now saw as having a deeper, even ominous significance.

Cara had been talking about historical and geographical context. The context of the ugly monument to Wilhelm I had altered out of all recognition in the one hundred and twenty or so years since it had been erected. A forest had grown around it.

Their context had changed geographically too. They had been in Bonn, far from Arras and their usual social setting: the school, their colleagues in the staffroom, their respective living arrangements (Cara's apartment, his room in the staff wing of the chateau). In Bonn they were out of context, alone together, sharing a hotel room, a bed, a bath and meals. For David, this new arrangement was exhilarating and he had presumed Cara felt the same way. She had given every indication that this was so. They had become closer, David felt. The context had changed, but the change was all to the good. It had raised their relationship to a new plateau.

Had Cara experienced the reverse? Had she felt the new context was all to the bad, that it had been negative, threatening? Did she feel that another new context, a river cruise, would make things even worse?

David could not believe this. To believe it, he would have to deny the evidence of his feelings, his senses, of Cara's tenderness and laughter.

And yet . . . what had happened?

No sooner was he back in Arras than he had driven to Cara's apartment. The door was locked and there was no response to his ring. He tried to peer through a gap in the garage door, but he could not make out whether her car was inside or not. All he could see was darkness. The apartment block had no concierge to talk to and he had no idea how to find her landlord. He visited a couple of letting agents but Cara's apartment was not on their books.

It was at this point that David realised just how little he knew about Cara Bernstein.

She was American but had spent much of her childhood in France, which explained her excellent French. Where exactly in France he had no idea. From what he had gleaned, the family had returned to the States where Cara completed high school and college. He was not exactly sure where, but he suspected California as he knew she had finished her postgraduate studies at Berkeley. But she had rarely spoken of her university days and he wasn't even sure of her major. She had never shown any interest in pursuing a PhD so he presumed she had finished after her master's.

Of her parents he knew even less. Either they were off limits or she simply had no interest in them. She had never mentioned brothers or sisters. He guessed her parents were — or had been — wealthy, as Cara lived well: probably far beyond what she earned at the Huntingdon International School. She drove, expertly, a late-model Peugeot RCZ. David had been somewhat surprised when she had agreed to travel with him in his clunky little Ford on their trip to Germany.

She did not seem to be ambitious as a teacher, happy with the role she had at Huntingdon. He guessed she would leave when she felt like it, but it wouldn't be for promotion. The only ambition he had been able to detect was her wish to be a writer. It was something she had alluded to from time to time, but the nature and subject of the writing was another taboo. He suspected poetry.

Also off limits was any discussion of previous relationships and former lovers. Despite his lingering anxiety, David could live with this. His short-lived marriage had given him some experience, but he suspected he was neither sophisticated nor especially adept as a lover, whereas Cara was clearly both. In the early days and even long afterwards he couldn't really believe he had fallen into a relationship with such a woman. She was not beautiful in any traditional sense, but she was fiercely attractive in a Charlotte Gainsbourg kind of way: slim, long brown hair, and with a confident demeanour only occasionally troubled by darkness.

He loved her. He could not recall ever loving another woman the way he loved Cara.

What had happened?

He had yet to approach Agnès, Michael's secretary and the school receptionist. Cara had joined the staff three or four years ago. Agnès, who guarded the school records, would have her application on file, containing personal information, references. Surely there would be some lead to follow in that file — some name, email address or number.

Whether Agnès Delon (*Madame* Delon!) would help him was hard to tell. She was prickly at the best of times, jealous of her status and beholden only to Michael. Still, she was just about the only source of information he had not tried.

Cara's Manuscript

Mathilde drew a chair closer to her grandmother.

'Oma, do you have another tale for me? It would be good to take something else to the brothers.'

The old lady glanced at her shrewdly.

'Only one tale?'

'Perhaps just one more for now.' Mathilde had the grace to blush and, aware that she was doing so, lowered her face.

So sweet, thought the old lady. One story, and then another. One visit, and then another. Those young scholars should be careful. I suspect Mathilde is longing to offer more than stories, even if she doesn't know so herself.

'What kind of story, child?' she asked.

Mathilde recalled their earlier conversation. 'A story set in a forest,' she suggested. 'A dark forest — and somewhere a sharp, shiny axe.'

'Perhaps the story of Little Redcap,' said her grandmother. 'I'm not sure you know that one.'

'Little Redcap?'

'It's a tale that could have been written about us,' smiled the grandmother. 'It features a sweet young maiden and a grandmother.'

'And an axe?'

'Oh yes, there's an axe. Most certainly an axe. A sharp, shiny axe wielded by a brave woodsman. He saves Little Redcap and her grandmother after they have been gobbled up by a wolf.'

Mathilde laughed, her eyes wide with anticipation.

'It sounds perfect,' she said, 'but don't start yet, give me time to fetch Helga and my quill and ink and some paper. I will write it down for the brothers.'

The brothers listened attentively to the story of Little Redcap, just as they had to Mathilde's first story. It was as though she had returned in time to the previous week, with no intervening days, hours or minutes. How many times had she pictured Jacob Grimm in that time? The man himself now sat in his chair as he had on the first occasion, eyes closed, leaning forward intently, his face bent into his outspread fingers. Brother Wilhelm stood as before, chin in hand, smiling lightly and studying her carefully.

Helga sat on the sofa, gazing up at her sister, as if hearing the story for the first time. In fact Mathilde had rehearsed her reading in front of Helga time and time again.

Mathilde read fluently, having learnt from her grandmother how to spin a tale to make it exciting, exploiting every tension and surprise the story held. She read as if to a child in love with magic and fear, a child ropewalking the thin line of hope.

When she had finished she lowered her script and looked at the brothers in turn, willing them to give her a more detailed response than the somewhat offhand reception she had experienced the first time.

Jacob opened his eyes, lifted his head and straightened. However, he did not look at Mathilde. Instead he gazed at his brother, who stared back, still smiling slightly.

Mathilde realised they seemed able to communicate without words, but exactly what they were saying she could not tell. Last time this exclusion had disconcerted her so much that she felt she must leave; this time she was emboldened, more determined to solicit a reaction.

'This story?' she prompted them.

Somewhat startled back into manners, Jacob now scrambled to his feet and turned to her courteously.

'You read the tale very well, Fräulein Heller,' he said.

'Very well indeed,' echoed Wilhelm.

Although she was flattered by this intelligence, it was not what Mathilde really wanted to hear. 'Thank you,' she said. 'But the story, was it new to you? Have you heard it before?'

The two men exchanged glances.

'We have, Fräulein,' said Wilhelm. 'It is not an uncommon tale. However—'

'There are elements in the version you read,' continued Jacob, 'that differ somewhat from other versions we have in our possession.'

'The coda particularly,' said Jacob.

'The coda?' asked Mathilde. 'I'm not sure—'

'The coda is the last bit,' explained Wilhelm.

'You see,' said Jacob, 'other versions of the tale end with the part where the woodsman cuts open the wolf's belly, freeing Little Redcap and her grandmother, and then the three of them fill the wolf's belly with stones and sew up the wound—'

'Yes, and the wolf dies when he has to run with all that weight in his belly,' Wilhelm adds. 'You read that part with great gusto, Fräulein Heller.'

'But your ending was new,' explained Jacob. 'The final tale about the second wolf who is tricked down the chimney to fall and drown in the boiling sausage water.'

'I rather liked the boiling sausage water,' said Wilhelm.

'So, in your version,' Jacob continued, 'two wolves, two endings—'

'But the same moral,' said Wilhelm. 'Just retribution for those who scheme to carry out evil.'

'Good will out,' said Jacob, 'even though this outcome does not seem to be assured until the very end.'

'So our visit was not entirely in vain?' asked Mathilde.

'On the contrary,' replied Jacob, surprised at the question. 'All grist to our mill. Anything you bring would be most valuable. It will either confirm a tale we have already, or it will offer, as this has done, a useful variant.'

'So—' Mathilde began.

'Indeed, yes,' said Wilhelm, anticipating the question. 'Please bring us any other tales you have. We would be—'

'From your grandmother?' Jacob interrupted.

'Yes, our grandmother. She knows many tales and has known them since she was a girl. Probably from her own oma.'

'And no doubt from that oma's oma before her,' smiled Wilhelm. 'These are precisely the tales we seek.'

Mathilde smiled. 'I will do my best to prise more stories from her,' she said, 'and bring them to you.'

'We would be glad if you would,' said Jacob, 'and especially pleased if you would write them down for us. Speaking of which—'

'Of course,' said Mathilde, handing over her script. 'Last time I took the story away. Would you like—'

'Most certainly,' said Jacob. 'We would be very pleased to have it.'

'I will bring it then,' said Mathilde, blushing slightly. 'Next time.'

As Helga and Mathilde made their way down the Königstrasse, Mathilde was scarcely aware of what street she was on or why. He had taken her hand. As he stood in the doorway, and though his eyes (his beautiful eyes) were downcast, he had taken her hand in a formal farewell. His soft hand, his soft scholar's hand. She had wanted her hand to linger there, but soon, too soon, she had to withdraw it and turn her back on his figure in the doorway, moving away from him until she sensed rather than heard him stepping back and closing the door.

He had asked her to return. He wanted her transcript — had expressed his desire to have her bring it to him — and other transcripts . . . She would keep taking him stories until she came across one he really treasured, a story he — they — did not know. A story whose novelty would delight him (them), a story that would prompt his gratitude, his admiration.

Oma must know of such a story.

She must know how important it was.

David's
Story

David Cunningham had grown up on Cashmere, that elegant anglicised Kashmir, the word probably too Indian for those who had built their two-storey villas a century and a half earlier, surrounding them with gracious gardens shaded by English trees. His parents had been driven to the hills by the asthma-inducing smog that regularly blanketed the city in winter. Here, high above the smog-line, they could breathe more easily and leave the coughing to those trapped below.

Christchurch, that ersatz-English English-speaking city with the English name, capital city of Canterbury, another English name, with its streets named after English dioceses, English poets, English worthies. At its heart Christ Church Cathedral, a Gothic pile that would not have been out of place in an English town.

David had followed his father into a college modelled on an English public school where he had learnt, as had his father, of the Battle of Hastings, the Battle of Agincourt and the charge of the Light Brigade, where he had learnt Rupert Brooke's 'Soldier' (*That there's some corner of a foreign field / That is for ever England. There shall be / In that rich earth a richer dust concealed; / A dust whom England bore, shaped, made aware, / Gave, once, her flowers to love, her ways to roam; / A body of England's, breathing English air . . .*), Wordsworth ('Daffodils') and Browning.

Thus, suitably equipped, he had embarked on study at the University of Canterbury then teacher training and, as soon as possible after graduation, set off on his Grand Tour, known as O.E. or Overseas Experience.

Naturally, he sought this experience in London, and managed to remain there for a couple of years (his visa courtesy of English grandparents) working in pubs, then moving into supply teaching.

The position at Huntingdon, when he saw it advertised, seemed too good to be true, but he applied anyway.

He didn't claim in his application to be English, though he wrote nothing that might suggest otherwise.

For all that, Michael Bastion had not been fooled.

'And where are you from, Mr Cunningham?'

'Christchurch, actually.'

'Christchurch?'

'In New Zealand, the South Island—'

'Oh, that Christchurch.'

Michael had glanced at the applicant. That explained the hard-to-place accent, not South African, not American, not quite Australian. New Zealand. Michael did not know a lot about New Zealand but felt that it was reasonably safe. The young man had supplied excellent references and he came across as pleasantly biddable, if a little gauche. Neither of the other shortlisted candidates had impressed. One, the man, looked to be a potential child-molester, and the woman came across as very capable, somewhat opinionated and highly intelligent — rather too intelligent for Michael's comfort. The New Zealander it would have to be, perhaps by default, but *c'est la guerre.*

'Anyway,' he said to Miranda that evening, 'they're almost like us.'

'What do you mean?'

'Their chap Hillary conquered Everest,' he reminded her, 'and planted the Union Jack on top. Icing on the cake for the coronation.'

'That was seventy years ago. They've probably changed a bit since. Besides, this chap isn't a mountaineer, is he?'

'Not sure. He didn't say so. The New Zealanders have a pretty good rugby team, too.'

'Weren't you after an English teacher rather than a rock-climbing rugby player clutching a Union Jack?'

'He has good references.'

'What about the other two?'

'The man was creepy; the woman was arrogant. She wouldn't have fitted in.'

'And this chap will?'

'Better than the other two.'

'From what I hear you saying,' said Miranda, holding out her glass for a refill, 'he sounds merely the best of a bad bunch.'

David's Story

As David had feared, Agnès Delon was not at all cooperative.

'I'm sorry, Monsieur Cunningham, but what you ask is impossible.'

'Please, Madame Delon, surely—'

'Quite impossible!' Agnès looked at him, unyielding.

'There may be some information on those files that could help me — help us — find Ms Bernstein. You know she's gone missing. We cannot get hold of her and need to contact family members.'

'That may be so, and there may be such information perhaps,' said Agnès, 'but those files are confidential. They are not to be shared with all ... all and—'

'Sundry?' suggested David.

Agnès refused to be helped.

'But Mr Bastion—' David attempted.

'I do know Monsieur Bastion is concerned that he has not heard from Mademoiselle Bernstein, with term starting so soon. He has, of course, told me so. If Monsieur Bastion wishes to consult her file that is, naturally, his right. But I repeat, it is not *your* right, Monsieur Cunningham, and I would also suggest,' Agnès added with a hint of venom, 'it is not *your* problem.'

David stared helplessly at Agnès's departing back. He might have appealed to her romantic side, but suspected she had none, ditto better nature. He might, as a senior teacher, have tried to pull rank, but knew that Agnès (*Madame* Delon!) in reality had far more rank than he.

Agnès was a dead-end street with a padlocked gate.

His only option was to go over her head, and that meant another interview with Michael.

'You have some news?' asked Michael once David was seated.

David shook his head. 'I'm afraid not.' He sighed. 'Everything has turned up a blank.'

'Everything?'

'Everything I've been able to think of. I have tried ringing, texting, emailing. I've even searched her name online. She hates social media so there's no point trying Facebook or Twitter. As far as I know she hasn't gone back to her apartment and there's no concierge to ask. I can't tell whether her car is in the garage.'

'You have no key to her apartment?' asked Michael delicately.

'I don't.'

'Nothing at this end, either,' said Michael. 'Miranda is of the opinion that there's not a lot to worry about yet. That she'll probably turn up in time for school on Monday. But . . .'

Michael's *but* was prompted by the fact that it was now Friday. Time was rushing by, and if Cara were not to turn up next week he would have to run on a barrel for some time before being able to secure a replacement. The ripple was threatening to become a wave.

'I know,' said David.

'I mean, she's always been most reliable. You know of nothing to suggest instability or anything like that?'

'Oh no,' said David. He gave a rueful grin. 'She was — is — quite the grown-up.'

'Despite the — what did you call it? — playfulness?'

'Despite that.'

There was a pause in the conversation. Michael waited. David had yet to reveal why he had sought this interview, especially as he had, by his own admission, nothing to report.

'I suppose I ought to tell you I approached Agnès,' David began.

'You did? Why?'

'You probably know that already.'

'She did mention something.'

'You see, despite our becoming close in recent weeks, I realise I have never known much about Cara's background. She's a very private person. It wasn't until I started thinking over things that I realised just how private. She's hardly ever revealed anything about her past. She lives so much in the here and now, it's almost as if the past is irrelevant. We've just never really gone there.'

'Go on.'

'I mean family stuff, for instance. I know next to nothing about her parents. I don't even know whether they're alive or dead, together or divorced. I have no idea whether she has brothers or sisters, and nothing about previous jobs, relationships, places she's lived.'

'A woman of mystery.'

'Yes, but it never appeared that way until now. I know it sounds strange but I've never even thought about it. I mean I've told her all sorts of stuff about me, my parents, where I grew up, my brother. I even told her all about Heidi.'

'Heidi?'

'My ex-wife.'

'Your ex-wife?'

'Yeah.'

'You were married long?'

'Not really — about three years. We got married not that long after we met. She just walked out one day, out of the blue.'

'Just like Cara.'

'Yeah . . . though not really. The point is, I told Cara all this stuff but I never noticed that she didn't return the compliment. I can't recall asking, if it comes to that.'

'I see.'

'That's why I asked Agnès . . . Madame Delon. I realised I didn't know the name of a single person from her past whom I could ask about her. Not one.'

'I see.'

'Then I suddenly remembered all that sort of information would be on file in the school office from when she applied for her job.'

'Naturally.'

Michael glanced at the young man, his earnest face now a scruffy ginger from not shaving for several days.

'Trouble is,' said David, 'Agnès — Madame Delon — is a stickler for protocol and I got my head bitten off.'

Michael assumed his headmaster mantle.

'And so you should have. Agnès was only doing her job. The staff records are highly confidential and you should not have tried to compromise her.'

David looked unhappy. 'Yes, but—'

'Your suggestion was sound, but there are proper channels. I'll look into it.'

'And let me know?'

'David . . .' There was steel in Michael's tone, and David knew at once that he had stepped too far. He lowered his gaze, abashed.

Michael could have told the young man that after Agnès's complaint he had instructed her to bring him Cara Bernstein's file and that, even as he and David were speaking, it was secured in his desk drawer. Later in the afternoon he would go through the file carefully to ascertain whether it contained anything that might be useful.

He stood up. David stood as well, still a little embarrassed at the rebuke. As if to mollify him slightly, Michael added, 'If you're not doing anything tomorrow evening, Miranda and I wondered if you might like to come to dinner. We've invited Angus and Eleanor. What do you say?'

David allowed himself a small smile of relief.

'Thank you very much. I'd like that.'

'Good. About seven? Don't bring anything.'

'David Cunningham sought out Agnès, asking to look at Cara's staff file,' said Michael. He and Miranda were having lunch.

'Good lord,' laughed Miranda. 'I'm sure that went down well.'

'He said she bit his head off, and next thing, of course, Agnès came storming in to me firing both barrels.'

'You appear to have survived.'

'It was a narrow thing. All the same, it wasn't a silly idea. I asked Agnès to bring me Cara's file and I'll look through it later. I might be able to go back to a couple of her referees, or her last school . . . Might find contact details for parents or siblings. Perhaps there is a pattern.'

'What sort of pattern?'

'You know — instability, unreliability.'

'She always strikes me as pretty reliable.'

'Me too. Until now.'

'What do mean? In what way exactly has she been unreliable?'

'You know — this disappearance thing.'

'I've said it before. This "disappearance thing" is a private matter between Cara and David Cunningham. As far as we know she hasn't "disappeared" at all. She just doesn't want to be in Cunningham's presence anymore. I find that perfectly understandable.'

'That's a bit harsh.'

'Not at all. Would *you* want to be his constant companion? I know I wouldn't.'

'That's not the point.'

'What is the point?'

'I have a school to run. Term starts in two days' time and I've no idea whether Ms Bernstein intends to show up for work. She still hasn't had the courtesy to reply to my emails.'

'Well, I think you're being a panic pants. She'll turn up. And even if she doesn't, the school won't fall over just because you're one teacher short. In any case, I'm a perfectly capable French teacher. I can step into the breach if there happens to be one, which I doubt.'

'I suppose so,' sighed Michael.

'I know so.'

'For all that,' added Michael, 'it looks as if Cara hasn't returned to Arras yet. David's been around to her flat and there's no sign of life. He couldn't tell whether her car was there either.'

'So she may have been out shopping?'

'Possibly.'

'Probably still clubbing in Berlin or somewhere.'

'I hope so,' said Michael. His tone suggested the hope was forlorn.

'Anyway,' said Miranda, changing the subject, 'did you remember to invite David for dinner?'

'Yes, and he said he'll come. I'm not sure why you wanted to ask him, given your obvious animus.'

'I merely observed that I wouldn't want him for a partner. I can cope with him as a dinner guest.'

'I hope so. I wouldn't want any discourtesy. All the same, I suspect you have a hidden agenda, don't you?'

'Of course, my dear. Of course I do!'

Michael drew the file out of his drawer. He had decided to ignore Miranda's views and proceed with his inquiry. He opened the file and took out Cara Bernstein's original application.

He remembered it now. Over the years he must have read hundreds of job applications. One developed an instinct for the genuine applicants and those who struck a wrong note. This enabled him to cast aside an application after little more than a quick glance. Those who affected an unfortunate chumminess, an informal intimacy quite out of place; those who gilded the lily, glossing faint achievements with the enamel of pretended accomplishment; the arrogant; the fawning; the near illiterate — ignorant about apostrophes and the distinction between subject and object pronouns; the stupid.

In a perverse way he rather enjoyed the stupid: these were the applicants who enclosed references so understated, often so deliciously ironic, it was perfectly clear the poor idiot applicant had no idea what was being said — or not said. He was suspicious, too, of the over-burnished testimonial that claimed the subject was a gift to the universe, worthy of a Nobel Prize, an Academy Award or sainthood. Michael read these for what they often were: an attempt to saddle him with some pathetic anorak his or her school was desperately keen to get shot of.

Cara Bernstein's application was none of these. Her cover letter was straightforward and to the point. She summarised her background objectively, listing her qualifications and experience. She omitted nothing he needed to know, and included nothing he did not need to know. She came across as brisk, businesslike and efficient. He'd liked that.

Her previous school, another international school near Paris, summarised her five years with them warmly and expressed regret that she had chosen to leave; her two referees, likewise, both senior teachers at the same school, had been unstinting in their admiration of her character and abilities, but not suspiciously fulsome.

It was only now, his antennae twitching, that he found it a little odd that Cara had focused so much on her immediate past in her application. He shuffled through the file for her CV.

Yes, there were earlier schools listed — in the US (California) and then in the UK (Chester, the Isle of Wight). Five or six in all. However, when he looked more carefully at the dates, he realised there were significant gaps. Two years, three years when Cara seemed not to have been employed at all.

At that point, remembering David Cunningham's revelation that he knew nothing of Cara's background, he went back to the file to look for personal information. Apart from her date of birth and the fact that she was an American citizen there was next to nothing. Of course there was no real reason why there should have been: they were looking to employ her, not her family. For all that, most applicants did provide a modicum of personal information, if only to give their application a human dimension. Some mention of partner if they had one, children if they had any, interests and passions beyond their immediate professional field.

Cara had proffered none of this.

It was slightly unusual but not a hanging offence.

What had he said to Cunningham? *A woman of mystery* . . .

Michael opened his laptop and went to his email.

He would write a note to the principal of Cara's previous school. Very professional, just gently enquiring. He would contact the referees as well. He doubted whether anything especially relevant would be forthcoming but he had been left slightly intrigued by rereading her job application. It had not provided any answers but had raised one or two questions.

Cara's
Manuscript

Mathilde and Helga were preparing for bed. Helga, already in her nightgown, was sitting cross-legged on their shared bed, her face shining in the flickering candlelight. As if by mutual consent, they had not spoken intimately of the visit to the brothers all afternoon and evening.

'And this visit?' began Helga, smiling. 'Did you still find Herr Jacob —?'

Mathilde nodded. 'When he took my hand I—'

Helga laughed. 'He took my hand too, Mathilde. I felt nothing except a hand!'

Mathilde shrugged.

'And isn't Herr Wilhelm just as attractive?'

Mathilde blushed. 'Don't be so wicked, Helga!'

'Why is that wicked? It's a reasonable question.'

'You are being foolish.'

'But isn't he?' Helga persisted.

Mathilde thought before she responded. 'Some would say so. Some might say more so. He smiles a lot more, doesn't he?'

Helga laughed. 'If he smiles on our next visit you can have Herr Jacob and I can have Herr Wilhelm!'

'Helga!' Laughing, Mathilde seized a bolster pillow from the chaise longue and threw it at her sister.

Helga laughed in turn and reached for the pillow to throw it back.

'Don't you dare!' warned Mathilde.

'Why not?'

'I need you to undress me.'

Mathilde unbuttoned and slipped off her gown, then backed over to her sister who, still smiling, began methodically unlacing her stays.

'When shall we return?'

Mathilde considered the question. The brothers' house on Bellevue-strasse was already familiar and they had been encouraged by the brothers themselves to return. All that was required was another story from Oma, who seemed delighted that Mathilde was delivering her stories to the young scholars. Mutti had so far not objected but might become less than happy if the frequency of the visits were to increase. Papa certainly would. Mathilde suspected he had yet to learn that they had visited the scholars at all.

Freed of her stays, Mathilde removed her chemise and shrugged on her nightgown. Helga made room for her and, after extinguishing the candles, Mathilde slipped into the bed and drew up the bedclothes.

'When?' whispered Helga in the darkness.

'When what?' asked Mathilde, who knew what.

'When will we go again?'

'Oma must provide another tale,' replied Mathilde, 'and then I must write it down. As you saw, the brothers need a written version.'

'When will that be?'

'Don't be so impatient!'

Even as she remonstrated with her sister Mathilde felt a twinge of hypocrisy. She herself was impatient. She knew it would not be politic to call upon the brothers again too soon. They might sense her neediness. She must maintain a reserve — a friendly reserve if that were possible. Her heart must not be on her sleeve. Was it already? Oma seemed to have a twinkling suspicion, and Helga was not fooled for a moment.

If these two had seen through her so easily, would the rest of the world?

Would Herr Jacob Grimm?

Helga whispered something.

'What was that?'

'Should I hurry Oma up?'

'No, don't do that. I will talk to her.'

She did need to talk to her grandmother. Mathilde needed not just a new tale, but one the brothers had yet to collect, one they would exclaim at, that would be a prize in their collection. She did not quite believe their reassurances about the value of retellings of tales they already had. They were probably just being kind, encouraging her in the hope that she would bring them something novel. Sooner or later, if she did not, they would become impatient, would prefer she not interrupt their valuable time.

Oma must have such a story, surely.

Mathilde would press upon her how important it was.

David's Story

'Now listen, everyone. He'll probably tell you all about it when he comes,' said Miranda, 'but David somehow managed to lose Cara Bernstein just before their cruise down the Rhine.'

She was passing around gin and tonics in the sitting room of the headmaster's lodge. Angus Paton, the art teacher, and Eleanor Klaus, a teacher in the junior school, were the only other dinner guests. Strategically, Miranda had given them an earlier arrival time than Michael had given David. She could then fill them in on the Cunningham/Bernstein situation in advance — on the off chance one of them might have something to add.

She liked them both.

Angus was a large, powerfully built redhead who could have been a rugby international, although his sporting interests went no further than the odd game of darts at the pub. Angus liked to say outrageous things, but so disarmingly that you could never be sure how serious he was. It was safer to assume he was being ironic, although Miranda suspected he often was not. She enjoyed having him at her table; he was sure to introduce an edgy element to prod even the stodgiest of her other guests into action.

Eleanor was an old friend who had joined the staff in Miranda's father's time and had grown with the school. She was loyal and discreet. Miranda valued her as a confidante, for she had never let her down. In the early days Eleanor had been a trusted babysitter for the girls, and now that they were teenagers they regarded her as an honorary aunt.

'Lose Cara?' Eleanor now asked. 'What on earth do you mean? Miranda, you must tell all!'

Miranda took a long sip and began. 'I'll tell what I know, although I warn you my version is already third hand. Michael can chip in if I get things wrong.'

'**M**iranda reckons it's some perversion of the frog prince story,' said Michael. 'Cara kissed her frog and promptly disappeared.'

'I didn't say that at all,' Miranda protested. 'I simply said that after the first few kisses Cara probably realised that David was never going to turn into a prince and so she—'

'Disappeared,' laughed Eleanor.

'I'm bound to say he's turning into something,' said Angus Paton. 'Not a prince, more Neanderthal. Have you seen him lately?'

'He's growing a beard,' said Michael. 'It's something he promised Cara.'

'So that's why she ran away,' said Eleanor. 'Ever been kissed by a scrubbing brush?'

'As my old father always said, why cultivate it on your face when it's growing wild round your arse!' said Angus.

'Your old father was a wise man,' observed Miranda tartly.

'Seriously, though,' said Eleanor, 'does anybody know why Cara just upped and left like that? It does seem odd.'

'Miranda has a whole raft of theories, don't you, darling?' said Michael. 'Some of them are even quite convincing. Go on,' he encouraged her.

Miranda outlined her various suspicions as she had explained them earlier to Michael. By and large he gave her free rein, only occasionally commenting. The other two heard her out in silence.

'So what do you think?' asked Michael when Miranda had finished.

'You should be a forensic psychologist!' said Angus. 'You've missed your calling completely.'

'Oh, I know it, I know it,' Miranda laughed.

'I go for the epiphany,' said Eleanor. 'She realised she had a frog in her bed. Too difficult to come clean, so she took off.'

'Typical woman,' said Angus. 'Cut and run.'

Michael shot him a warning look.

'Sometimes,' said Eleanor, 'you have to be cruel to be kind.'

'Both probably,' said Angus. 'But, Miranda, for all of your theorising, impressive though it is, you've left out the most likely explanation.'

'Which is?'

'Cara Bernstein is obviously a sleeper agent. Somewhere in the graveyard she came across, or arranged to meet, her minder and was activated. David was lucky she didn't do him in before she left. You know — what do they call it? — collateral damage!'

'Sleeper agent? For whom?'

Angus shrugged. 'Does it matter? She's American, so probably the CIA. Could have been a double agent, of course. There's a lot of that about. Could be one of Putin's stooges.'

'A trifle far-fetched, Angus,' said Michael. 'Have another drink.'

'Don't mind if I do,' said Angus, handing his glass to his host. Warming to his theory, he added, 'Could be Mossad of course. Check her CV, Michael. See if it mentions Mossad.'

Michael, busy refilling drinks, chose not to mention that he had already revisited Cara's CV.

While he was out of the room Miranda turned to Angus, smiling disarmingly. 'Anyway, Angus, surely you have something more interesting to tell us than fairy stories about Mossad and the like?'

'How do you mean, Miranda?' Angus asked, with a quick glance at Eleanor, whose face remained impassive.

'Would you perhaps have known Cara better than most?'

'I'm not sure I know what you're getting at.'

'Didn't you and she, you know, have a little fling at one stage?'

Angus shook his head. 'Not my type.'

Michael returned with the tray of drinks. Sensing an atmosphere in the room he asked, 'Have I missed something?'

'Not a thing,' said Angus.

'But didn't you?' Miranda pressed home.

Now Eleanor was faintly smiling.

Angus shrugged, grinning. 'Let's put it this way, I did have to find out whether or not she was my type, didn't I?'

As he reached for his drink, he gave Michael a quick glance. Michael raised his own glass to Angus's in a wordless toast.

It was precisely at that point that the doorbell rang.

'Michael cooked,' announced Miranda, once the guests had been seated. 'His specialty: *daube Provençale*. Bon appétit!'

'My mother would have said beef stew,' said Michael self-deprecatingly.

'Come on, old man, beef casserole at least,' said Angus.

Steam rose from the large terracotta casserole dish as Michael lifted its lid. 'Pass me your plates,' he said. 'It'll be easier if I serve from here.'

Angus half stood to peer into the dish. 'Amazing,' he exclaimed. 'You have excelled yourself, headmaster. I wish my mother had put a beef stew like this on our table.'

He sat down and looked about his fellow guests before continuing. 'To tell you the truth, she never put a beef anything on the table. Lifelong vegetarian. That's probably why I hate them so much to this day!'

David joined in the laughter, but half-heartedly. He felt uncomfortable. He had borne the inevitable teasing about his embryonic beard but had found it difficult. The trouble was, he knew the teasing was justified. His face hadn't seen a razor for over a week now, and his whiskers had gone from the designer stubble stage to the Skid Row stage. He suspected that if he sat down in one of the Arras squares, people would throw money into his hat.

Beyond that, he invariably felt uncomfortable in Miranda's company. He didn't really like her. He sensed her disapproval somehow. Whenever he had been invited to the headmaster's lodge, which was not often, Miranda had come across as the perfect hostess, yet somehow managed to give the impression she regarded him as some kind of challenge. With him, it seemed, she always tried just a little too hard. She tinkled too loudly at his attempts at humour and would gaze around the table at the others as if encouraging them to laugh too. It was patronising; it was hard not to feel diminished.

Luckily, he would not be under any pressure to crack jokes tonight. Angus would have that covered. With some relief, David decided he could safely fade into the background.

However, he soon discovered that fading into the background was not an option. It became clear that it was Cara's disappearance that had prompted his invitation, and Miranda was not going to accept silence on his part. After a modicum of ice-breaking banter she began directing questions at him about what *exactly* had happened in Bonn, and David was compelled to reprise the whole story.

He imagined there was an element of concern, as well as curiosity, in the interrogation. These, after all, were his colleagues. But it didn't feel that way. He'd actually felt more comfortable in the slightly more formal atmosphere of Michael's headmaster's office.

'Why did you return so quickly?' asked Miranda. 'Surely—'

'Because I saw no reason to stay,' David explained. 'I mean, she'd left the hotel. She'd packed up and checked out. I saw no point in staying there by myself.'

'She left no note?' asked Eleanor. 'She's not texted or phoned or anything?'

David shook his head. 'Nothing. Nada.'

'Was there anyone with her when she checked out?' asked Miranda.

'How would I know?' asked David, a little irritated by the implication. 'I wasn't there.'

'Did you ask the person at reception?'

Again, David shook his head. 'I'm sorry, no. Why would I? I'm sorry, I was all over the place, not thinking straight at the time. It didn't even occur to me. To tell the truth, I'm still not really thinking very straight.'

'Be honest, Cunningham,' grinned Angus. 'When did you ever think straight?'

'Yeah, fair comment,' said David ruefully, and taking the opportunity to fork some food into his mouth.

'Why didn't you go to the police?' Miranda was not letting it go.

David, looking up over his fork, observed Michael give her a warning frown.

He glanced at Miranda, recognising her hostility. Patiently, he said, 'Why would I? Cara had simply checked out of the hotel. There was no suggestion she'd been abducted, kidnapped or sold into white slavery. What grounds did I have for going to the police?'

Miranda didn't flinch. 'David, don't get me wrong. I'm not getting at you. As you said, you were clearly disconcerted, not thinking straight. I'm only looking at things from, perhaps, a more objective point of view. I know you said there was no suggestion Cara had been abducted, but did you feel she might have been, or that something like that may have happened?'

David allowed himself to chew for some seconds, both on the daube and the question. Had he? He wasn't sure. 'That didn't even occur to me,' he said at last. 'I mean, when people are kidnapped, abducted or whatever, they're usually snatched off the street or hijacked in some way, aren't they? Kidnappers don't normally escort you to your hotel room and wait patiently while you pack up and check out.'

'Don't ask me,' said Angus. 'I've not kidnapped anybody yet. Thought about it often enough, though.'

'David's right,' said Eleanor. 'If you were to abduct somebody you wouldn't go about it like that.'

David gave her a quick, grateful smile.

Michael raised the bottle of Languedoc he'd chosen to accompany his daube. 'Top-up, anybody?' Once he'd refilled the glasses he said, 'I'm certain we can rule out abduction. Why would anybody want to abduct Cara?'

'Ransom?' suggested Angus.

'Well, naturally,' said Michael. 'But then they'd need to know who she was and whether she was rich — or her family was rich. I mean, *we* don't even know that. Moreover, they'd need to know how to get in touch with her family in order to present their demands. And again, we don't even know that.'

'It would be easy enough to find that out,' said Angus. 'All you'd need is a sharp knife or a knitting needle.'

'Angus!' protested Miranda. 'Too much!'

'Anyway,' added Angus, 'people aren't necessarily kidnapped for money.'

'No?' asked Eleanor. 'What other reason is there?'

'The white slave trade,' said Angus.

'You're getting carried away, Angus,' said Miranda. 'Stop it.'

David closed his eyes as he took a sip of wine. He was finding Angus quite tiresome and Miranda insufferable. He wanted to leave.

He had barely reopened his eyes when she started in on him again.

'You must have had an argument. Nothing else makes sense.'

'Miranda . . .' said Michael.

David closed his eyes again. 'Your second statement I quite agree with. As for your first — nothing could be further from the truth. We were having a happy day.' He was certainly not going to mention his marriage proposal in this company. He would be laying himself wide open, to no good effect.

'Let's change the subject,' said Eleanor brightly. 'This is not getting us very far.'

'Couldn't agree more,' said Michael.

'Neither could I,' said Miranda. 'It's all quite academic anyway. Cara starts work again on Monday and we can ask her ourselves what happened.'

The following morning Michael checked his emails to find two responses to his note about Cara: one from the principal of the previous school and the other from Louis de Verre, one of her referees.

The principal's note was professional and perfunctory:

> In response to your query re Cara Bernstein: I can only
> reiterate what was said at the time she applied for a
> position at your establishment. We were sorry to lose
> Madame Bernstein. She was a most competent teacher,
> a person of high integrity and an agreeable colleague.
> I have had no intelligence since her departure that
> would cause me to modify this view.

Louis de Verre, on the other hand, was a little less stiff and a trifle more forthcoming:

> Hi Michael. You were very circumspect, but I imagine
> from the tenor of your note you have experienced

some difficulty with Cara. At the time I wrote
her testimonial I did mean every word, and were
I to write her a testimonial again today, I'm certain
I'd say exactly the same things. We worked together
for a number of years in a relatively small school
and I like to think we came to know each other
very well. So much so, I came to regard Cara as
one of my closest friends. However, at this point
I must add a qualification. This does not affect
or alter anything I said in her support. It is more
personal. I must say, *entre nous*, that it seems I was
quite mistaken about the nature of our friendship.
Since her departure north I have emailed her a
number of times, friendly chatty notes as you would
to an old friend with much in common, but not once
have I received a reply. I imagine Cara has returned
to Paris at odd times, but again not once has she
made any attempt to contact me. I should add that
as far as I know, she has made no attempt to get in
touch with any of her former colleagues, nor with
the school. It seems she has rather expunged us all
completely from her present.

Michael read this with growing interest. He sensed Louis de Verre's
deep hurt and wondered whether his relationship with Cara Bernstein
had gone beyond friendship. It sounded as if it had. And now David
Cunningham had been expunged (good word) as well. And Huntingdon?

It was Sunday morning. Term began tomorrow. Although it was not a
requirement, most teachers put in an appearance quite some time before
term began — to prepare lessons, review their courses and programmes,
or just to get into back-to-school mode. Some, indeed, would spend
much of the week before term began doing this. Cara Bernstein had
been diligent in the past, but so far: no show.

What had Angus Paton said last night?

Cut and run.

Suddenly Michael felt a little depressed. Cutting and running, according to de Verre's plaintive note, did seem to be a pattern. Miranda's

breezy confidence, he sensed, was quite misplaced. She'd better start dusting off her old lesson plans. It looked as if Cara Bernstein would not be putting in an appearance in the morning.

He replied briefly both to the principal and to Louis de Verre, thanking them for taking the trouble to respond but still without elaborating on the reasons for his enquiry. In thanking de Verre he did not allude to the man's obvious pain.

It was while composing these replies that Michael decided to email Cara herself directly once more.

Dear Cara . . .

At lunch he thought it best to tell Miranda about his recent correspondence and subsequent misgivings, partly to prepare her for the likelihood that she would be taking Cara's classes in the morning.

She heard him out, eyes widening as the full implications became clear.

'Fascinating,' she said.

'My view, too.'

'She and this de Verre chap — were they an item do you suppose?'

'Who knows? It does seem they were very close. "One of my closest friends" he called her.'

'Perhaps she felt he was getting too close. Perhaps that's why she left Paris.'

'Could be.'

Miranda was thoughtful. 'So it could be that she considered Cunningham was getting too close.'

Michael nodded. 'Sounds a bit like a pattern.'

'In which case—'

'She's cut and run,' said Michael.

'Oh, lord,' said Miranda. 'It pains me beyond measure to say this, Michael, but just for once you may be right.'

Michael smiled. It was a rare concession. 'Anyway,' he said, 'I've sent her yet another email. Quite friendly, but I did insist she let me know ASAP whether she intends coming to school tomorrow.'

'When did you send it?'
'A couple of hours ago.'
'No reply?'
Michael pulled out his phone and examined it.
'Not a whisper,' he said.

Cara's Manuscript

'But it's so difficult, dear girls,' said Mathilde's grandmother. 'How can I possibly provide you with a tale that will be new to the brothers when I have no idea what tales they have already heard?'

'But you know so many stories, Oma,' said Mathilde. 'There must be one that's little known.'

'A strange story, Oma,' added Helga. 'A haunting, mysterious story.'

'Perhaps one you scarcely know yourself,' suggested Mathilde.

'If I scarcely know it myself,' said the old lady drily, 'I can hardy tell it to you.'

'The oldest story you know,' said Mathilde, remembering Wilhelm's comment about stories from her oma's oma, and from that oma's oma before her.

Their grandmother smiled indulgently, 'You know, my dears, most of my tales are like that. And I'm afraid most of my tales will be well known. They've been around for so long.'

She eased back into her wing chair and closed her eyes. Helga and Mathilde exchanged a glance. This was not going to be as easy as they had hoped.

Then suddenly it became even more difficult.

The door opened and their mother entered. She saw her mother sitting back with her mouth open, her eyes closed, and wagged a warning finger at her daughters.

The old lady opened her eyes. 'They're all right, Gretchen.'

'No, they're not, Mutti, they're annoying you. You're tired.'

Now that her mother was awake, Gretchen felt able to clap her hands at her daughters. 'Out!' she ordered. 'You can see how tired Oma is. You should not be pestering her like this!'

'But Mutti—' cried Helga.

'No buts,' said their mother firmly. 'Go to your room!'

As soon as they were out of the parlour their mother closed the door firmly.

'Oma was going to tell us a story!' protested Helga.

'Oma is going to have a nice long rest,' said their mother. 'In any case, you're too old for stories.'

'What shall we do?' asked Helga.

'What can we do?' replied Mathilde.

'Oma is always tired. It could be days.'

Mathilde shrugged. 'We just have to wait.'

Helga fell down on the chaise longue, pouting. Mathilde slumped into her chair and picked up a book, flicking through its pages. She was equally frustrated but did not want to show it. She had revealed too much to Helga already, she had decided, and was determined from this point on to adopt an outward show of *sang-froid*. It was difficult to do, as inwardly she was seething.

For some time there was silence. Helga stretched out on the couch, staring at the ceiling; Mathilde, having found her place, read her book.

Then Helga said, 'Why do we have to wait?'

'Because we don't have a story,' said Mathilde patiently.

'We don't need a story,' said Helga.

'What are you talking about?'

'Didn't the brothers ask you to take them your written script of the first story? Surely we can deliver that?' And she added, in a slightly calculated manner: 'When we get another story from Oma, we'll have a reason to go again!'

She was right. There was nothing to stop them delivering the story. 'I suppose so,' said Mathilde, trying to sound as though she were conceding a point. 'We could. There's no reason not to.'

Helga laughed. 'Good!' she cried and clambered off the chaise longue to hug her sister. 'What shall we wear?'

They stood once again before the door of the house in Bellevuestrasse. Last time she had been at this door, Mathilde remembered, he had held her hand, however briefly, however formally, however tentatively — he had held her hand. And she had held his, briefly, tentatively — his soft scholar's hand. She could almost feel it still as she reached up to pull the cord on the doorbell.

Helga looked about her. The street was lovely. Such trees. Living here would be like living in a park. And so close to the centre as well. With her family, she disapproved of this French king, Jérôme Bonaparte, and his Frenchifying of their ancient town. These French names — Bellevuestrasse! However, she had to concede he did have an eye for beauty; already parts of Kassel had become so much more beautiful.

The smile Mathilde had prepared as she heard footsteps approaching faded as the opened door revealed neither Jacob nor his brother. Instead, a young woman stood there, observing the two visitors with curiosity.

'Good afternoon,' Mathilde faltered. 'Is Herr Jacob Grimm able to see me? I have something for him.'

Helga's face fell as she beheld the young woman. She was clearly not a maid. Could she be the wife of Jacob, or of Wilhelm? It had not occurred to the sisters that either, or both, of the scholars may have been married already. This woman was young, but young wives were not uncommon.

Her relief was almost palpable when the young woman replied, 'I'm sorry but my brother is not at home right now.'

Mathilde tried once more. 'Would Herr Wilhelm be available?'

'I'm very sorry,' replied the young woman, 'but he, too, is out. My brothers are both working at the Royal Library. Can I help you, Fräulein . . . ?'

'Heller,' said Mathilde. 'I am Mathilde Heller. This is my sister, Helga.

I have been able to share some of my oma's folk tales with your brothers.'

'Of course,' said the young woman. 'They have mentioned you. Won't you come in, Fräuleins. I am Charlotte but my brothers call me Lotte.'

She smiled more warmly now and ushered them inside the house. She led them through the entrance hall to the already familiar parlour.

'I'd like to say my brothers will not be long,' said Lotte, once they were seated, 'but I'm afraid they often work extremely long hours at the library.'

'They must be very busy,' said Mathilde, bitterly disappointed but somewhat mollified by being able to make the acquaintance of the sister.

'They are,' smiled Lotte. 'But just between ourselves, it is not work for King Jérôme that keeps them busy. To be honest, I'm not sure he has any real work for them now that they have organised all of his books. He has so many! There are thousands of books, I understand, but he rarely reads any of them.'

'But they are still very busy?' asked Helga, puzzled.

'Can't you guess with what?' asked Lotte. 'You of all people must know, Fräulein Heller,' she added, turning to Mathilde.

'Oh,' Mathilde said as it dawned on her. 'Stories?'

'Of course,' said Lotte. 'They are working for Herr Brentano. You know of him?'

Mathilde shook her head.

'He is a poet and a scholar. You must know he has collected folk songs. "The Boy's Wonder Horn"?'

Mathilde shook her head once more. 'I'm sorry . . .'

'Herr Brentano is keen to publish a collection of folk tales to go with his collection of songs. He has asked my brothers,' she added proudly, 'to gather stories for him. That is why they are so busy in the library. Scouring the king's books for material. And they have asked people to bring them stories, people like yourself.'

Mathilde smiled.

'Already they have hundreds of stories,' said Lotte. 'They are so industrious. And they will be sorry to have missed you.'

Mathilde and Helga exchanged a quick glance. They, too, were sorry.

'You said you had something for my brother Jacob?' asked Lotte.

Again, Mathilde and Lotte exchanged glances. Mathilde gave her sister a small frown and closed her hands around her reticule.

'I did, Fräulein Grimm. It was just another story our oma has told us.

A strange little story, but unfortunately I have yet to write it down.'

Lotte's face fell. 'Oh, a pity. They will be disappointed. Could you not tell it to me? I could take notes and—'

'I think,' said Mathilde hurriedly, 'it would be best I told it to your brothers myself. I mean, if I told it to you it would be third hand before they heard it and—'

'Of course,' agreed Lotte. 'And they are great sticklers for accuracy.'

'If we could come again,' said Mathilde, warming to the white lie, 'I could write it down and leave it with them.'

'That is an excellent idea,' said Lotte. 'I will tell them to expect you.'

The sisters stood to take their leave. Lotte stood as well, and reached for their hands. 'I'm sorry. It was remiss of me. I offered you no refreshments—'

'Not at all, Fräulein Grimm. It is we who must apologise for arriving at your doorstep unannounced.'

'We were just passing by,' said Helga.

'I will tell my brothers,' Lotte said again. 'I know they will be sorry to have missed you.'

'She was not unpleasant,' remarked Helga as they walked back to their home. 'You didn't tell me the brothers had a sister.' She gave a little laugh. 'I was quite startled to see her. I imagined at first she must be a wife!'

'I didn't know they had a sister either,' said Mathilde. 'The brothers didn't mention her, did they?'

'They didn't,' said Helga. 'I'm sure.'

It occurred to Mathilde that there were a lot of things the brothers had not mentioned to her. Had they spoken of this Herr Brentano? She had a vague recollection they might have. They had talked about the library of course. The green stockings. But little else of a personal nature. Did they live with their parents? They were quite young, possibly not yet thirty, although they did have a scholarly seriousness that gave the impression of their being much older.

Helga's comment just now had startled Mathilde, as she realised it hadn't even occurred to her that they might be married. She had assumed they were single. She gave a rueful smile, remembering how the brothers seemed able to communicate with each other without speaking, almost like a married couple.

The sister was nice, though. Clearly she admired her brothers. All the same, their absence had forced Mathilde and Helga into deception. Was that what happened when your need to see somebody again became so great? Did honesty go out of the window? Mathilde considered herself an honest person. And yet, almost without compunction, she had just told not one but two falsehoods. She *did* have the copy of the story hidden in her reticule. And she did *not* have another story to bring them. Helga, too, she had—

'Mathilde!' Helga's voice was sharp.

'What is it?'

'I was talking to you.'

'I'm sorry. I was thinking. What did you say?'

'I asked whether it's possible they are already married?'

'I'm sure they're not,' said Mathilde, convincing herself even as she tried to convince her sister. 'Lotte would have mentioned it or alluded to it somehow. Besides,' she added, 'how could they have wives?'

'What do you mean?' said Helga.

It was with an aching pain of realisation, the sudden awareness of the impossible difficulty of her project, that Mathilde explained.

'They could hardly have wives. When they are together it is almost as though they're married to each other.'

David's
Story

Cara Bernstein was conspicuously absent from the staff meeting on the Monday morning. Michael made passing reference to the problem by way of a general appeal to any staff who might know of her intentions. Would they 'pop in' to see him? The matter was quite urgent, he added. He did not mention that he had tried several times to contact Cara but she had not responded.

Nobody volunteered any information at the meeting; nor did anybody, that day or in the following days, 'pop in' to see him.

David Cunningham said nothing. He spent most of the meeting with his eyes fixed on the handouts the headmaster distributed outlining the term's events and deadlines. Even so, he was aware that he was the subject from time to time of curious glances, so he guessed that most people had caught up with what happened in Bonn. Angus, probably. He wasn't a man to sit on a good story, especially one he could embroider.

David was grateful, when the meeting concluded, to be able to hurry to the relative normality of his classroom. He passed Miranda in the corridor and remembered that, unusually, she had been at the staff meeting. Of course, he realised — she would be substituting for Cara. He gave her a fleeting smile when their eyes met, and she gave him in return a small, distracted wave of her hand.

Miranda as colleague, rather than as the headmaster's wife, fellow administrator and daughter of the founder, was not such a bad thing. It put them on a more equal footing, albeit temporarily.

However, the days that followed disabused him of that hope. Miranda clearly did not see herself as one of the staff and made no pretence at refashioning herself that way. She avoided the staffroom and had little interaction with other staff members, except for those such as Eleanor Klaus and Angus, whom she regarded as personal friends. Although David had been a recent dinner guest she ignored him completely.

David sensed her negative influence below the surface. Few people had broached the Bonn situation with him directly, but he was not unaware that there was gossip: shared glances in his direction, conversations broken off at his approach. Apparently Cara's no-show was something to do with him — somehow he had caused her disappearance. Any blame attached not to Cara, but to him. It was uncomfortable, awkward, and he found himself resenting the innuendo, all the more because there was nothing he could do to change what was happening, to dissipate an atmosphere (miasma?) he suspected had been generated by Miranda.

David's earlier return to Huntingdon had been a disconcerting experience on so many levels: the awkward interviews with Michael; the toxic dinner party; above all, his sadness at Cara's absence and his preoccupation with discovering what had happened. Added to this had been the holiday-time strangeness of the largely deserted Huntingdon itself, with its alienating silence and disconcerting echoes as he walked along its tiles or closed its doors.

He had anticipated that this strangeness would dissipate with the return of the students: their post-holiday exuberance, the laughter, the shouting, milling and jostling as they crowded the corridors and tumbled in and out of classrooms.

But it had not. If anything, in a perverse way all the energy, bustle and life merely threw Cara's absence into even sharper relief. There was no possibility of a glimpse of Cara's face among the thronging faces, of the flash of Cara's smile among the dozens of smiles, or of Cara's voice breaking through the hubbub of conversation.

Miranda, now reincarnated as not-Cara, irritated him beyond measure. Each time they passed in the corridor as she made her way towards Cara's classroom with her expensive briefcase he felt affronted.

He suspected Miranda felt much the same about him. Her smile was tight. His nod was curt.

'Hello, David. Mind if I join you?'

David looked up. He'd been leafing through *The Guardian* in the staffroom. Teaching was over for the day — for the week, in fact — and he was too tired, too low, to do anything other than slump with a cup of coffee and a newspaper.

It was Arlene Abramson, smiling her bright enamel smile.

He did mind but wasn't able to summon the bluntness to say so. Instead, he laid down his paper and murmured, 'No problem,' hoping body language might do the trick.

It didn't. Arlene took the chair beside him and smiled again.

David, suspicious, found the smile unnerving.

Arlene taught senior mathematics, but by dint of having read a lot of Fritz Perls, Carl Rogers and Eric Berne's transactional analysis in her youth, fancied herself as an expert on behaviour and psychology. Somehow, at some stage, she had persuaded Michael or perhaps even his father-in-law — she had been at Huntingdon that long — to appoint her school counsellor. There was in fact little call for a counsellor at Huntingdon, but, even so, roughly half of Arlene's hours were devoted to the task and she had been given a small office to accommodate her in this role.

One of Arlene's particularly irksome claims was that she was *a whole-school counsellor*: in other words, her skills and understanding were at the service not only of the students, but the teaching staff, the administration staff, even the gardening, cleaning and maintenance staff.

Few, if any, had ever taken up her offer, but this did not stop Arlene from attempting to make herself available whenever an opportunity arose.

David suspected she had heard about Bonn and was unable to resist. He guessed that trying to put her off may prove very tiresome.

The wait before she said anything was becoming even more unnerving than Arlene's smile. Was it some practised technique to reduce people to jelly? If so, David had apparently been sufficiently jellified, for Arlene finally leaned towards him confidentially and whispered, 'I wonder, David, if it might be possible for you and I to have a little chat.'

David swallowed, leaning away from her. 'Sure,' he said, 'fire away.'

Arlene leaned further towards him to close the gap David had just created.

'Not here,' she said. 'Perhaps somewhere more private?'

Oh god, thought David. She's won, just like that. What was wrong with him? Why couldn't he just tell people what he wanted to say, what they needed to hear?

'Might be possible,' he said, after a pause. 'Your office?'

She shook her head.

'Somewhere else,' she suggested. 'My office might make our talk seem dreadfully *official*.'

And isn't it? David refrained from asking. He suspected that Michael, or even Miranda, might have unleashed Arlene on him in order to probe his story.

He shrugged. 'Okay,' he said. 'Where?'

'How about your room?'

'My classroom?'

'No, your apartment in the wing. If you're free this evening, I could come up after dinner.'

David considered this. Arlene had her teeth latched on to his ankle. He may as well get it over with as soon as possible.

'Okay,' he said. 'Come up about eight.'

Arlene gave him a quick, grateful smile and squeezed his hand.

'Thanks,' she said. 'I'll see you then.'

David watched as she walked away. He didn't know what to make of the encounter. Arlene was a known do-gooder busybody, but this didn't seem like her usual approach. It was a little more mysterious somehow. And what to make of her not wanting the interview — he suspected it was to be an interview — in her office? Arlene was proud of her counsellor's office. It gave her considerable cachet and she liked to flaunt it. As for inviting herself to his rooms — that was head-scratching stuff. It wasn't flirtation. She was old enough to be his mother — not that she wasn't a striking woman with her height, and her steel-grey hair worn in a buzz cut rather like one of those female collaborators at the end of World War II.

The more he considered the matter, the more unlikely he thought it that Michael or Miranda had instigated her approach. He suspected it was her own initiative, but he couldn't for the life of him think why.

Across the room he noticed Angus Paton grinning. He had clearly observed the whole thing. Angus raised his coffee cup in salute and said loudly, 'Lucky man! You've scored there, old son!'

David gave him an amiable two-fingered salute and picked up *The Guardian* once more.

'You haven't told me your latest on the Cara Bernstein situation,' said Miranda, easing her skirt down and off, and carrying it to her wardrobe.

'What latest?' asked Michael.

It was Friday evening; the school week had ended, and Michael and Miranda were preparing for bed. There had been no word from Cara all week.

'I mean, how long are we going to carry on with this running on a barrel? Are we going to replace her?'

'I thought you were enjoying those classes.'

'That's not the point. I do have a life, you know, and it doesn't include full-time teaching. I do enjoy it — sort of. I'd just like to know how long I'm expected to do it.'

'It's a little tricky,' said Michael.

'Tricky? How?'

'Well, she hasn't actually resigned or anything. Officially, she's still employed and I'm not sure I have grounds to dismiss her yet.'

Miranda looked at him in surprise. 'She hasn't reported for duty for a whole week! What other grounds do you need?'

Michael was already in bed, ostensibly reading. He had laid aside his book when Miranda entered the room, largely because he always privately enjoyed watching his wife undressing. She continued this while waiting for his reply, peeling off her tights.

'The trouble is,' he explained, 'we don't know the reason for her failure to turn up. I mean, she may have had an accident or something. There may be some quite legitimate reason. I don't want to run the risk of a wrongful dismissal case.'

'If she has a legitimate reason, what could that be? Illness? Death in the family? In either case she would have been in touch. She hasn't even had the courtesy to reply to your emails, for god's sake.'

'That's just my point. She may not be *able* to reply to my emails.'

'Whyever not? Can you please pass me my nightgown.'

Michael reached under Miranda's pillows, located her nightgown, bundled it and threw it at her. 'I don't know. There could be a host of reasons. A coma, for instance.'

Michael, with a twinge of disappointment, watched Miranda as she carried her nightgown into the ensuite.

'So how long do you expect this coma to last?'

Michael did not reply. Biting back a sarcastic rejoinder, he reached for his novel once more. Sometimes Miranda could be bloody impossible.

David had almost forgotten about his tryst with Arlene Abramson when there was a soft knock at his door.

There she stood, a bottle of red wine in hand.

'It's good of you to see me,' she said. 'I brought a little something . . . by way of a thank you.'

'That's very good of you,' he said, taking the bottle, anticipating embarrassment and tedium. 'Come in.'

He ushered her to a seat and went to open the wine, returning with two glasses, which he had filled.

'Have you heard anything?' asked Arlene, reaching for the proffered glass. 'I assume you haven't.'

David shook his head. 'Not a thing.'

His fears were realised. Arlene was clearly here for a *tête-à-tête* about Cara's disappearance and had nothing to offer apart from some pointless platitudes. In exchange she would suck his emotions dry. Oh, how wearisome.

'So strange,' she said. 'So out of character.'

'Is it?' David found himself asking.

Cara's disappearance had compelled him over the past few days to reassess his understanding. A woman of mystery, Michael had said. Now, David was recognising that the mystery extended far beyond biographical data; it embraced Cara's very being. Perhaps, he wondered, that was why he was so attracted to her.

How selective she had been, how deceptive. She had revealed her body (so beautiful), her wit (so clever), her sense of fun (so enjoyable), but these things had blinded him to the fact that she had revealed little else. What, for Cara, was 'out of character'? He had no idea. What lay beneath? What were her dreams, her ambitions, her fears, hopes . . . ?

For that matter, what did she really think of him? He had been brave enough on occasion to use the word *love*, but she had only smiled in a Mona Lisa kind of way and said nothing. His gratitude for the smile had been enough to satisfy him. He now realised how adroitly she had skirted the issue. What was her real opinion of him? If it came to that, what was her opinion of anybody they knew?

What he had always admired as Cara's non-judgemental nature, her refusal to gossip, he now understood as secrecy, inexplicable privacy. Of course she had joked about politicians, celebrities, but they, not being in her orbit, were not really people, only names. The closer people were to her, the less willing she was to express an opinion. These things, along with her hopes and fears, he realised he had been forced to infer. Everything was always veiled. What misguided audacity had possessed him that he had actually asked her to marry him? He didn't know her at all.

What had he been thinking?

David raised his glass and took a large mouthful of wine.

'Thank you,' he said. 'This is a nice drop.'

'I like it too,' said Arlene. 'Not too sweet, not too dry.'

She had learnt the counsellor's art of listening, of waiting.

'The *via media*,' smiled David. 'That's how we're supposed to live, isn't it?'

'I guess it's a way of keeping us out of trouble,' said Arlene.

'Perhaps I should try it,' said David, rubbing his incipient beard.

'What did you mean by asking "Is it?" just before?' asked Arlene.

'Well, you suggested that Cara's vanishing was out of character and I suddenly wondered whether that were true. I mean, how much do we know of Cara's character? I've been thinking about this and I've come to see that I don't really know that much. You know, the basic things we come to find out about our close friends.'

'You were that close?'

David shrugged. 'As close as you get in a few weeks,' he said.

'I meant,' said Arlene carefully, 'that her leaving without saying anything was odd and so unexpected, given what we know of Cara. She was always so friendly and cheerful — bubbly even.'

'True,' admitted David, adding sourly, 'Mostly, anyway. We could have been seeing the sizzle, though, not the sausage.'

'So you're saying,' said Arlene, with an encouraging smile, 'we haven't got a sausage?'

David glanced at Arlene. That little flash of wit was unexpected.

Emboldened a little by the wine, David asked, 'So what's the gossip in the staffroom? What are they saying about all this?'

'You probably know that. I mean, you're in the staffroom too.'

'I may be, but people don't talk about it with me. Some seem to be avoiding me altogether as if I had the plague or something.'

'So, you really want to know what people are saying about *you*?' Arlene asked.

'That too,' David said.

Arlene considered the question. 'All sorts of things. Most people I guess are at a loss. They don't know what to think. Of course there are a few theories.'

'Convincing?'

'Take your pick. Miranda has a whole pile.'

'I can imagine,' said David bitterly. 'She's even shared some with me. I suspect Miranda believes I hit Cara over the back of the head with a shovel and threw her into the Rhine.'

Arlene smiled but did not comment.

'So what are the theories?'

'I think most people believe you had a quarrel and she stormed off. Or that she just switched off because for some reason she needed time out.'

'It's probably what I'd think as well if I weren't so closely involved,' David said. 'What pisses me off, though, is that this scenario, especially the argument bit, casts me as a liar. Cara and I did *not* argue. It's not easy having half your colleagues thinking that you're a bloody liar.'

'I can understand that,' said Arlene. 'I'd hate it too.'

'Where do you stand?' David asked suddenly. What did he have to lose? He had a sudden suspicion that Arlene knew more than she was letting on. There was something a little contrived about all this.

'Oh, I have my theories,' she said mysteriously, then fell silent. She sipped the last of her wine thoughtfully and sat quietly, not even glancing at David. A counsellor's silence.

'Another glass?' he asked.

'Why not?'

When David returned with the bottle he said, 'I'm not going to let you away with not sharing these theories of yours. What do you reckon happened, Arlene?'

'Everybody believes it must have been something emotional,' she said. 'Some disagreement, what have you. But you say there was no argument.'

David was about to remonstrate when Arlene quickly leaned over and pressed her hand down on his.

'Don't get me wrong, David. I *believe* you. I believe you utterly. But people who *do* believe you — there are others, you know — think that Cara must have suddenly had a change of heart, suddenly decided she didn't want to be with you anymore. Rather than have it out with you and explain, she took the chicken's way out and fled.'

'Is that what you think?'

Arlene shook her head. 'Actually no. That makes no sense to me. People don't spin one hundred and eighty degrees on the spur of the moment. Cara is a confident, forthright young woman. Nothing about her suggests she would run away rather than tell you her true feelings.'

David was no longer so sure. 'So?' he asked.

'So I don't think it was emotional. I don't think it was psychological. This might sound far-fetched, but it's the only thing that makes sense to me — in my view it was something *physical*.'

'Physical? What do you mean?'

Arlene didn't reply, and David wondered whether she felt she might have lost it completely. Nonetheless, he pressed her. 'Go on.'

Arlene looked up. For a few moments she still did not reply. David was not sure whether she was struggling to find the words or didn't want to say anything at all.

Eventually she said, 'I mean she could have had an event of some kind. A stroke, a seizure.'

This was something of an anti-climax. 'Unlikely,' David murmured. 'She was fighting fit.'

'Could she have had an attack of amnesia? It's not all that uncommon. All at once she has no idea who she is, where she is, or how she got there.'

David shrugged.

Warming to her theme, Arlene went on. 'Catatonia.'

'Hardly, said David. 'If she'd shown those sorts of symptoms she wouldn't have been able to check herself out of the hotel. I believe she was quite rational when she did that. Besides, a sudden onset of amnesia would have alarmed her — all the more reason to stay put. She would have known she had a companion in the hotel room from my luggage and stuff. Wouldn't she have waited until her companion returned to help restore her memory?'

'Perhaps,' said Arlene, as if reluctant to give up her theory. Again she lapsed into silence.

David sat waiting, and when it became clear that Arlene had nothing more to add he said, 'Anyway, Arlene, don't you think it's time you came clean?'

'Came clean? I don't know what you mean.'

'I think you do. You didn't really arrange this little meeting just to talk about amnesia and catatonia, did you?'

Arlene shook her head, smiling ruefully. 'Not really.'

'Well?'

'Well, you know how you said earlier that you didn't really know much about Cara?'

David nodded, looking at her with sudden interest. 'Go on.'

'I heard something recently and I've stewed about it quite a lot, but I do feel the right thing to do is to pass it on.'

Now David was intrigued. 'Okay, shoot.'

'I'm guessing one thing you don't know is that at one time Cara had quite a close relationship with Angus Paton.'

David was astonished. 'Good god,' he said. 'Angus! I did not know that. How do *you* know?'

'I don't really know first hand,' Arlene admitted cautiously. 'It surprised me too. I always understood Angus had a thing for Kate Garner. Eleanor told me that.'

'Eleanor Klaus?'

Arlene nodded.

'And how on earth did Eleanor know?'

'Through Miranda, apparently.'

David experienced a surge of resentment. Bloody Miranda. It always came back to bloody Miranda!

'In that case,' said David levelly, 'Miranda is probably making the whole thing up. She loves to stir the pot.'

Arlene shook her head. 'No, no. I don't believe so. According to Eleanor, Miranda challenged Angus about it and he more or less confessed.'

'And how does Eleanor know all this?'

Arlene looked miserable and took another sip of wine.

'So Angus confessed he'd had a thing with Cara? In so many words?'

'More or less, I believe.'

'Less, I reckon. Much less.'

'Perhaps.'

'Does Michael know about this?'

'I'm not sure.'

David considered this new information. All in all, it didn't amount to much. A third-hand rumour, which may or may not have been confirmed by Angus himself. Angus may well have tried his luck with Cara — he was flirtatious, chauvinistic and impetuous, albeit in a calculated way. He liked to give the impression of being that somewhat old-fashioned character: a bounder.

But would he have succeeded?

David thought it unlikely. If Angus had conducted an ongoing liaison with Cara, it hadn't been apparent at any stage. Whenever he'd seen them together, socially or at school, they had never given the least indication of being more than colleagues. He had never observed a brush of hands, a private shared look, an intimate glance. His own growing relationship with Cara, by contrast, had been quite open, apparent to all.

Bloody Miranda.

Arlene was speaking again.

'I'm sorry,' said David, focusing on her again.

'I asked if you were aware that Cara had written a novel.'

'What? You mean published?'

Arlene shook her head. 'Oh no, not published. Only a draft. A young adult novel from what I understand.'

'Have you seen it?' How do you know?'

'Apparently it's based on a story by the Grimm brothers. You know it, perhaps — "The Frog Prince".'

David shook his head. 'Only vaguely. But you've seen this novel?'

It was astonishing to him that Arlene Abramson of all people should have known about and possibly read a book Cara had written, when he . . .

'You didn't know about it?'

He shook his head again. 'I knew Cara had writing ambitions. She talked about wanting to be a writer. But, you know, only in a roundabout kind of way. She never showed me anything she'd actually written. I guessed she must have been writing poetry or something. Personal stuff.'

'She might write poetry,' said Arlene, 'but she's also written this other thing.'

'You haven't told me how you know, or whether you've—'

'Indirectly,' said Arlene. 'From Steffi Fox, as a matter of fact.'

'Steffi?'

Steffi Fox was a senior student, probably the best English student David had in that year, or in many previous years. It wouldn't have surprised him to hear Steffi herself had written a young adult novel. He expected she would one day. Cara had taught Steffi French for two or three years so probably knew her well.

'According to Steffi, Cara sought her out, for a young person's perspective and that sort of thing.'

'Why Steffi?'

'Because she's literate and in the target audience, I guess.'

David considered this surprising news. Was he surprised? Certainly.

Was he surprised Cara had not told him? Not really, not anymore. Would he like to see it? Certainly.

'You don't have a copy?'

Arlene shook her head. 'Sorry.'

'Does Steffi?'

'I imagine so. At least she'd have earlier drafts. You want to see it?'

'Of course.'

'You could ask Steffi. She may of course have been sworn to confidentiality.'

'That's possible, especially if it's still incomplete. All the same, I'll ask her.'

'Do you think it might have anything to do with . . .'

'Cara doing a runner? I very much doubt it. But I have to say I'm curious.'

He was, too. He would ask Steffi Fox as soon as an opportunity presented itself.

Cara's
Manuscript

— KASSEL —

Mathilde was drowsing in bed early in the morning when she was startled by an unearthly scream.

Helga, jerked into wakefulness, suddenly sat up.

'What was that?'

'Was it Mutti?'

Before they had reached the door the scream had given way to an inconsolable wailing.

'It's Oma's room!'

The two sisters, barefoot, hurried along the upstairs passageway to their grandmother's open door.

Their mother was kneeling beside Oma's bed, her shoulders shaking, and she was wailing. It was a strange, vaguely animalistic sound. Oma's breakfast tray was upended on the floor, a cup broken, the rug stained with spreading brown liquid.

Some days later, a plain pine coffin on a bier mounted on a covered black carriage proceeded at a walking pace towards the Lutheran burial ground. Two black-suited figures sat in front of the wagon, one holding the reins of two black horses. The sides of the carriage were open so that the coffin could be observed by passers-by, who invariably stopped in respect as the tiny, mournful cavalcade passed by: women bowing their heads, men removing their hats, children moved to stillness and silence.

Behind the carriage walked Papa, Mutti clutching his arm, and behind them Mathilde and Helga, arm in arm. All were in black, and Mutti was veiled in dark lace. Following these were other relations and friends, twenty or thirty in all.

Mathilde was still in a state of shock.

She kept her eyes steadfastly on the ground as she walked. It was a street she knew, as familiar as her childhood, but a street now foreign to her, as were the buildings, the trees and the sky. She could not lift her eyes to the relentless reality of that wooden box positioned on the horrid black wagon just in front of her.

It could not contain Oma. Such a loathsome thing could not contain Oma. Oma was too large for it, too soft, too alive. Only days ago Mathilde had sat at Oma's knee and the old lady had rested a hand on her head. Oma's hand . . . Mathilde could not bear it. As long as Mathilde had been alive, Oma had lived in their house, had eaten with them, dreamed with them, told them stories. Such marvellous stories. In that time Oma had scarcely grown older. Of course her hair under her white cap had grown a little greyer, her face a little more lined, her hands trembled a little more at her needlework. And she had been so tired of late. However, these had been such small, incremental alterations they were hardly noticeable. In that same time Mathilde had grown from a baby to an infant to a girl to a woman. Helga, too. Oma, on the other hand, had seemed untouched by time.

At the graveside the sexton and his assistants gently lowered their awful cargo into the even more awful hole. Mathilde, feeling Helga beside her shudder, gave a gasp before both were overcome with weeping.

David's
Story

'Here's a strange thing I've only just noticed,' said Miranda. It was Monday and she and Michael were lunching in the lodge.

'Mmm?'

'You know, I've been in Cara's classroom all week and the whole time I've been niggled by something odd. This morning I realised. It suddenly occurred to me that there is no trace of her anywhere.'

'No trace of her? I don't follow.'

'You know what I mean. You've been a classroom teacher. Your room becomes your castle, doesn't it? You usually go to some lengths to personalise it. You know — pictures on the wall. A frieze perhaps. Posters, quotations, signs, that sort of thing.'

'I suppose you do,' Michael agreed, and gave a provocative little smile. 'Especially if you're female. So?'

Miranda ignored the provocation. 'So, Cara's been with us now for three or four years or thereabouts, and in that time you would expect her to have made some effort to stamp her personality on her room. But there's none of that.'

'Cunningham says she's a very private person—'

'It has nothing to do with privacy. It's to do with decoration, homeliness. But there's no *stuff* there.'

'Stuff?'

'Stuff belonging to Cara. There's not one book with Cara's name in it.

The only books in the rooms are texts and reference books belonging to the school.'

'You checked?' Michael sounded surprised.

'Certainly.'

'Why?'

'Because of that niggle.'

'It may not mean much.'

'Perhaps not, but I became intrigued. The drawers to her desk were locked, so I went to Kate for the spare key.'

Kate Garner was the school's first assistant.

'You did what? I wish you'd checked with me first.'

'Don't be so pompous, Michael,' said Miranda icily. 'I had every right.'

'And?'

'And nothing. Nothing in the drawers at all. Whatever had been in them has been removed. They have been stripped bare.'

Michael considered this. 'Perhaps she never used them in the first place.'

'Unlikely. Anyway, it seemed so strange to me that I had another, more systematic search through the room. Cupboards, the filing cabinet — another key from Kate — and there wasn't a *smidgeon* to indicate that Cara Bernstein had been anywhere near the place.'

'It may mean nothing.'

'It may mean a lot. Think about it. Anyway — and note, I'm asking your permission now — I'd like to ask Kate for the key to Cara's locker in the ladies' cloakroom. We need to look in there.'

Michael glanced at her determined face and nodded. 'Of course. Yes, we should do that.'

'There's another thing. David Cunningham told you he'd been to Cara's apartment and it was locked and he couldn't tell whether her car was in the garage. Is there some way we can find out whether she still has the lease? Or whether she has left Arras altogether?'

'How might we do that?'

'Perhaps through Jules . . .'

Not a silly idea, thought Michael. Jules Ferrer was an old friend who worked at some bureaucratic job in city administration. Town planning, was it? From time to time he had been able to help smooth out difficulties between the school and local authorities. He would possibly know how they could find out.

'Good idea,' said Michael. 'I'll give him a call this afternoon.'

A young adult novel . . .

This newly discovered snippet intrigued David. He longed to find out more and resolved to speak to Steffi as soon as he could. Not in the crowded corridors; he would have to snatch a few moments after a class with a break following.

However, even as he thought about Steffi he felt a pang of misgiving. Every now and again since the term began he had become aware of a subtle shift in Steffi's attitude towards him. Previously, if their paths had crossed in the corridor, Steffi usually in the company of a group of friends, she would treat him to a small complicit wave, sometimes a larger smile, and on the odd gratifying occasion a smile that was actually radiant. This, David understood, was because of her favoured student status: he tremendously admired Steffi's academic ability, her maturity, imagination and dedication. She was a star in his eyes and he had no hesitation in letting her know.

Perhaps because of this, Steffi had often indicated — subtly — how much she relished his classes and his style of teaching.

But since the start of this term he had sensed a standoffishness. In the corridors there were no waves or smiles. Rather, a quick averting of eyes, a loud comment to a friend or another student passing by, allowing her to ignore him. In class she was as attentive as ever, but offering nothing more than you would expect of a diligent student. He somehow sensed that his chances of getting any information out of Steffi had taken an inexplicable dive, and along with them his hopes of getting hold of the draft manuscript.

Of course it could all be his imagination. He comforted himself that his suspicions may be quite groundless, and he was determined to try.

In the meantime he would look more closely at the Grimm Brothers' tale.

Despite the quite large sums parents and caregivers shelled out in fees, Huntingdon had a somewhat inadequate library and David was unable to find a copy of *Grimms' Fairy Tales* on its shelves. However, the internet provided more information than he needed on the Brothers Grimm and the frog prince story Cara was allegedly basing her novel on.

He did not have to search far. In every edition of the tales he came across, 'The Frog Prince' was the very first story featured.

David was puzzled. He had hoped — foolishly, he now realised — that her choice of story might have been a subtle key of some sort; might suggest something about Cara herself, her obsessions, her feelings about life and love. Some clue.

Fiction upon fiction upon truth.

An utterly foolish wild-goose chase, of course.

'The Frog Prince' was full of the usual folk-tale tropes: deep, dark forests, princes and princesses, enchantment and metamorphosis, and above all: Happy Ever After.

Could he have been a frog Cara had magicked into a prince? Wishful thinking, he saw immediately. Whatever he was to Cara, it hadn't been a prince. He may well have been a frog, but then Cara's manuscript had no doubt been written before they became an item. Not a prince. Probably not a frog . . .

If there was a key to Cara in all of this, it had long been lost down the back of the sofa.

Futility ruled.

He really needed to see Cara's manuscript to have any hope of making sense of this.

Which, of course, led back to Steffi Fox.

Shortly after lessons ended for the day Miranda went to her husband's office.

'Anything?' she asked.

'I was just coming to look for you,' he replied. 'I've not long heard back from Jules. Cara has done a bunk.'

'Of course she's done a bunk!'

'He managed to find the name of the landlady. Cara must have come straight back here from Bonn. She told the woman that her father had had a severe stroke in the States and was hospitalised, and that she had to leave France immediately to care for her mother. She offered to pay quite a sum to escape the lease at such short notice. Jules said she loaded her car and left more or less the same day.'

'That would have been when?'

'Early last week. Probably just before David Cunningham got back.'

'Curiouser and curiouser.'

'I suppose we've sorted out one thing,' said Michael. 'It doesn't look as if she intends returning to Huntingdon.'

'Certainly doesn't look like it,' said Miranda.

'But why not tell the school about this personal drama with her parents? Why tell the landlady all that and tell us zilch?'

'I suppose if she wanted to get out of the flat she had to come up with some kind of reason. She had no need to tell us anything.'

'Still, it's odd.'

'It's only odd if you believe the story.' Miranda gave a wry laugh. 'Typical landlady. If Cara had hoped the sob story might have got her off paying the penalty she must have been pretty quickly disabused.'

'I suppose you have checked her locker?'

'Clean as a whistle. Everything gone.'

'I see.'

'Kate said she was certain Cara kept stuff in the locker. Some wet-weather gear: boots, a raincoat and a brolly. She thought another coat and a puffer jacket. That sort of thing.'

Michael pondered the implications of this before looking up at his wife. 'Beats me.'

Miranda, who was way ahead of him on that front, said, 'I know one thing: Cara Bernstein planned to do a runner long before she went off with poor old David Cunningham to Bonn. She must have cleared all of her stuff from her classroom and the locker before she went on leave.'

'Unless she's had someone else do it for her.'

'Who? You don't believe that.'

'I suppose not.'

'If she'd done this after she came back from Bonn, surely somebody would have seen her — or her car. You've been here, and Kate, quite a few of the other staff.'

'Quite so,' said Michael. 'She's not been in.'

'So this means,' said Miranda, 'that her disappearance was not the sudden, spontaneous thing everybody's been puzzled by. It's something she carefully planned. And that's another reason why I take the father-in-hospital-with-a-massive-stroke story with a massive grain of salt!'

That Friday night David had persuaded himself that Arlene Abramson's story of Cara and Angus Paton having had some sort of affair was so unlikely it was almost certainly some fabrication of Miranda's. The account of Angus's alleged confession he put down to Angus's typical mischief-making and delight in mixing it.

However, over the weekend the story preyed on him; he agonised that there might just have been a grain of truth in it. Part of the problem was Cara's hermetic nature. If there had been an affair, it would not have been within her to allude to it in any way. The possibility now began to gnaw at him.

He didn't believe it likely, and yet, and yet . . .

The shock of her leaving had forced him to adjust all that he had thought real, as if he could no longer rely on the evidence of his senses. In one fell swoop everything had turned upside down.

As he had become increasingly attracted to Cara he had focused almost every thought on her: her manner, her words, her movements, her clothes even. Surely, during this period of growing infatuation he would have been especially alert to any rival. But he had noticed nothing.

And yet, and yet . . .

Perhaps infatuation itself had blinded him.

As lessons ended on Monday, he felt an urge to find Angus and talk to him. He knew this would be delicate, and that he was opening himself up to possible ridicule, but he *needed* to know.

David left his classroom and made his trepidatious way to Angus's art room. Ordinarily he liked art rooms. He liked their colourful chaos, the evidence of practical, hands-on work everywhere: splatters, marks and stains; and he liked the smell of paint and turpentine. He had always enjoyed art and considered himself to possess something of a talent. However, his father had not been encouraging. Whenever he'd visited Angus in his art room, David always felt a wistful nostalgia.

Today, however, the awkwardness of his purpose had wiped away any nostalgia. He merely felt apprehension.

Thus it was almost with a sense of relief that he discovered the art room deserted. No pupils had stayed behind to work on some masterpiece.

Angus was quite relaxed about students working in his room out of class time; in fact he encouraged it.

The man himself was nowhere to be seen either. He had most likely retreated to the staffroom for a coffee, David decided.

He really should have made for the staffroom himself to find Angus but he was reluctant. There would undoubtedly be others there as well, and a private talk with Angus would be difficult. Particularly since Angus loved an audience. He could see David's fumbling questions (David knew he would be fumbling) as an opportunity for mockery. Public mockery.

Another time perhaps.

Still he lingered. Angus might not be long. David wandered about the room studying the art on display. It was impressive. Angus was an excellent teacher who brought out the best in mediocre students and brilliance in the talented.

In one corner of the large room was a glassed-in inner sanctum: Angus's office. The door was open and David went in. He would wait there for Angus's return. There was Angus's office chair and a desk, a large table really, covered with paper, sketchbooks and all manner of equipment. Angus was a believer in the principle that creativity springs out of chaos.

David sat down on the tall, leather-covered stool that Angus kept for visitors and for students he needed to interview. Perched up high, David felt almost like a student again.

There was a cabinet beside Angus's table. It was far and away the neatest thing in the room: a white enamel set of document drawers, probably for housing artwork. David glanced at his watch, wondering whether he was wasting his time. Perhaps he should cut his losses and leave. At that point, curiosity overcoming him, he crossed to the cabinet and pulled open the top drawer.

Almost immediately he realised that this was Angus's own work. He worked in chalk, occasionally augmenting it with subtle pastel colouring. There were twenty or so drawings, separated by large squares of soft crêpe paper. Angus was no modernist; the drawings were without exception realistic. Buildings mainly, some of which David recognised from Arras, others presumably of places in local villages: a barn, a small patisserie, a picturesque church.

They were very good. Despite Angus's personal extroversion, the drawings were muted, delicate and softly refined. David was surprised.

He opened the next drawer.

He drew in his breath. The top drawing was of a nude woman lying on her back. One leg was drawn across the other, knee uppermost, artfully hiding her pudenda. Her large-nippled breasts rose proudly but her head was turned to one side, as if not wanting to observe the artist as he examined her nudity. Her dark hair was arranged in a full chignon, but wispy at the edges and somewhat messy, as though ready to fall.

David placed the drawing on top of the cabinet to study the next one.

It was the same woman, this time kneeling and facing front. Her hands were pushing up her breasts provocatively. She was staring directly at the artist this time, her expression challenging, a sardonic pout, and her hair had been set free so that it tumbled about her shoulders. It was almost a soft-porn pose and David felt a little contaminated by it.

The third picture was drawn from an unusual angle. Again the woman was on her back, her head in the foreground, her body stretched away. The artist had sketched from above her left shoulder. This time the head was leaning back, the hair falling on either side, the lips half open, the breasts splayed, the legs languorously spread, the dark thatch of pubic hair carefully crayoned in — no artistic concealment this time.

David felt a choking tightness in his chest.

In each drawing it had been the same woman.

Cara Bernstein.

'Quite beautiful, isn't she?'

David had not heard Angus's approach.

He spun around guiltily. Then he turned back and hastily gathered the drawings off the top of the cabinet and returned them to the drawer.

'Sorry, Angus. Didn't mean to pry. Dropped in to see you—'

'Yeah, I can see that.'

David turned to face Angus, who was looking at him with a quizzical expression.

'It's Cara, isn't it?'

'Is that a compliment to my skill? If so, thank you. Glad to accept it.'

There was a silence.

'I didn't know,' David said.

'Didn't know what?'

'That you had . . . that she . . .' He was fumbling. He knew he would fumble.

'Had posed for me?'

David nodded. It wasn't what he had meant but he nodded all the same.

'No reason why you would.'

David turned again and pushed the drawer shut.

'So, what was it?'

'I'm sorry?'

'You said you'd dropped in to see me. Why?'

David felt the deep hostility in Angus and his mouth became dry. This had been the worst possible start and he had no idea how to go on. Angus took a mouthful of his coffee. His expression had become more mocking. He had the upper hand and they both knew it. Angus was clearly enjoying himself.

Finally David managed to say, 'Arlene came to see me the other night.'

'Lucky old you!'

'Yes . . . She told me that you and Cara were—'

'Were what?'

'I mean, she said Miranda thought—'

'Miranda thinks lots of things,' said Angus. 'Most of them are stupid, and when they're not stupid they're usually unpleasant.'

'Probably,' said David.

'Not probably, Davy boy, certainly. She's said some pretty choice things about you and all, by the way.'

David, not terribly surprised, said nothing.

'So, you came hot-footing along to the horse's mouth to check his teeth, did you?'

'I wouldn't put it like that—'

'How would you put it?'

'It just occurred to me—'

'What just occurred to you? That Cara Bernstein actually had a life before you and she started cavorting with unicorns and bluebells? What *do* you want to know? That she goes off like a rocket? You of all people shouldn't have to ask that, or didn't you get that far?'

'There's no need—'

'There *is* a need. Who gave you the right to come into my office, open my drawers and perv through my drawings like some *Penthouse*-obsessed teenager?'

'I didn't mean—'

'Of course you bloody meant.'

'Okay, okay. I ought to go.'

'You absolutely should. But to satisfy your prurience, yes, we did have a whatever word you were struggling to find. And very pleasant it was, too. I should add that by mutual agreement we didn't feel like flaunting it before the world, especially before this shitty little hothouse called Huntingdon Interpenetration School. Savvy?'

David nodded, unable to meet Angus's eyes.

'Or not,' said Angus.

'What?'

'Or we didn't. Savvy?'

'I don't understand.'

'We did . . . or we didn't. We remained chaste as holy nuns the whole fucking time.'

'I'm not sure—'

'What I'm saying is, believe whatever you want to believe. I don't give a sod either way!'

David could find no response.

'Happy?'

'Not really. I'm sorry, Angus. I've kind of fucked up, I know. I'm not really—'

'What are you really?'

'It's just that . . . if you had been close to Cara you might have some idea why she took off like that.'

'Didn't we thrash that out at dinner the other night?'

'Yes but—'

Sorry, old son. Nothing to add. Your guess and all that.'

Cara's
Manuscript

In her dream Mathilde was lost in the forest but strangely unafraid. There were paths going every which way but Mathilde knew it mattered not which path she followed. They were like the lines on Oma's face — all paths would lead her to safety, although there may be unexpected encounters, adventures even, along her journey.

Somewhere, too, she knew there would be her prince, the one who would shepherd her home. She knew she would not recognise him at first, but that did not matter, for ultimately he would be revealed.

And so, like Little Redcap, she lingered in glades gathering wildflowers — violets, golden cinquefoil, the bluest of bugloss, yellow larkspur, red poppies, white asphodel — until she had an armload. Then, shedding flowers as she wandered, she took a random path once more. Even though the dark trunks pressed ever closer together and the shadows grew ever deeper, she felt no apprehension.

Shapes moved. Things scurried up the trunks of trees. Squirrels, or creatures more sinister, she did not know. There were noises, too. Snuffling, shuffling, the snap of twigs, but these did not alarm her.

Her prince, Jacob — for although he had not appeared, he had been revealed — was near, she knew, just off the path, tracking her journey. She was comforted by this, exhilarated, and even in her dream she felt herself smiling as she broke into a run, shedding more flowers as she ran ever deeper into the deepening darkness.

Helga and Mathilde, in black mourning, were enduring a long afternoon in their bedroom. Mathilde was trying to read a novel; Helga, chin in hand, leaned on the windowsill gazing out at the street. Her expression was morose.

Finally, she turned and asked her sister, 'Do you think Mutti would object if we were to visit the brothers?'

Mathilde glanced up at her. 'You know she would. In any case, Papa certainly would not allow it.'

Helga turned, slumping back on the windowsill.

'This is so frustrating. It feels like . . .'

'What?'

'That we are prisoners in our own home.'

Mathilde felt her sister's frustration but saw no point complaining about it. She turned back to *The Sorrows of Young Werther* but found herself reading the same paragraph over and over. She cast the book to one side and sighed.

'We told their sister we would come back with that story,' said Helga.

'There's nothing we can do about it right now,' said Mathilde.

Helga shrugged. 'We could write to them,' she said.

Mathilde started. In her misery this was not something she had considered, but it was an excellent idea. Lotte may be wondering why they had not returned, the brothers too. It would be polite to offer the brothers an explanation and a reassurance that their errand had not been forgotten, but that unforeseen circumstances had intervened.

Tragic circumstances.

Oma's death.

Mathilde's brow furrowed.

'Well?' demanded Helga.

'Yes,' she replied. 'It's a good idea, an excellent idea. But, Helga, it must be carefully done.'

'Carefully done?'

Mathilde pondered the problem. It was delicate.

'It might be best,' she said, 'that we do not mention Oma's death. It might be better to say only that there has been a death in the family.'

Helga looked at her curiously. 'Whyever?' she asked.

'Think about it,' said Mathilde. 'Oma supplied our stories. We were delivering Oma's stories to the brothers. If they learn that she has passed away they will probably feel we do not have a lot more to offer.'

'And they would be right,' said Helga sombrely.

Mathilde nodded. 'Poor Oma. Why did this have to happen?'

Dear Herr Grimm, wrote Mathilde, then, reconsidering, reached for a second sheet of paper.

> My dear Herr Grimm,
>
> We (my sister Helga and I) were very sorry to miss you the morning we called and met your dear sister.
>
> It was our intention, as we told your sister, to return with the story — the first story — I had written out for you.
>
> Alas, I must tell you there has been a death in the family and this has prevented us from fulfilling our promise to your sister and, through her, to your brother and yourself.
>
> Please know, dear Herr Grimm, that as soon as it is appropriate, my sister and I will present ourselves at your house to deliver the promised manuscript.
>
> Until that time I remain your most faithful servant,
>
> Mathilde Heller

Jacob Grimm read the letter with some puzzlement and passed it to Wilhelm.

'What do you make of this, brother?'

Lotte had told them of the sisters' visit and how they hoped to return with the text of the original story. The fact that they had not actually turned up had hardly registered. Now this letter . . .

Wilhelm studied the note and smiled at Jacob.

'It would appear that you have an admirer, brother.'

'Would it?'

'See for yourself: "My dear Herr Grimm", "dear Herr Grimm". When did you become so dear?'

'A little excessive,' agreed Jacob, 'but mere politeness, surely.'

'Perhaps, but it occurs to me that this Fräulein Heller would rather fancy herself as your most faithful servant, don't you think?'

'Fiddlesticks!'

'I don't believe so.'

'It's just the way people end letters.'

Wilhelm read the letter once more and added, 'And another thing puzzles me.'

'Which is?'

Wilhelm tugged at his chin. 'Why, if she sent you a letter, did she not enclose the text of that story? If it comes to that,' he added, 'why did she not give the story to Lotte to hand on to us when she last visited?'

'I have no idea,' said Jacob.

'I believe Fräulein Heller is laying siege to you. I believe she is orchestrating another reason to return to the house.'

'Again, fiddlesticks!'

Wilhelm passed the letter back to his brother. 'I do hope that this death in the family is not that of the grandmother. I was quite intrigued by that variant of the Little Redcap story Fräulein Heller brought us. The old lady promises to be a most valuable source.'

'Amen to that,' said Jacob.

'Mathilde, what are we going to do?' asked Helga. There was a note of trouble in her voice.

'How do you mean?'

'I mean, with that story you've written out we have a reason to call on the brothers — once we are allowed to leave this wretched house. But how can we contrive to visit them again after that?'

'I suppose we must find another story.'

'How? From whom?'

Mathilde did not reply. It was a problem she had been pondering. How would they find another story? Oma had been the only one of her generation in their immediate family. Mutti was not much interested in stories and Mathilde was quite certain Papa did not even know what a story was. Only *facts* were worthy of his attention; novels were the exclusive domain of women and thus unworthy of serious attention.

She stared helplessly at Helga. Their own little store of half-remembered nursery tales from Oma's whispering them asleep when they were young was useless. Those they could remember in their entirety would already be in the brothers' collection, and scattered fragments would not interest them.

'What can we do?' Helga would not let it go.

Mathilde could think of nothing. She smiled. It seemed Helga's need to see the brothers was as great as her own. Then again, how could it be? Mathilde had touched his hand, held his fingers, looked into his eyes. Her need was so strong she could almost touch it, squeeze it, hold it to her breast.

It was Helga who, eyes shining, came up with the solution. Brilliant, clever Helga!

Two days later. Two long days, two long evenings later they were in bed, the candles extinguished. Mathilde was on the verge of sleep when she became aware that Helga was whispering her name.

'What is it?'

'Are you asleep?'

Mathilde turned to her sister, rubbing her eyes. 'I'm not now,' she grumbled. 'Why aren't you asleep?'

'Because I've been going over and over in my mind how we can find a story for the brothers.'

'And?'

'I do know the way, and it's so obvious!'

Helga's excitement was infectious. Mathilde sat up. 'Tell me!'

'We write one ourselves!'

'Ourselves? But—'

'Don't you see? We know the sort of stories Oma told: forests, witches, wolves, princesses and princes. We could write a story like that!'

'But it wouldn't be an ancient tale. The brothers—'

'How would they know? It would sound like an ancient tale.'

Mathilde lay on her back staring at the ceiling. It might work. In fact in many ways this would be better than trying to find a genuinely ancient tale. With an old story there was every likelihood the brothers would have recorded it before. A story she and Helga wrote would be a complete novelty to the brothers. Almost certainly they would be delighted with the find, would treasure it, would be grateful to them for bringing it, would almost certainly beg them to bring more.

There was very little possibility of sleep after that. Mathilde's mind was racing with story ideas. She tried to remember dreams she had had; she suspected many of the tales Oma told them had their origins in dreams. In any case they were dreamlike, full of strange juxtapositions — marvellous creatures, talking animals, magic and miracles.

As her mind scurried over possible scenarios, another idea began to take hold. This idea had its source in her wanting to impress Jacob, to earn his gratitude. Somehow, her story could be a parable. It could include a secret message pertaining to her secret love. The story could contain a seed . . . No, the story could *be* a seed, a seed that could sprout and grow, tall and green and mighty, the tallest tree in the forest.

The wonder of it excited her and she rolled to one side, then to the other and back again until Helga murmured grumpily, 'For goodness' sake, sister, go to sleep! You're keeping me awake.'

After breakfast they excused themselves and returned to their bedroom.

Earlier, a little breathlessly, Mathilde had described to Helga the idea that had come to possess her so strongly it had kept her awake much of the night: the idea of a story containing a hidden message.

'Like a parable?'

'More an allegory, or perhaps an analogy would be even better,' replied Mathilde, smiling.

'Could we do this?' Helga asked.

'We could try,' Mathilde laughed. 'It could be wonderful. It could be a seed.'

'Or a key,' suggested Helga.

Indeed, a key: a key to the closed-up Jacob. It was a delicious metaphor. Could they do it?

Mathilde, in her excitement, was sure they could.

Now, with quill, ink and a sheet of paper they sat down together at the little escritoire in their bedroom.

'First of all,' Helga mused, 'obviously you must be in the story and so must Herr Grimm.'

'Of course,' agreed Mathilde. 'What of Herr Wilhelm?'

Helga shook her head. 'No,' she said. 'Too complicated. Let's keep things simple so the message is not compromised.'

'You're quite right. The message must not be compromised. But what is the message to be?'

Helga laughed. 'Don't be silly! It is the oldest message: love conquers all! Write it down!'

Mathilde smiled at her sister, dipped her quill in the inkwell and carefully inscribed: *Love conquers all.*

'Next problem,' said Helga, 'is how does love conquer all?'

Mathilde closed her eyes considering this, and what it might be that love had to conquer. She tried to recapture some of the fleeting, evanescent images and story ideas that had flickered through her racing brain the previous night.

'There has to be an obstacle,' Helga said.

'Or obstacles.'

'Probably.'

'Clearly, too,' said Mathilde, 'the maiden must rescue the prince.'

'Maiden? Prince?'

'Haven't we decided that? I must be the maiden and Herr Grimm must be the prince. I must rescue him.'

'Must you? Could not Herr Grimm, I mean the prince, rescue you?'

After considering this briefly, Mathilde shook her head. 'No, it's best that the prince should be grateful to the maiden, rather than the maiden grateful to the prince. It is a much better message.'

'So,' asked Helga, 'who should this maiden be? A poor girl? One who lives near the forest like Little Redcap?'

Again, Mathilde shook her head. 'No, Little Redcap would be too young, too poor. When love conquers all, she would be too beholden to the prince for elevating her. To my mind, the heroine must be a princess.'

'Of course. The prince's equal.'

'Quite so. But you were right to remind me about the forest. We must have a forest. The maiden must be a princess who lives in a castle near the forest.'

'Write it down!'

Mathilde bent again to the paper.

'So,' Helga continued, 'there must be an obstacle or obstacles. The prince, I imagine, must have a problem. Something the princess can rescue him from.'

Mathilde nodded, smiling. This was fun.

'What's it to be, then?' continued Helga. 'Is he a prisoner? Is he trapped in a tower? Perhaps he could be the captive of a witch in her creepy cottage in the forest.'

'These are excellent ideas.'

'I'm just trying to think of obstacles.'

All at once Mathilde saw a way through. 'Of course!' she said. 'He is enchanted. The prince is enchanted!'

'You mean enchanting?'

'No, enchanted. The prince is under a spell, and the princess is somehow able to release him from it.'

'Wonderful!'

'It would mean magic.'

'And cleverness.'

'Metamorphosis!' declared Mathilde, things becoming even clearer in her mind.

'Metamorphosis?'

'The prince has been changed into something and the princess somehow manages to restore him.'

'But into what?' asked Helga. 'A tree? A statue? What about a bird?'

To each of these suggestions Mathilde shook her head.

And all at once — complete clarity.

'I have it,' she said with excitement. 'A frog!'

David's Story

In the two and a half years he had worked at Huntingdon, David Cunningham had come to enjoy the region of northern France surrounding Arras. Arras itself he found a fascinating little city. Largely destroyed during the horrific battles of World War I, it had painstakingly rebuilt itself so that its squares, churches and public buildings, even its terraced shophouses, betrayed no sign that they had not been there for centuries. It was as if the war had never happened.

This was, however, misleading, for the war was still omnipresent in the vast memorial cemeteries with their endless geometries of white crosses; geometries that might have appeared monotonous were it not for their implications, their reality so throat-catching.

There were the more architectural memorials: Vimy Ridge with its soaring wings of white stone, Delville Wood, Amiens, Albert and literally hundreds of others, including the beautiful Memorial to the Missing in Arras. All white, all reverential.

If these weren't enough, the very landscape — although softened, of course, after more than a hundred years with grass and trees — was scarred and dimpled by the years of shelling and slaughter. In places trenches remained and some fields were still fenced off by barbed wire because beneath their soft green grass lay sleeping munitions liable to burst into life and murder.

He had discovered that to be a New Zealander in Arras was to have a special distinction. Near the town was the Carrière Wellington, a museum built on the site of an ancient chalk quarry. Here, five hundred or so New Zealand miners — coalminers from the West Coast and Otago, goldminers from the Coromandel — had been recruited to dig tunnels beneath the German lines so British troops could attack the German front lines. They dug kilometres of secret passageways beneath no-man's land. They needed to do this particularly quietly because of the enemy overhead. British miners joined the New Zealanders in this work: small, wiry men from the Midlands, from Midlothian.

The project was dangerous and difficult, but the enterprise was successful — initially at least. Eleven thousand troops used the tunnels to launch a surprise attack in early April 1917, pushing the Germans back several kilometres. However, as was typical in trench warfare, the attack soon bogged down into stalemate and the casualties grew to horrific proportions.

David had visited the museum on a number of occasions. It was not so much a museum as a *son et lumière* display. A small section of tunnel had been restored with displays and sound effects. A lift took visitors underground, where they followed a guided pathway. Graffiti from the time was preserved: drawings and, with especial resonance for David, place names given to stations along the tunnels: Christchurch, Dunedin, Wellington. There were sound effects and illuminations, dioramas and relics. The effects were subtle and convincing and the experience very moving.

When he had let slip on his first visit with Cara that he was from New Zealand he was all at once welcomed like an old friend. It was almost as if he himself had toiled underground on the brave project to save France from *le Boche*.

Being a New Zealander at Huntingdon, however, held no such special cachet. What had Angus called the place? A hothouse.

Even in his agitation at the time of his humiliation, David recognised the truth of this description. Huntingdon *was* a hothouse. Mainly this was because most of the staff lived in small apartments in the residential wing of the chateau. Only a few, such as Cara, lived in Arras or in one or other of the small towns in the neighbourhood. This meant there was a forced togetherness. Working together, dining together, gathering in the school staffroom or the common room in the residential wing: there was a claustrophobia about this that drove him out to his regular explorations of the countryside.

He had made few, if any, real friends. There had been Eric Wilson, another English teacher, an Australian with whom he had established a superficial antipodean bond. But Eric had left a year ago and the emails soon petered out.

The exception was Cara Bernstein.

He had been curious about her. As he grew familiar with her he grew to like her, and then to like her more and more.

*C*ontext changes.

Sometimes Cara would join him on his sightseeing trips.

'This isn't too morbid for you?' he asked as they wandered around yet another memorial site on a former battlefield.

'Not morbid,' Cara replied, 'but unsettling.'

'I know what you mean.'

'Do you really? I mean, it's the contrast between what this place has become and what it must have been like in 1917. It's so utterly beautiful today, isn't it? The trees, the grass, the silence.'

'I suppose that's the point.'

'But is it the right point? Just imagine what it must have been like, this very spot. The destruction, the carnage, the barbed wire, the mud, the blood ... There probably wasn't a blade of grass left, let alone a tree.'

'The noise, too.' David all at once remembered Wilfred Owen. 'You know, shrill demented choirs of wailing shells. Was that it? And gunfire and screaming, no doubt.'

'And now what? Birds, rustling leaves and visitors whispering,' said Cara.

David glanced at her, nodding. She was quite right. Almost instinctively, the serenity of the place had caused them to speak softly. He couldn't imagine anybody shouting here; it would somehow define sacrilege.

'Should it be more like it was back then?' he asked. 'Barbed wire, mud and shell holes?'

She considered this. 'No,' she said. 'I don't think so. I'm not sure what I want, really. It's just that ... I mean, this place is not a lie, I'm not saying that. But it is somehow denying reality.'

'I don't think that's what it's trying to do. Isn't its purpose to remember and respect the poor sods who died here and what they did — you know, *supreme sacrifice* — by giving them a beautiful resting place? A pilgrimage site of sorts for their families and descendants, and for visitors like us?'

Cara did not immediately respond. She had walked some metres ahead down one of the endless lines between the identical white gravestones. Now she turned back and said, 'That's why it's so unsettling. They're still *here*. All those thousands of dead, the named and the unnamed. They're still here. We're walking among them.'

'Resting in peace,' said David, 'in a place of beauty fit for heroes.' He wasn't trying to be ironic.

'Don't be such a sentimentalist. They weren't heroes. I mean, some of them were, no doubt. Most were probably teenage boys scared out of their wits. None of them wanted to die. They were just cannon fodder.'

David remembered the Dawn Parades at the Christchurch Cenotaph. He had attended with his mother when he was young, and later on his own — on those occasions when he could be arsed getting out of bed early enough. His grandfather, his mother's father, had served in Egypt and later in Italy. His father, on the other hand, never observed Anzac Day. The old man didn't talk about it much, but David had worked out that it had something to do with Vietnam.

On those cold, sometimes wet, grey mornings he knew he was supposed to feel gratitude towards the fallen for falling, and on those mornings, red poppy pinned to his jacket, he mostly did.

'And anyway,' said Cara, returning to him, possibly to avoid raising her voice despite their being the only visitors to the cemetery that morning, 'the dead *aren't* resting. The dead are dead.'

David did not reply but reached for her hand. *This place is getting to you*, he thought and wanted to comfort her.

For some time they walked in silence hand in hand until Cara said, 'I need coffee and I need food. Had enough?'

He had. 'Sure. Me too. Let's find some cheerful little patisserie with excellent coffee and great pâté.'

'We're in France,' said Cara, smiling. 'Could be difficult.'

As they left the cemetery, through a gateway built to resemble a miniature Arc de Triomphe in white marble, Cara made an odd observation.

'Do you know what these places remind me of?'

'I'm sure you're going to tell me.'

'Refrigerators.'

'What?'

'I don't know — they're so clinical, so clean, so white and mechanical.'

'But—'

'And designed to preserve.'

'Do you really—'

'And another thing, isn't it weird how the temperature always seems lower in these places? Even on a warm day there's a slight chill.'

David was about to remonstrate, tell her not to get carried away, when he realised that he felt that too. The day did feel warmer once they had passed out of the entrance.

A few days after his conversation with Arlene Abramson, David noticed that Steffi Fox was still packing her bag after most of the other seniors had left the classroom. This was the opportunity he had been waiting for. Every other day this term she had hurried away after class with a uncharacteristic alacrity.

'Steffi?' he said.

She looked up. Steffi was usually a reserved, serious student, her manner a little at odds with her great flounce of Little Orphan Annie red hair.

'Mr Cunningham?'

'I wonder . . . could we have a word?'

Steffi glanced at the door, which was still wide open.

'Sure.' She zipped her backpack, slung it over her shoulder and approached David's desk. Everything in her actions told David she intended the interview to be a very short one and he wondered why.

He waited until she reached the desk before saying, 'I was speaking to Ms Abramson the other day and she mentioned that Ms Bernstein had written a book. She said you had been helping her.'

Steffi nodded: waiting, not helping.

'I wondered whether you'd be able to tell me about it. You see, I knew nothing about it and—'

'Why?'

David was finding this difficult. 'It's just that we — Ms Bernstein and I — we were really good friends and I was a little surprised to hear about the book and . . .'

He petered out. Steffi glanced again at the door.

'What is the book about?'

'It's about "The Frog Prince".'

'The Grimm story?'

'Yes.'

'So is it about the story itself, or a version of the story or—'

'Mr Cunningham, why don't you ask Ms Bernstein—'

'I would if I could, Steffi. Trouble is, I'm not sure where she is.'

She frowned at him. 'But if you were really good friends . . .'

Somehow Steffi managed to give *really good friends* an oily flavour.

David shrugged. 'I know . . . Do you have a copy of the manuscript?'

Steffi nodded again but did not elaborate. Instead she said, 'Is the fact that you were *really good friends* the reason she left?'

David noted Steffi's resentful face. This is the reason, he realised. I'm being blamed.

'Why do we have to have Mrs Bastion?'

'I've no idea why Ms Bernstein left,' David said. 'I wish I knew. But I'm absolutely certain it had nothing to do with me.' In the face of Steffi's sceptical look he felt obliged to amend this. 'I'm sorry, *very little* to do with me.'

Now David glanced at the door. How did I get into this? Just a friendly little chat about Cara's book and I'm being interrogated by a student about my bloody love life.

'Could you please let me see it?' he asked once more, knowing even as he asked what the answer would be.

Steffi adjusted her bag. Clearly for her, the interview was over. 'I couldn't do that, Mr Cunningham,' she said. 'That's not my decision. It'd have to be Ms Bernstein's.'

Context changes. It was one of the few lines David regularly recalled from their conversation in the forest at Venusberg. He couldn't help but be reminded of it as he wandered yet again around the Memorial to the Missing in Arras.

It, too, was beautiful. They were all beautiful. Particularly this long building with its colonnades and cool cloisters like a parenthesis wrapped around the pattern of full stops that were the white headstones. So many of these were for New Zealanders. At least their nationality was known even if their names were not.

'Aren't you a little obsessive about these places?' Cara had asked him on one occasion. 'Wouldn't you rather be in Paris?'

'We've been to Paris.'

They had, too. Twice. Once in Cara's Peugeot and once on the intercity TGV.

'You're avoiding the issue.'

David thought. Was he obsessive? Why did he visit and revisit the sites?

'I reckon it's because,' he said slowly, 'they're sort of good for me in a spiritual sense.'

'God help us,' laughed Cara. 'That sounds so hair-shirty!'

'Don't tease. I mean these places put everything in perspective, don't they?'

'Do they?'

'They really do. How can you be depressed about stuff in your little world — you know, pissed off with the kids you teach, with the fools at work — when this . . .'

He gestured about him. Cara waited.

'There are just so many of them. So many thousands upon thousands who all had lives, dreams cut short.'

Cara looked at him.

'You know, David, sometimes I can't work out whether you're Hamlet or Pollyanna.'

'Oh, Pollyanna probably,' said David. 'If there's a difference . . .'

Now, with Cara vanished from his world for over a fortnight, he was discovering that the *putting things in perspective* theory just wasn't working any more. He found it a little ironic that he had arrived at the Memorial to the Missing in the hope of finding some relief. Cara's being absent from his life loomed as large ever, despite his wandering the long cloisters with their views of the serried headstones. His own pain and confusion had not been alleviated one jot; in fact he was about to leave, wondering why he was wasting his time, when he heard a voice.

He didn't recognise it at first, but when he looked up he saw Arlene Abramson waving at him. He waved back, surprised to find that he rather welcomed her interruption.

'Hi, Arlene.'

'Fancy meeting you here,' she said, coming up to him. 'Have you been here before?'

'I do come occasionally,' he said. 'You?'

'Not often, but yes, from time to time.'

'Actually I was just leaving,' said David, and then, because it might have seemed as though he were giving her the brush-off, he added, 'I thought I might grab a coffee. Like to join me?'

Arlene gave him a quick, gratified smile and said, 'Why not? Sounds very pleasant.'

As they walked to the carpark she named a bistro that David was familiar with and it was agreed.

A little later, over their coffee, she said, 'I suppose you go because of the Kiwis?'

'Kiwis?'

'The New Zealanders buried there.'

He glanced at her. 'Not really, no. I guess they're incidental. I go because of the atmosphere, I suppose. It's usually calming.'

'Usually?'

'Not today.'

'Still no word?'

David shook his head. 'I left her about my seventeenth voicemail in the middle of last night when I couldn't sleep. I don't know why I'm bothering.'

'I believe Michael's going to advertise Cara's job.'

'But has she resigned?'

It was Arlene's turn to shake her head. 'Not as far as I know. I understand Miranda's been on her case and is putting pressure on Michael. I imagine they've decided that she's *de facto* resigned by not turning up, and maintaining a radio silence.'

'I suppose so.'

They sat quietly for some time. It was the first time they had spoken alone together since Arlene visited David in his rooms to tell him about

Angus. David wondered whether he should tell Arlene about having gone to see the art teacher, though he wouldn't have been surprised to find she already knew. The jungle drums at Huntingdon were usually quite alert to sensation.

Nevertheless, he did tell her, but without mentioning the chalk drawings.

'I have to say it wasn't a very comfortable interview,' he said. 'I didn't go about it very well.'

'But he did own up to it?' asked Arlene.

'Oh, yes,' said David. 'Yes, he did. In rather graphic terms. Or rather he did and then he didn't. His ambiguity may have been designed to piss me off.'

'So did you come to a conclusion?'

David considered this, all at once realising that he had.

'I don't believe they did,' he said. 'When he told me they had had something I think it was because he was angry with me. He said it to goad me.'

Arlene reached over and, as she had in his rooms, rested her hand over his. 'Poor boy,' she said. 'But in a way, I have to say I'm a little relieved.'

'Relieved? How so?'

'I've been worried that I may have unnecessarily alarmed you, that I may have been spreading malicious tittle-tattle that contained not an iota of truth.'

'You don't need to worry about that,' said David. 'There probably wasn't an iota of truth. Just Miranda stirring—'

'So did he say anything that might help us understand why she disappeared like that?'

'Not a thing.'

'That's something, I suppose,' said Arlene.

'He would have said, I think. I managed to make him angry, but I don't think he was holding anything back. He has no more idea than I do why she walked off or where she might be. I'm sure of that.'

He sipped his coffee. Arlene had finished hers but showed no signs of wanting to leave.

'Remember you told me Cara had written a novel?' David asked.

Arlene looked at him with some interest.

'That's right. So I did.'

'Yes. Well, actually, I had a word with Steffi Fox.'

'And?'

'The proverbial concrete parachute. I got the impression that Cara's senior French class consider me the big bad wolf.'

'Why on earth?' Arlene seemed surprised.

'Because they have the idea that I had something to do with Cara's disappearance. That, and the fact that they're not mad keen on her replacement. My fault as well, apparently.'

'I see. They know about you and Cara?'

'It wasn't exactly a secret. I did tell Steffi that Cara and I were pretty good friends but I don't think I was telling her anything new.'

'We kid ourselves, don't we,' observed Arlene, 'that the students don't know what's going on. We think we lead private lives, but really we live in a glasshouse.'

'Huntingdon certainly seems to be a glasshouse. At least some of the time.'

'Some of the time the students have help, of course,' added Arlene mysteriously.

'How do you mean?'

'You know — in the war they called it the fifth column.'

'Oh, right.' David realised what she was getting at. 'You think some of the staff—'

Arlene laughed. 'David! Don't be naïve. I *know* some of the staff. If it comes to that, I'm sure that even present company is not always as discreet as it should be.'

This comment irked David a little. He always maintained, he believed, a *professional* discretion. 'So, apart from present company and everybody else, anybody in particular?'

Arlene smiled a little mischievously. 'Well, my first port of call would be their present French teacher.'

Miranda. Of course.

David felt a welling resentment. He had always liked Steffi Fox and thought she liked him. In fact he had been sure of it. It was so disheartening that someone like Miranda Bastion could so easily have sabotaged their relationship.

'So did she tell you anything?' Arlene asked.

'What?'

'Steffi. About Cara's book.'

'Not really. She didn't want to talk at all. She confirmed there was a book and it had something to do with that Grimm brothers' story. Oh, and she did say she had a copy.'

'Is she going to let you see it?'

'No way. She got a little holier than thou and said she could only let me have it with Cara's express permission.'

'Oh.'

There was a silence for some seconds before Arlene said, 'Has Steffi heard from Cara?'

'Oh Christ,' said David. 'It didn't occur to me to ask.'

As he drove through Arras on his way back to the school, a sudden impulse took David back to the street where Cara's apartment was. He stopped the car on the road opposite, looking up at her window on the first floor.

There was a bill posted there:

À Louer
To Let

David climbed out of the Ford and stood for a moment looking at it. Then he took out his notebook and wrote down the name and details of the letting agency.

Cara's
Manuscript

Mathilde tickled her nose with the quill before dipping it once more into the inkwell.

> Once there was a king who had three beautiful
> daughters, but the youngest daughter was the
> most beautiful, with golden hair and a laugh
> that was like music. Close to the king's castle was
> a dark forest and in this forest was the young
> princess's favourite place. A deep pool in a glade.
> There was a well nearby under a . . .

'Linden tree,' suggested Helga, who was standing at her shoulder, reading.

. . . *linden tree* . . . wrote Mathilde.

'Where does she find the frog?' asked Helga. 'The pool or the well?'

'The well,' said Mathilde. 'The well sounds deeper and more mysterious.'

'There must be something to bring them together,' said Helga.

Mathilde considered this. 'I know, a ball,' she suggested. 'She could be playing with a ball and it somehow falls down the well.'

'A golden ball!'

'Excellent!'

'She must be dancing,' said Mathilde. 'Dancing suggests energy and spirit. Throwing her ball up into the air and catching it.'

'And she throws it too high and before she can get to it, it falls down the well,' said Helga. 'Splash!'

'The deep, mysterious well.'

'She would be upset.'

'Of course, she would weep and cry out, "My ball! My golden ball! Who can help me retrieve my golden ball?"'

'Enter the frog!' said Helga.

'Enter the frog,' said Mathilde. 'Exactly.'

Together, the two sisters worked up the story. The frog — large, green, incredibly ugly — would appear after being roused by the cries of the princess. He would leap up onto the edge of the well and ask her why she was crying. She would tell him her precious golden ball had fallen into the well and she had no way of retrieving it. *I could help*, the frog would offer. *How could you help?* the princess would ask, drying her eyes, hope springing in her heart.

I can help, the frog would repeat, *but what would you give me in return?*

The princess clasped her hands together and did a little skipping dance of delight.

'Were you to retrieve my golden ball, dear frog,' she cried, 'I would grant you anything you asked!'

At this promise, the frog leapt from the edge of the well and dived deep, deep into its dark, mysterious waters.

A few moments later his green head and shoulders broke through the surface and he leapt once more onto the brick wall of the well.

In his arms he held the golden ball of the princess.

She was overjoyed and could not help but break into another dance of delight. Then she turned back to the ugly green frog, still squatting upon the edge of the well.

'But what would you ask of me, dear frog?' she asked. 'Now that you have retrieved my golden ball?'

'Very little,' croaked the frog. 'Merely a simple kiss from your lovely lips.'

The princess blanched, for the frog was very ugly,
wet and cold. Yet she remembered that a promise is a
promise, a pledge is a pledge, and so, closing her eyes,
she leaned towards the frog and kissed him gently.
There was a noise she could not identify and,
startled, she opened her eyes.
Standing before her she beheld the most handsome
prince she had ever seen,
He was smiling, but his eyes were filled with tears
of gratitude.

Mathilde read over what she had written, frowning slightly.

Helga, sensing her disquiet, asked, 'What is wrong, sister? It reads very well.'

'It does,' agreed Mathilde, 'but it's too easy. It's all over too soon.'

'More obstacles?'

'Yes,' said Mathilde, turning to her. 'There must be more twists and turns. We don't yet have a story that would convince the brothers.'

'You mean one particular brother, do you not?'

'I do, Helga, I do. One particular brother.'

Mathilde glanced at her sister, smiling, and she tickled her nose with the feather end of her quill as she read through their story once more.

David's Story

— ARRAS —

'**Y**ou did *what*?'

Michael was unconscionably angry. Miranda, for her part, was not in the least abashed.

'I have no idea why you're taking it like this,' she said, assuming that patient tone used to placate a child having a tantrum. The effect of this was to fuel Michael's temper. 'It seems to me a perfectly reasonable thing to have done. The woman has gone missing and put us in a difficult situation. We have no idea of her intentions. It could be that she's had an accident . . . or worse,' she added ominously.

'There is no suggestion she's had an accident!'

'How on earth do you know? This is the whole point. We know nothing, and as her employers we're entitled to know. Surely you can see that?'

Michael was not appeased. 'You should have talked to me about it.'

'I would have,' said Miranda, 'but it was a spur-of-the-moment thing.'

'All the more reason. Spur-of-the-moment things are usually recipes for disaster.'

'Oh, for god's sake, Michael, don't catastrophise. Look, I ran into Jules Ferrer in town and I took the opportunity to thank him for finding out about Cara: you know, the apartment business. We got chatting about it all and he asked whether we'd talked to the police. I hadn't really thought much about that, but he seemed to think it was important we should.'

'There is,' said Michael, 'the small detail of her checking out of the hotel *voluntarily*.'

'If we accept that story,' said Miranda.

'I wish you'd let it alone,' said Michael. 'You really seem to have it in for poor Cunningham.'

'Not in the least.'

'I suppose you suggested to Jules that it was probably white slavers who moved her stuff out of her apartment, paid off her lease and stole her car?'

'Don't be childish! Anyway, Jules said it would be possible to make an *unofficial* inquiry. He said there were things the police could find out quite easily that might allay our fears.'

'Miranda, I don't have any fears.'

'You might not, but *I* naturally have worries.'

'Naturally?'

'In fact Jules came with me. He said he knew people at the station and could help make sure everything was done discreetly.'

'Thank god for that,' said Michael. 'The last thing I want is for any parent to see Huntingdon crawling with police. They might think we're harbouring a murderer, or riddled with drugs or something.'

'You've progressed from childish to ridiculous,' said Miranda, angry herself now. 'They're not likely to send in a SWAT team.'

'So what did they say?'

'We had a private chat with the *commissaire* himself. He was quite intrigued.'

'And did he then ask you to leave?'

'Not at all. He didn't think there was a lot they could do, but they might be able to find out whether she's left the EU. Or possibly whether she's had an accident of some sort.'

'So that's it?'

'Not quite. He said he'd send a lieutenant to talk to people here at Huntingdon who know Cara.'

Michael shook his head wearily. 'Miranda, I do wish you hadn't! This whole thing has been disruptive enough without some bloody Inspector Clouseau coming in and stirring things up.'

'Nothing's going to be stirred up. The *commissaire* promised they would be very discreet.'

'So, any idea when this very discreet lieutenant is going to turn up?'

Miranda studied her phone. 'In about half an hour,' she said brightly.

Inspector Clouseau turned out to be a youngish woman in plain clothes. Shortly after ringing through, Agnès escorted her to Michael's office. He stood up to welcome her before coming around his desk to shake her hand.

'Lieutenant,' Michael said, studying her card.

'Véronique Robert,' said the officer.

Michael guessed she must be in her thirties, nearer thirty than forty. Her dark hair was cut quite short, and she had an olive complexion. Possibly Mediterranean. She was elegantly dressed in a subdued way, and Michael was relieved at this. Anybody seeing her being brought to his office would assume she was a job candidate heading for an interview.

Michael ushered her to a seat and returned to his own.

'I'm bound to say, Lieutenant,' he said, 'that while we're all very concerned at Cara Bernstein's disappearance, I personally did not really believe it a matter that should concern the police.'

Véronique Robert took this with equanimity. 'I quite agree, Monsieur Bastion,' she replied. 'And it doesn't really concern the police yet.'

'But you're here?' Michael said.

'Of course,' said Véronique Robert. 'My visit is quite unofficial. Were it to be official, it would have to have been sanctioned by a magistrate who was convinced that a crime had been committed.' She smiled, and Michael was suddenly taken by her charm. 'And of course,' she continued, 'there is no suggestion of a crime, so . . .' She shrugged.

'So?'

'So I am here simply because the *commissaire* gave an undertaking to Madame Bastion that we would look into the matter. It's not because we feel there is anything to worry about.' Again she smiled.

'In that case, what do you intend to do?'

'There is not a lot we can do,' she said. 'We can try to trace her movements through the document trail. That is the quickest and easiest way to ascertain whether we should be concerned. However, it would be also useful to talk confidentially to Madame Bernstein's friends and colleagues. Some may know more than they have been prepared to let on so far.'

Michael doubted that. He also doubted that Lieutenant Robert would be the one to whom they would open up, given that the gossip machine hadn't already loosened their tongues.

'What can I do?' he asked.

'I hope you will give me the names of those people. I presume you will know who I should speak to. I'd also like you to introduce me to them or, if you're busy, delegate somebody to do that.'

'Of course.'

Michael thought. He could do it himself, but really had better things to do. Agnès Delon would resent being asked and would make her resentment felt.

Miranda. Miranda would be ideal. She had unleashed this whole silly police thing; she could see it through.

'I'd suggest my wife,' he said. 'She's been most concerned about Cara. That's why she went to the police in the first place. She'll know the people you might find it useful to talk to. I'll have my secretary take you to her.'

He stood up, and Véronique Robert stood as well. She's very tall, Michael realised as he reached to shake her hand.

He led her down the short corridor to Agnès's office. 'I'm sorry, Lieutenant,' he said, hand on her elbow, 'but I do rather feel this whole thing is a waste of your time.'

Miranda paused, pen in hand, considering who to add to the list. She and Lieutenant Robert were sitting in the drawing room at the headmaster's lodge. Coffee had been prepared and Véronique Robert sipped at hers thoughtfully. She agreed with the nice headmaster: this was in every way a waste of her time. Still, it was rather pleasant sitting in this comfortable room drinking excellent coffee. She would have a number of fruitless conversations with a number of confused and confusing schoolteachers, then return to the station to find out that the woman had left Europe on the first available flight and returned to her home in the States. What had she told her landlady? Her father had had a severe stroke?

Miranda quickly added two more names then handed her list to Véronique.

'I think this will be it,' she said. 'We're a close, friendly staff so a lot of people knew Cara, although some more closely than others.'

Véronique glanced at the list, her heart sinking. There were probably twenty names on it.

'Is it really necessary to interview so many, Madame Bastion?' she asked. 'Perhaps I will focus on those who knew Madame Bernstein better?'

Miranda, feeling slightly rebuked, stiffened. 'Of course,' she said. 'We should start with those. If you pass me the list I will highlight them.'

Véronique picked up the word 'we' and smiled wryly. Surely this woman didn't think she was going to take part in the interviews? She waited.

'All right,' said Miranda, handing back the list. 'With whom do you want to start?'

Véronique Robert smiled. 'It seems to me, Madame Bastion, that while we're here, I should probably start with you.'

'I've told the *commissaire* all I know already,' said Miranda. She had not realised that she herself would need to be questioned, and rather resented the implication. However, she soon sensed the chance to air some of her suspicions and ideas and she relaxed.

'You have some doubts about Monsieur Cunningham?' the lieutenant asked carefully once Miranda had completed her outline.

'Well, I'm not really trying to suggest anything, but . . .'

'But?'

'There are a couple of worrying things,' said Miranda, entering her element. 'I mean, it does seem to me that he didn't do a lot to find out what had happened before he left Germany. He just up and left straight away.'

'Did he?'

'Pretty much. You must ask him.'

'I will,' said Véronique, 'but what else, in your opinion, should Monsieur Cunningham have done in Bonn, Madame?'

'Oh, I don't know,' said Miranda airily. 'Something, anyway.'

Véronique Robert waited.

'Well,' Miranda said, feeling it incumbent upon her to come up with something else. 'He could have gone to the German police, for instance.'

'But why would he do that?' asked Véronique.

'Oh, I don't know,' repeated Miranda, a little irritated by such wilful obtuseness. 'Because her leaving like that was so out of character; it was such an odd thing to do.'

'I see,' said Véronique Robert, closing her notebook. She stood up.

'Thank you for your time, Madame Bastion. Who do you recommend I see now? Monsieur Cunningham, I expect?'

'He may be teaching,' said Miranda.

'Does that matter? I won't need long. Besides, I imagine that most of the people on your list would be teaching, wouldn't they?'

Miranda knocked on the door of David's classroom and entered. Véronique Robert waited in the corridor.

The class watched Miranda curiously as she strode quickly over to whisper in David's ear. He listened to her hissed message with growing surprise and stood up. Miranda did not attempt any explanation. She merely told him that there was a police officer waiting in the corridor who would like a few words.

The students nearest the teacher's desk clearly heard what was said, and turned to whisper to each other. Miranda then announced that she would be looking after them while Mr Cunningham left to attend to urgent business. David flashed her a frown. She had made it sound as if he were likely to be absent for some time.

He had been expecting a uniformed gendarme rather than the young woman in civilian clothes who waited for him in the corridor.

'Monsieur Cunningham?'

'Yes?'

'My name is Lieutenant Robert. I am with the Arras Police Nationale.'

'Yes?'

'Would we be able to talk somewhere more—'

'Of course. The staffroom?'

'That would be fine.'

David led her to the staffroom, where they sat down.

'Please don't be alarmed, Monsieur Cunningham. This not an official investigation, but there have been some questions raised about the disappearance of your friend—'

'Cara Bernstein?'

'Yes, Madame Bernstein.'

Miranda, thought David angrily. More of her bloody mischief.

'What about her?'

'Would you like to tell me about the circumstances surrounding her disappearance?'

David shrugged. 'If it would help.'

Véronique Robert nodded.

'So you and Madame Bernstein became separated while you were viewing the graves?'

'I wasn't really aware of it at the time,' David said. 'It was just that at some point I realised Cara wasn't with me. I wasn't concerned. I assumed she'd just wandered off to look at different things. It's quite a large area, on several levels. Easy to get lost in. I have a bit of a thing about cemeteries,' he added, 'and Cara sort of humoured me.'

Véronique made a note.

'Eventually I realised it was getting late and thought I should try to find her. I tried phoning and texting but got no reply. So I began to search more systematically, up and down the rows, calling out, but she was nowhere to be found.'

'Did you see any other people?'

David shook his head. 'No, the place was deserted. Eventually I assumed she must have gone back to the hotel. Perhaps she had been looking for me but gave up and went back.'

'So you yourself returned to the hotel?'

'I did. I wasn't especially concerned at that point. But then I asked at the front desk whether Cara was back and I was gobsmacked to be told she'd checked out.'

'*Gobsmacked*?'

'Very surprised. Astonished.'

'Did you ask when Mademoiselle Bernstein had checked out?'

'He said about an hour earlier.'

'And your reaction?'

'As I said, utterly astonished.'

'What did you do?'

'The first thing I did was to hurry back to our room. I still hoped the guy had got it wrong — was confusing her with somebody else or something. But as soon as I got to the room I saw that all of her stuff was gone. Her clothes, toilet gear, suitcase and carry bag. There was nothing of Cara's in the room.'

'And then?'

'So I rushed back to the front desk to ask whether she had left any message for me. It seemed inconceivable that she would just check out without telling me why. I mean, you know, we had ongoing tickets booked and all that.'

'And there was nothing?'

David saw the concern in her eyes and felt she understood how distressed he had been. He shook his head. 'Not a thing. I tried phoning her again, and texting, but nothing.'

'And then?'

'I felt utterly bereft. I had no idea what to do, where to go, who to ask. It was my first visit to Bonn and I knew nobody. I decided the only thing I could do was cut my losses and come back to Arras. Perhaps Cara had been called back to Arras, you know — something so urgent she had no time to tell me.'

After David had returned to his classroom, Véronique remained in the staffroom waiting for Miranda to reappear. She gave a little half-smile as she thought how common it was for people after life-changing episodes to try to change their appearance: a woman might buy a new outfit, radically change her hairstyle, arrange a tattoo. Men, too. This could be the reason this David Cunningham was growing a beard. She was not convinced it was a good idea.

'You knew Madame Bernstein well?' asked Véronique.

'As well as most,' said Angus Paton. 'Better than most, I dare say.'

'Better?'

'She'd posed for me.'

'Posed?'

'For some art studies. Chalk drawings.'

'So you were good friends?' asked the lieutenant drily.

Angus shrugged. 'We were friends — I wouldn't say good friends — and then we were not friends. That's what happened.'

'I'm not sure exactly what you mean.'

'I mean the light was on, and just like that Cara switched it off.'

Véronique nodded.

'That's just the way she operates, I guess. That's what probably happened with that poor sod Cunningham.'

'You mean that she—'

'Do you know the word "succubus"? I have no idea what it is in French.'

Véronique shook her head. 'Tell me.'

'As far as I know it's some sort of female demon that comes in the night with a lust for sex with sleeping men, and leaves only when she's sucked the life and soul out of them.'

Véronique Robert looked at Angus with surprise and some distaste. 'That is rather dramatic, isn't it? Is this your view of Madame Bernstein?'

Angus laughed. 'Sorry, probably a little harsh.'

'*Certainement.*'

'So, try this one. It's one of Miranda's theories. Miranda Bastion, wife of the headmaster?'

'Yes, I know.'

'Miranda thinks . . . you know the old story about the Frog Prince?'

'The Grimm brothers?'

'That's the one. Miranda has this idea that with Cara it's like that story, except in reverse. Her men are kind of like princes for a while but all at once, when she kisses them, she opens her eyes and realises they're frogs.'

'And she leaves?'

'That's the ticket.'

'That happened to you?'

'I would have preferred the succubus story if it had got that far. No idea about David Cunningham. Probably the frog story with him!'

Angus laughed, but Véronique did not. She closed her notebook, thanked him formally and left the art room office to find Miranda Bastion once more.

Cara's
Manuscript

— KASSEL —

'Perhaps,' said Mathilde, puzzling over how to make the story more complex, 'the frog should have more requests. A request for a simple kiss is not enough.'

'Perhaps it could build up to that?' asked Helga. 'There should be intervening stages?'

'I think so. Somehow there must be a way—'

'Perhaps she should be more reluctant at first,' suggested Helga. 'After all, kissing a frog is quite grotesque really.' She shuddered.

Mathilde considered the problem. 'Yes. You're right. We should somehow have her finding the kissing thing quite repugnant but slowly, gradually, the frog manages to persuade her.'

'Her essential sweetness and kindness shine through!'

'Precisely,' Mathilde smiled. 'Now, how do we do that?'

'Let me be your friend,' croaked the frog.

In her delight at having had her golden ball returned, the beautiful princess had quite forgotten the frog, had quite forgotten the one who had returned the ball to her.

She now turned back to the creature still squatting on the brick wall of the well.

'I could come to visit you at your palace,' croaked the

frog. 'I could share your breakfast. I could play with
you in your garden . . .'

'I could go to bed with you and sleep beside you,' suggested Helga,
giggling.

'Helga!' Mathilde pretended to be shocked.

'But why not?' asked Helga. 'Don't forget your hidden message.'

'Yes, but—'

'Don't you want to have Herr Grimm see you in a certain way, a certain
light?'

Mathilde turned to her sister, considering the idea. A certain light.
Candlelight in the bedroom? It was daring but could be — must be —
perceived as innocent at the same time.

'Why not?' she whispered.

'I could go to bed with you and sleep beside you,'
croaked the frog.
The beautiful princess found all of these suggestions
unpleasant, but she reminded herself of her promise
and swallowed. 'If you really wish it, frog,' she said.

The long days of mourning passed slowly. Gradually the sisters were
permitted to return to the world outside, but they would be required
to wear black for some time yet.

Despite not having anything much to add to what she had said in her
previous letter, Mathilde had written again to Jacob Grimm, ostensibly
in response to his quite professional reply. At length she wrote yet again,
this time requesting a time he would be at home to receive the long-
delayed manuscript of the first story she had read to the brothers. She
did not mention the story of the princess and the frog. She hoped to use
that story to engineer yet another visit.

'She is quite persistent, brother,' said Wilhelm, smiling at Jacob.

'It does appear so,' said Jacob. 'It would be useful to have that manuscript, though. And she did hint that her grandmother had other stories.'

'Why not,' suggested Wilhelm, 'have her come at the same time as Dortchen? She has told me she will visit on Tuesday morning with some more tales she has unearthed.'

Dortchen Wild was a family friend and a regular source of the stories for the brothers' growing collection.

'A good idea,' said Jacob. 'Two birds with one stone.'

'You could say that,' laughed Wilhelm, 'but I might have rather said, more water in the wine!'

David's Story

On impulse, David rang the number of the letting agency.

'Yes, monsieur, the apartment is still available.'

Without really intending to, he found himself making an appointment to view Cara's vacated apartment after school the following day.

He glanced at his phone briefly in surprise, as if what had just happened were the phone's fault. Realising what he was doing, he grinned and shrugged. *Oh well, go with the flow, I suppose.*

Why on earth had he done that? He had no interest in taking the flat. Perhaps it was curiosity — or maybe nostalgia. The apartment was furnished and there would be so many familiar associations: carpet, sofa, table, bed.

And he was increasingly resentful and disenchanted at living in school. Maybe taking the flat wasn't such a bad idea? He was still astonished that Miranda had gone to the police, had come into his classroom and more or less told the entire class the police were waiting for him outside the door.

Bloody nuts, she's bloody nuts.

Then there was his falling out with Angus Paton. And, on top of all this, the whole Greek chorus thing of whispers and nudges from other staff members. Not even his new friendship of sorts with Arlene, or Michael Bastion's studied professionalism, did much to improve things.

'I'll take it,' he said.

Even as the words came out he was conflicted, suspicious of his reasons. Taking the apartment would be expensive and inconvenient. Living in the staff wing was relatively cheap, and his classroom and office were both minutes away. He smiled wryly, remembering how he had often ribbed Cara for being disdainful of her workmates, for setting herself apart. However, he had thoroughly enjoyed the privacy from prying colleagues when he visited Cara, and her apartment became a retreat and ultimately a love nest.

For it *had* become their love nest. Was that the reason for this urge to repossess it? He followed the agent through the suite of rooms he knew so well, the agent pointing out familiar features, extolling their virtues. David could hardly help smiling. He had had no intention of taking the flat, but there was a wicked pleasure in the deceit, in asking questions he knew the answers to, in plumping himself down on a sofa he had sat on so many times, in opening cupboards, in patting the bed he had slept in naked, arms and legs wrapped around a naked Cara.

Once he had had his fill of memories he would thank the agent warmly, tell him he would consider it, and later send him a regretful email.

Yet, even before the end of the tour, he found himself reaching for the agent's sleeve.

'I'll take it.'

He was honest enough to recognise that the idea of some stranger living here was unbearable, something he must forestall at all costs. In the brief weeks of their relationship this apartment had become a sanctum. A private, somehow holy place. Cara's place. Cara had never permitted him a key, but it was here that she had given him her body. There was a bitter irony in the fact that now that Cara had gone, it was possible to buy the key.

'Davd Cunningham's moving out of the staff quarters,' said Michael. 'He is?' asked Miranda. 'Why on earth?'

'He didn't say in so many words,' said Michael. 'I rather understood he wanted a little more privacy.'

'So, when?'

'Quite soon. He's taken up a lease on an apartment in Arras. He's asked to leave more or less as soon as he's settled the paperwork. He asked for a reference.'

Miranda said nothing for a few moments, apparently concentrating on her pasta salad. Eventually, though, she caught Michael's eye. Over her fork, she said, 'You think this has something to do with me?'

'I said not a word.' It was Michael's turn to pause before adding, 'Why ask? Feeling guilty?'

'What on earth do I have to feel guilty about?'

'You have been rather down on him. He's a good teacher. He doesn't deserve your distrust.'

Miranda didn't reply.

'And of course there was that stunt with the police. That wouldn't have helped.'

'My going to see the police was not a stunt,' said Miranda evenly. 'I was following sound advice from Jules. You know that.'

They continued to eat in silence, neither wanting to increase the tension in the air. Eventually, to placate a little, Michael asked as neutrally as he could muster, 'In any event, have you heard anything from the police?'

Miranda looked up. It did not seem to be a trap. 'I have, actually,' she said. 'Just this morning I had a call from Véronique.'

'Véronique?'

'The police officer.'

Michael had forgotten her name.

'She told me that while they could not divulge any details, there was no indication that Cara had got into trouble of any sort.'

'Trouble?'

'You know — she hasn't been in an accident, or been arrested for robbing a bank or committing a series of murders.'

'I suppose that's something.'

'In some ways it was most unsatisfactory, but she says she is hamstrung by privacy issues and the fact that there is no official inquiry. You know, no magistrates involved. But she wanted to reassure us that she believes we have nothing to worry about.'

'So there was no real point going to the police at all. We learnt nothing and we were probably never going to learn anything.'

'We learnt that much, and something more,' said Miranda.

'What's that?'

'Véronique said that the one thing she could tell us was that it seems Cara has not left the EU.'

Michael put down his fork. 'But . . .'

She nodded. 'That's right. Shows a great deal of concern for her stricken father, doesn't it?' said Miranda.

'So she's been telling porkies,' said Michael.

'Which begs the question,' said Miranda, 'why did she leave the apartment in such a hurry?'

'It doesn't beg the question, actually. It *raises* the question.'

'Pedantic pillock!' said Miranda. 'Must be why I love you.'

She took another mouthful of pasta salad, relishing it. She was in good spirits once more.

Cara's
Manuscript

— KASSEL —

Mathilde and Helga stood again at the door of the house in Bellevuestrasse.

Despite their sombre black dress, each was excited, albeit in a different way. Mathilde was almost sick with apprehension. The relief she had felt at finally being able to re-establish physical contact with Herr Jacob was all at once dissipated by fear that her hopes may be dashed. She had tried to persuade herself that the passion she increasingly felt for the older brother must surely be reciprocated — if only he could be brought to recognise it somehow — but now on his doorstep, only two or three rooms away, the bright light of the pretty street became the cold light of reality. He did not love her; he might never love her. He hardly knew her and could have no inkling of her feelings. If he did, he might be more embarrassed than anything.

Helga was under no illusion that Wilhelm felt anything for her. It was a game she had gone along with for Mathilde's sake. She had no feelings for Wilhelm. Her excitement was simply anticipation — the anticipation that a project was about to begin.

While they waited for the door to be answered, Helga flexed and unflexed her knuckles. Mathilde wanted to thrust her knuckles into her mouth.

As on the previous occasion, Lotte Grimm opened the door. She tempered her smile of welcome at the sight of the mourning garb, but the smiles of the two sisters assured her that there was no special need for solicitude and she relaxed.

'Fräuleins, welcome. Come in. My brothers are expecting you.'

Helga and Mathilde shared a brief glance of reassurance, greeted Lotte and thanked her. As before, they were ushered into the house.

As they were led into the sitting room, the two brothers rose to greet them. However, the brothers were not alone in the room. Seated between them, smiling curiously at the newcomers, was a pretty young woman. She looked to be about the same age as Helga. She was not wearing a cap; instead, she had an elaborate hairstyle in which her long plaits had been wound into a kind of turban on top of her head. Her frank, amused expression and apparent familiarity with the brothers immediately disconcerted the sisters. All at once, each realised, the dynamic would be different and they would have to adjust.

There was a momentary pang for Mathilde as she noted that neither brother offered a hand. They did nod formally, however.

After acknowledging Helga, who said how sorry they were to have missed the brothers on their previous visit, Wilhelm said, 'I know, Fräulein, we were at the library. Work, you know. Work, work, work. Our sister told us of your visit and, of course . . .' at this point he smiled at Mathilde 'there were your letters.'

He turned an amused glance to Jacob, who appeared a little embarrassed. Mathilde experienced another pang. What was it about her letters that might have provoked this conspiratorial exchange?

'Oh, and I am being remiss. Please allow me to introduce our very good friend Fräulein Wild. Dorothea, Fräulein Heller and her sister have been providing us with stories, as you have.'

The young woman smiled up at them and extended her hand. 'Please, let it be Dorothea. Or Dortchen if you like; most people call me that.'

The introductory pleasantries over, Helga and Mathilde were ushered to the small sofa and Lotte departed to prepare some coffee.

'So, you have joined the army?' said Dorothea Wild.

Mathilde was a little nonplussed. 'Army?'

Dorothea laughed. 'I call it that. I mean the army of friends and helpers who have been enlisted to gather stories for Jacob and Wilhelm. I know he's just complained about work, work, work, but *entre nous* I believe it's people like us who do all the real work.'

'Dortchen,' protested Wilhelm. 'Do you know how many books there are in the king's library? Each has to be carefully studied and catalogued.'

'Thousands,' laughed Dorothea. 'I know. You've told us thousands of times. And also, that King Jérôme has never opened the cover of any of them. But we know you're not really cataloguing the books; you're only hunting for stories. You two have become obsessed.'

'What slander!'

This easy banter alarmed Helga. She looked from one to the other, her tongue frozen. How could they intrude on this familiarity? What could they possibly say?

Mathilde, too, was alarmed, but her anxiety was focused on Jacob, who seemed unwilling to meet her eyes, to acknowledge her in any way. Wilhelm, meanwhile, was outgoing, charming and far friendlier than the somewhat aloof presence she remembered from their last encounter. She suspected this might have something to do with the presence of Dortchen Wild. Nobody had made them unwelcome in any way, but it was as if she and Helga had been reduced to irrelevant ciphers, spectators at a performance.

As for Jacob — with a vulnerability and intensity she was convinced only her tenderness could assuage — he might as well not have been in the room.

'So, Fräulein Heller, you have finally brought us the story,' said Wilhelm, turning to Mathilde at last. Suddenly a look of consternation replaced his cheerfulness, as if the colour of her dress all at once reminded him of her reason for not delivering the story earlier. In a much more sombre tone he said, 'But forgive me, Fräulein, I had forgotten. Please allow us to express our condolences.'

Helga and Mathilde lowered their heads appropriately for a moment or two, and when they lifted them once more Mathilde said, 'Thank you. It has been a most sad time for us.'

Wilhelm waited for a second or two to see if there was to be any elaboration. When it was apparent that there was not, he added, 'Forgive us, please. Your letter did explain and we were both very sorry to hear of your loss.'

He glanced at Jacob, who nodded imperceptibly in agreement but did not take the trouble even to murmur a few words.

To allay the slight awkwardness that had overtaken the gathering, Mathilde fumbled in her reticule and withdrew the story. She wanted to pass it to Jacob but clearly the older brother had relinquished all leadership in this matter to Wilhelm. Jacob remained to one side, hands behind his back.

'Thank you,' said Wilhelm. 'This will be very helpful.'

'Work, work, work,' laughed Dorothea. 'What did I tell you? We are the slaves who do all of the work!'

Mathilde smiled at her. 'It was no trouble. No work at all really. It was something I enjoyed doing.'

'See, Dortchen?' smiled Wilhelm. 'Some people understand the importance of this enterprise.' He turned back to Mathilde. 'And how is your grandmother, Fräulein? Has she managed to remember any more tales?'

Helga and Mathilde exchanged an uncomfortable glance. Mathilde swallowed and took refuge in the second question. 'There is another story, Herr Grimm,' she said. 'I am writing it out for you at the moment but it may need a day or two yet.'

It was the brothers' turn to exchange glances and once again Mathilde picked up the slight conspiratorial air.

'Might I ask what it is about?' asked Wilhelm cautiously.

Mathilde paused, unsure how much to reveal. 'It is about a princess and a frog,' she said.

'A princess and a frog? Really?'

All at once Wilhelm's manner changed slightly. The instinct of the collector gripped him and his focus sharpened. 'I'm not sure that I . . .'

He looked at Jacob. He too was at once more alert. He shook his head. 'No.'

Mathilde felt emboldened to elaborate. 'And a golden ball,' she said.

Dorothea Wild sensed the changed atmosphere. 'I have not come across such a tale.'

Helga relaxed, smiled at Mathilde and reached for her hand.

'If you'd like, I could bring it to you quite soon,' said Mathilde. 'It would give me great pleasure to read it to you, especially if . . .'

'If?' asked Jacob.

He had spoken to her!

'If you have not heard the story before,' said Mathilde.

'We would like that very much,' said Wilhelm.

And although he spoke no more, Mathilde was gratified to see Jacob nodding his head, even permitting himself a small smile.

It was at that point that Charlotte Grimm and a servant girl returned to the room with trays bearing coffee and cake.

The sisters did not talk a great deal on their walk home, each processing the shifting events of the morning in her own way.

It was not until they were back in their bedroom after luncheon that they broached the subject. Their description, to their parents, of the morning's visit had been necessarily perfunctory.

'She's very pretty, isn't she?' Mathilde suddenly asked.

'Who?'

Helga knew exactly who Mathilde meant.

'Fräulein Wild. Do you think she might be a relative?'

'A friend, Wilhelm said.'

'Our very dear friend,' said Mathilde.

'No, sister,' Helga corrected her. 'He said our very *good* friend.'

'What is the difference?' asked Mathilde. 'Very dear, very good . . . and so very, very pretty.'

'You are pretty, too,' said Helga.

'You are kind, but I am not as pretty, and she is so bright and cheerful. I would like to dislike her but—'

'I'm not sure why you need to be so wretched. There is nothing to suggest Fräulein Wild is anything other than an acquaintance, admittedly a close one. I'm sure she would have many admirers! You seem to be suggesting she is already affianced to Jacob or Wilhelm.'

Mathilde, after a few moments, said, 'I suppose you're right. I'm building mountains. Besides, it could be Brother Wilhelm she's affianced to. Did you happen to notice whether she was wearing a ring?'

Helga laughed, and Mathilde made as if to throw a book at her sister. 'Stop teasing me!' she said.

If not on account of Dorothea Wild, why had Jacob been so standoffish, all but unfriendly? And neither brother had seen the sisters to the door, nor had they taken their hands when they made their farewells. Those duties had been delegated to their sister Lotte.

What had happened?

Had it something to do with the letters she had sent?

There had been some puzzling glances between the brothers when the letters were mentioned. She tried to remember what she had said in the letters but had not kept copies. She was sure she had been scrupulously polite and businesslike: friendly, of course, but not overly so.

It was so lucky she had thought to mention the new story. How the atmosphere had changed then. She mentioned this to Helga.

'I know,' Helga said. 'It was as if we'd been transported into a different place. I felt they were quite excited.' She giggled. 'They have taken the bait, but don't forget, we have not yet completed the fish!'

'It must be a perfect fish,' said Mathilde softly. 'It must—'

'Swim in deep waters?' suggested Helga.

'Oh, Helga,' whispered Mathilde, all at once feeling guilty that somehow they were betraying their oma. 'Never mind the fish; I wonder if it is we who are swimming in deep waters.'

David's Story

D avid had been living in the apartment for just over a fortnight when he heard the sound of the doorbell. There had been no callers until now, not that he expected any. He had not made much of his move, even though he suspected it had aroused plenty of comment.

It was a Saturday afternoon and he was marking papers. He put them to one side and went to the speaker in the small lobby.

'Yes?'

'David?'

'Yes.'

'It's Angus. Mind if I come up?'

David was surprised and immediately wary. How did Angus know where he was? People knew he had moved into an apartment in Arras, but nobody beyond Michael Bastion and the administration had been given the address. Since their altercation he and Angus had spoken little. David had tried to avoid the art teacher, more out of embarrassment than animosity, although he still felt a deep and abiding resentment.

For all that, he couldn't come up with any reason on the spur of the moment to refuse Angus entry. Besides, he was a little curious.

'Sure. Hold on.'

He pushed the button releasing the outside lock and shortly thereafter heard Angus's footsteps on the stairs. David opened the door in anticipation, watching the big man as he climbed the last few steps.

'Hi,' he said.

'Hi,' said Angus with a faint smile. He was carrying under his arm a six-pack of Affligem Blond.

'Come in.'

'I've brought you a house-warming present.'

David was a little taken aback but decided to accept the gesture at face value. 'Nice idea. Take a seat and I'll find some glasses.'

'Good man. Not the sort of stuff to drink out of the bottle.'

David returned with a couple of glasses and a bottle-opener. Angus passed him a bottle.

'I'm not sure . . .' David began.

'I know, I know,' said Angus. 'Call it guilt. It's been exercising me that the dust-up we had in the art room might have been the reason you moved out.'

David shook his head. 'No, no. There's no denying I've been uncomfortable about that but, no, it was nothing to do with that.'

Angus seemed relieved and raised his glass. 'Good, good,' he said. 'Well, good health and good luck to the new quarters and all who sail in them!'

David joined in the toast.

'But how did you know I was here?'

'Quite intuitive,' said Angus. 'Cara moved out. You moved in. I put two and two together.'

'Smart work,' said David. 'Most people get five when they do that.'

'True,' said Angus, 'but I'm not most people, thank Christ.' He eased back in the armchair, quite relaxed, and looked about the living room.

'You've been here before, haven't you?' said David, realising.

'I have,' said Angus. 'But let's not go there again.'

It was clear that he wanted reconciliation, and David discovered he wasn't inclined to resist.

'You've not heard anything, I suppose?' ventured Angus.

David shook his head. 'Didn't think so,' said Angus, 'although I did wonder when you moved out.'

'Wonder what?'

'Whether you and she, you know, were moving in together somewhere.'

'I wish,' said David. And added, more for politeness' sake: 'You haven't heard anything?'

'God no!' laughed Angus. 'Why would she get in touch with me unless she wanted those drawings back?' Then, realising, he added, 'Sorry—'

'Not a problem. I'm getting used to it.'

'Anyway,' said Angus, 'getting to be chums again wasn't the only reason I wanted to talk to you. I do have some intel you might not have heard.'

'Do you? Sounds intriguing.'

'Perhaps, perhaps not. But it does give me great pleasure to spill a few beans.' Angus carefully filled himself another beer and said, 'Madame Bastion had another dinner party last night. For some bizarre reason I was invited again.'

'Lucky you. I wasn't.'

'No, well . . . However, your good name did come up.'

'How surprising. My *good* name?'

'A figure of speech, dear boy.'

'It's called a lie.'

'Anyway, the charming Miranda, plied by my good self with a few too many glasses of her excellent Côtes du Rhone, became quite expansive. Cara's disappearance has really sent her imagination into overdrive — not to put too fine a point on it, she's become a smidgeon obsessed.'

'Tell me about it.'

'I am, *mon cher*, I am. You, of course, are the villain of the piece.'

'Not you?'

'Miranda feels I am the wronged husband. The cuckold, when you came along, and thus an object of sympathy. Personally, I reckon it should be scorn, but there you go. No accounting for tastes.'

'Go on.'

'She's a determined old thing, our Miranda, and she has uncovered a couple of very interesting things.'

David sipped his beer, trying not to let his impatience show. Angus loved playing to the gallery, but to do so for a gallery of one was not really necessary.

'In the first place, she has managed to find out why Cara left this place — or at least the reason she gave her landlady.'

This *was* interesting. David leaned forward.

'Apparently her father in the States was suddenly stricken — struck? — ill. A massive stroke, Cara said. So she had to drop everything and rush back to California or wherever to help him and her mother.'

David looked at him in astonishment. 'Bloody hell! This is the first

I have heard. Why wouldn't she have said so? Sounds like utter crap to me. She'd never ever mentioned her father.'

'Never mentioned any parent,' agreed Angus. 'I always assumed she didn't have any. Just emerged somehow fully formed. You know Botticelli's *Birth of Venus*?'

'How does Miranda Bastion know all this anyway?'

'She and Michael have a friend in the Hôtel de Ville who spoke to the landlady. And that's not all — the plot gets thicker.'

'It does?'

'Remember that pretty gendarme, the one Miranda set on to us?'

David nodded.

'Apparently, despite all those interviews and probing and prodding, they only told Miranda one thing.'

'And that was?'

'That there's no evidence that Cara has left Europe.'

David shrugged. 'That doesn't really surprise me. Why would she?'

'To attend to her sick father?'

'I'm calling bullshit on that story.'

'Why?'

'Because if that was the reason she suddenly upped tent and left Bonn she would have told me. I mean, if this stroke thing really happened I totally understand her feeling she needed to go to him. But I reckon she would have found five minutes to give me a call, or even flick me a text or email to let me know, to explain why we needed to cancel the cruise.'

Angus shrugged.

'I mean, we're in Bonn. She gets a message: *Dad's really sick*. We have a car with us, my car. Wouldn't she just have said, David, this has happened, I need to get back to Arras straight away to sort things out and fly off to California or wherever. And I would have said, of course. We'll leave right away.'

'Makes sense,' agreed Angus.

'No,' said David, 'there's something else.'

'If it comes to that,' said Angus, 'if it was a life-or-death matter and she had to be in California pronto, why would she come back to Arras anyway? Why not fly directly out of Bonn?'

'And why vacate the apartment?' said David. 'Think of the hassle of moving out, finding storage for her stuff before she flew out. Where is all her stuff anyway? Where's her car? Why not just leave it all in place until she knew exactly what was going on at home?'

Angus shook his head. 'Weird.'

'It's only weird if you buy the bullshit story of father Bernstein having a stroke.'

'But why—'

'That's easy: it was a fabrication to explain why she had to decamp at short notice.'

'You're right, of course,' said Angus. 'Which leaves us with the burning question.'

'Yeah, the burning question.'

They opened another bottle each and drank in brooding silence for some time until Angus said, 'Oh shit, I was forgetting.'

'What?'

'Miranda in her Sherlock mode did mention something else she'd discovered.'

'Yeah?'

'Did you know that Cara cleaned out all of her personal stuff from the school —from her classroom and her locker — *before* she went on leave?'

David allowed the implications to sink in.

'No,' he said. 'I didn't know that.'

'You know what that suggests?'

'Yes,' said David slowly. 'Yes, I do.'

Angus glanced at him. 'Uh oh,' he said. 'Doesn't sound good.'

'Actually, I have some news too, relating to Cara,' said David. 'At least it was news to me. You may have known.'

'Try me.'

'Did you know Cara has written a novel?'

Angus looked surprised. 'No, I didn't. What sort of novel? Not a — what do they call it — *roman à clef?* That could be tricky.'

David shook his head. 'No, that's hardly the sort of thing Cara would write. Apparently it's a young adult novel. Something to do with a Grimm brothers' story about the frog prince.'

Angus exclaimed, 'No, not really!'

'What?'

'Sorry, I don't mean to doubt you or anything, but speak of the devil. That's the one about the princess kissing the frog or something, isn't it?'

'Yes, sort of,' said David. 'It's kind of a weird story. She's supposed to kiss the frog but she actually hurls it against a wall.'

'Miranda again, I'm sorry, old son. You know Miranda has it in for you. One of her many theories about Cara's hiving off is based on that frog prince story. She laid it out at the first dinner party, before you arrived.'

'You're dying to tell me, aren't you?'

Angus grinned, refilling his glass. 'According to La Miranda, there are two possible versions. Cara saw you as the frog in her life who could be transformed into a prince with a simple kiss. Alas, when she did kiss you, you steadfastly and perversely remained the frog you always will be. Bitterly disappointed, disillusioned, what have you, Cara left on the instant.'

'To search for another frog, I suppose. That was pretty compelling. And the second theory?'

'Just as flattering. In this version you were her prince in shining armour. But when she kissed you — whammy and abracadabra! —you turned into the frog you really were underneath all that shining armour. And—'

'Disappointed and disillusioned, Cara hives off?'

'Precisely.'

'Sounds to me like Miranda should be writing a novel,' said David.

'Chock full of novel ideas, anyway. So who told you about Cara's novel? I'm guessing it wasn't Miranda.'

'It was Arlene, actually.'

'Arlene? She's a dark horse. Has she read it?'

'No, she doesn't really know a lot about it, except that Cara gave a copy to Steffi Fox.'

'Steffi Fox? There's a pretty little thing. Pretty smart, too.'

David nodded. 'Agreed. I understand Steffi was brought in as a sort of technical adviser. As a representative of the target audience.'

'I'd like to read that manuscript,' said Angus.

'Me too,' said David.

'I assume Steffi's read it.'

'Oh yes.'

'So borrow her copy.'

'I tried that. And essentially had my head bitten off. I'm suddenly the bad guy, the one who drove Cara away. She said that letting me read it was not her decision; it was Cara's. She suggested I ask Cara.'

'Tricky. She has a point, I suppose,' said Angus. 'However, points can be bent.'

'What do you mean?'

'Steffi's copy would be electronic?'

'I assume so.'

'So it would be on her laptop?'

David was beginning to understand what Angus was driving at.

'You don't mean—'

'We know Steffi's username. All we need is her password.'

'But that's—'

'Perfectly in alignment with internet safety at Huntingdon. Can't have students accessing child porn and the like.'

'But how would you—'

'Leave it to Uncle Angus. There are ways and means and there are other ways and other means.'

Another bottle later and David was mellow enough to share confidences.

'I asked her to marry me, you know.'

Angus took a deep draught of beer. 'You mad romantic fool. Why on earth did you do that?'

'It seemed a good idea at the time. Besides, I loved . . . love her.'

'That's no reason to marry her.'

'I even bought a ring.'

'A fool and his money,' said Angus.

'That's the second time in as many minutes you've called me a fool.'

'There may be a message there.'

'Cara told me I was a sentimental bear.'

'That was kind. Other descriptions spring to mind.'

'I suppose they're much of a muchness, sentimental and romantic.'

'You're the English teacher, old petal. I avoid both. Not a romantic bone in my body.'

David shook his head, remembering the chalk drawings of the countryside. To probe a little, he ventured, 'Stops you from being hurt?'

'Stops me from being stupid. More beer?'

David, not usually much of a drinker, found himself proffering his glass. After pouring, Angus glanced at him. 'Is that why she scarpered?'

'What do you mean?'

'You asking her to marry you?'

David shook his head. 'No, no, no. I've agonised a bit about that. But I think she thought it was a bit of a joke.'

'The proposal?'

'No, the idea of getting married.'

Angus considered this. 'So that shoots one of Miranda's theories down in flames.'

'What?'

'The frog thing. That relied on Cara taking you seriously.'

David felt a twinge of bitterness. He didn't find Miranda's theory as amusing as Angus clearly did.

'What about you, then?' he asked. 'Did Cara find out you were an incurable frog as well?'

Angus laughed. 'No, I'm a toad through and through, and Cara never thought otherwise.'

'A toad?'

'Also known as a bastard,' said Angus with a short laugh. Clearly, he didn't believe that was such a bad thing.

'So did you?' David ventured, emboldened by the beer. 'I mean you told me you'd had a thing. Did you—'

'Also known as a bullshit artist, my old flower,' laughed Angus. 'Hold on, I'll open another bottle.'

Before Angus left, the two men embraced and David said, 'Thanks for coming.'

'Good to clear the air,' said Angus.

As they walked together to the door, Angus scanned about him again as if absorbing the apartment. David had a sudden realisation.

'Those drawings,' he said. 'The ones of Cara? You did them here, didn't you?'

Angus nodded. 'Naturally,' he said. 'Not really the sort of thing you could do at school.'

'I guess not,' said David, and he found he was able to grin.

'I actually thought of bringing one as a peace offering,' said Angus, 'instead of the beer.'

'The beer was good,' said David.

'School on Monday, then. And as soon as Miranda finds out what's happened to Cara, I'll let you know.'

'You do that,' said David warmly.

And he closed the door.

Over the next few weeks there was no indication that Miranda had discovered what had happened to Cara. David settled in to the apartment and began to enjoy living in the town, close to bistros, bars and a Carrefour supermarket. The prickly atmosphere at Huntingdon in the wake of Cara's disappearance gradually subsided, and good humour returned to his senior class. From time to time he and Angus Paton would share a drink or a meal in Arras, and on one of these occasions Angus added a postscript to their conversation about Cara's novel.

'You didn't!'

Angus grinned, nodding.

'How?'

'The old Paton charm and a little emotional blackmail.'

'Say no more.'

'I don't intend to.'

'And?'

'A blank, I'm afraid. We've been outfoxed by the Fox.'

'How so?'

'Steffi had a folder in her files named The Frog Prince, but when I opened it the folder was empty. She's cleaned it out. Probably moved it to a pen drive and lodged it in a Swiss bank account.'

'So that's that.'

'That usually is, old son,' said Angus. 'Sorry.'

David still thought of Cara much of the time, although the pain had reduced to a dull ache. Whenever he checked the mailbox at the apartment there was a small thrill of anticipation that there might be some letter for her, even an overdue account. There never was. He had given up leaving messages on her phone.

Life for Miranda returned to its usual orbit after the wobbles of *l'affaire Bernstein*. The indeterminate and deliberately vague report from Véronique Robert had effectively closed the door on any possible police revelations regarding Cara and, apart from a residual inquisitiveness, Miranda gradually lost interest.

Michael had appointed a new French teacher, putting an end to her brief sojourn in the classroom. She was surprised to find herself a little disappointed; she missed the interaction with the young people. But that faded as well and normality gradually returned.

Cara's Manuscript

The brothers' reaction to her announcement that she would deliver them a new story both excited Mathilde Heller and filled her with foreboding. They had clearly, as Helga observed, taken the bait. The problem now was to deliver. It would not be easy, for she and Helga had undertaken to tell a story that achieved many things. First, it had to have the feel of a genuine folk tale, a story that could easily be a first cousin to 'Little Redcap'; second, the language had to suggest an ancient lineage — a story passed down through generations; and finally, but most importantly, it had to be the vector of a hidden message that Jacob Grimm would sense but not necessarily be able to articulate: that Mathilde Heller was the princess capable of transforming him into the prince he truly was.

Initially, these hurdles seemed challenging but straightforward. The first was actually turning out to be fun; she and Helga were hugely enjoying putting the tale together. The second, too, was largely a process of imitation and was enjoyable. All they had to do was imagine their grandmother telling the story, and write it down the way Oma would tell it.

The third element was much more difficult. The hidden message could not be too obvious or the brothers would see through it in an instant and the whole building would fall down. But neither could it be too subtle or it would be lost completely.

But the prize was so great that it was worth the struggle to overcome these challenges, and ultimately the sisters felt confident enough in their achievement.

Now that it was time to deliver the story to the brothers, however, Mathilde had lost that confidence.

The shadow of guilt she had experienced when dissembling, first to Lotte Grimm and later about her grandmother's death, had grown into a dark cloud that quite occluded her purpose. The cloud was not going away. Her story was a lie. What especially troubled her was that Oma had hated lies.

She had not actually lied to the brothers when they asked about her grandmother, but she had not told the truth. In avoiding the question, she had implied that Oma was still alive. Did that count as a lie? Not quite, surely. However, worse was their implication that the next story they delivered came from their grandmother. There was no escaping this. This was a real lie, even if not spelled out.

Moreover, it was a betrayal of their grandmother. Oma had *not* told them the story: this was a fabrication, a confection.

Further disconcerting her was the manner of Jacob Grimm, who had not even looked at her on their last visit. At no stage had he leaned his lovely neck towards her, smiling and murmuring *Fräulein Heller*.

He had changed. Or something had changed him.

She was now convinced Jacob Grimm would not be in a sufficiently receptive frame of mind to read between the lines of the princess and the frog story, no matter how brilliantly she and Helga constructed it.

'We cannot do this, Helga,' she whispered.

'Cannot do what?'

'Finish this story and take it to the brothers.'

Helga looked at her in astonishment.

'Whyever not?' she demanded. 'You saw how enthusiastic they were at the prospect. We have them wriggling on our hook!'

'You and your silly fish analogies,' said Mathilde sadly.

Helga examined her sister more closely and saw her seriousness, her resignation. 'What is the matter?' she asked. 'What has happened?'

Mathilde did not reply and nor could she meet Helga's eyes.

All at once, Helga realised. 'It's him, isn't it? It's Herr Grimm, your Jacob.'

'He's not my Jacob. You saw that.'

'He was very reserved.'

'He was *too* reserved. I don't mean he was effusive or outgoing the first time, but he was dignified and quite friendly.'

'But yesterday he was different, wasn't he?'

'He was unfriendly. Quite unfriendly.'

'He brightened when you told him of the new story.'

'Yes, he did, but it wasn't anything to do with me. He brightened at the prospect of the story.'

'Then we must give him that story,' said Helga firmly.

'He won't read it,' said Mathilde, who had lost all hope. 'Not properly. He will not be in a frame of mind to read what it is *really* saying!'

'So that must be our task,' said Helga, moving to her sister and covering her hand with hers. 'We must invest the story with sufficient magic to enchant the man, no matter how resistant he is!'

Mathilde smiled at Helga, appreciating her efforts at comfort. But her smile faded and her brow darkened once more. 'You're forgetting Oma.'

Helga looked confused.

'What are you talking about?'

Mathilde explained her anxieties about the injury to their grandmother's memory, caused by their creating a lie in her name.

'But all stories are lies,' said Helga. 'Where is the truth in "Little Redcap"?'

'You're missing the point. "Little Redcap" is a genuine folk tale. Our story is an imitation.'

'That's only an accident of age,' said Helga. 'Our story will be five hundred years old one day.'

'In five hundred years' time?' said Mathilde with a faint smile. 'But you must see what a terrible thing we are doing. We have led the brothers to believe we heard the story at our Oma's knee when we did not. She would be most unhappy.'

Helga looked at her sister crossly. 'That cannot matter to Oma now,' she said. 'Think about it.'

Mathilde looked back, not willing to believe what she had just heard, the enormity of it.

Seeing not only Mathilde's shocked expression but also the tears welling in her eyes, Helga turned away.

'Oh, my dear Helga,' whispered Mathilde. 'How could you possibly have said such a thing?'

We all live in the forest.

Mathilde remembered Oma's words. Had she and Helga wandered into the forest? She felt the darkness, the pressing down of tall trees, and could not understand why Helga had not felt this — until Mathilde remembered enchantment. Helga had used the word. Had they been enchanted by possibility, so enchanted they had lost their way?

She had hoped their story would enchant Jacob Grimm. By this she did not mean she wanted their story to delight him. No, she meant *enchant* in its older, darker sense. This prospect had enchanted Helga. It had, she knew, enchanted her. It still did. Was it that which was troubling her?

Through the story, Jacob needed somehow to be held in thrall. Her thrall — Mathilde's thrall.

There was an irony there, she understood. The prince in the story they were devising had himself been enchanted. Somehow, by some device they had not yet engineered, their prince had been turned into a frog. Some witch? Some enchanter?

Their princess would un-enchant him, would break the spell, would return him to the prince he genuinely was. And her reward, of course, was that the prince would gift himself to her.

And yet . . . and yet . . .

They trusted that their story would enchant Jacob. Would turn him into something he quite palpably wasn't. Were they not turning Jacob into a frog? The idea troubled her so much she tossed and turned until Helga grumbled sleepily and ordered her to stop wriggling.

Dorothea Wild was on an errand with her mother on the Königstrasse in Kassel when she saw a familiar figure up ahead on the footpath. Under his arm he carried a bundle of books secured with string. It was her old playmate and now good friend, Wilhelm Grimm.

'Wilhelm!' she cried. 'Wilhelm!'

He heard her voice and turned. Peering down the road he recognised her and waved.

'Dortchen! Frau Wild!'

He hurried in their direction, even breaking into a run as if he worried she were about to turn and scamper away from him.

Dorothea stood waiting, smiling reprovingly.

'You must not do that,' she said.

'Do what?'

'Run like that. It could bring on your asthma. Another attack and you could be in bed again for months.'

Wilhelm, despite being slightly short of breath, beamed at her, smiling away her fears. How had his effervescent childhood friend turned into a reproving elderly aunt?

'It's not amusing, Wilhelm.'

'I'm sure the exercise is very good for my lungs.'

'We will tell Father,' Dorothea warned. 'Won't we, Mutter?'

Her father, Rudolf Wild, was an old family friend and neighbour of the Grimms. He was also the apothecary who had treated Wilhelm's asthma over the years with various remedies, including *Datura*, which he had encouraged Wilhelm to smoke in a clay pipe.

'How is your father?'

Dorothea's smile faded. 'He is not well, but he is in good spirits.'

Her mother nodded. 'He is always in good spirits, poor man,' she said.

'And what was your opinion of the Fräuleins Heller, Dortchen?' asked Wilhelm, changing the subject suddenly. 'Remember? The young women who brought the story they had found for Jacob and me.'

Dorothea remembered. She searched his face for any clue that there was some implication in the question, but he remained impassive. 'The younger one was rather quiet,' she said, 'but Mathilde was pleasant. The story she mentioned, the new one, sounds quite fascinating.'

'It does,' agreed Wilhelm. 'Jacob and I will be very pleased to see it.'

'It's not one I've come across before.'

'No. The other two stories their grandmother provided were quite familiar.'

'So sad that there will be no more, then,' said Dorothea.

Wilhelm looked puzzled. 'Why will there be no more?'

'Did you not know?' asked Dorothea. 'I mentioned to Father about meeting the Fräuleins Heller and how they were in mourning, and Father said they must be the daughters of Thomas Heller, an acquaintance of his, whose wife's mother had recently passed away. A fine old lady, apparently.'

'This is very interesting,' Wilhelm said. 'It was not the impression they gave us.'

'What do you mean?'

'You heard. When we asked about their grandmother the girls dissembled.'

Dorothea frowned, trying to remember what had been said. 'I cannot recall.'

'I can,' said Wilhelm. 'I asked directly how was their grandmother and they, or Mathilde specifically, deflected. She did not answer. Instead she talked about the new story. Surely her response should have been to tell me the old lady had passed away?'

'But why would she not say that?'

'I can think of only one reason,' said Wilhelm. 'They did not want us to know about their grandmother's death because there would be no more stories.'

He bowed to Dorothea, and then to Frau Wild who had waited patiently throughout.

'Thank you, Dortchen. This is most fascinating intelligence. I must away to Jacob. He will be equally intrigued.'

'We must take them the story,' said Helga.

'Why?' asked Mathilde.

'Because they are expecting it!'

'That is not a reason.'

'It's a very powerful reason. Do you want to let them down?'

Mathilde shrugged. She felt so compromised it hardly mattered to her now whether or not they delivered the story. She could not understand why it mattered so much to Helga. 'We *can't* take them the story.'

'I feel I'm running around in circles,' said Helga, exasperated. 'Why not?'

'Because we haven't finished it yet!'

'So we must finish it,' Helga said. 'We must finish the story and deliver it to the brothers.'

'And have them believe we were told it by Oma?'

'If that's what's worrying you, we can tell them we got the story from some other source.'

'Where?'

'I don't know. Great Aunt Hedwig?'

'We don't have a Great Aunt Hedwig — and, anyway, that's just exchanging one lie for another.'

Helga was silent for some time. Then she said, 'Let's finish the story anyway. It's been fun, hasn't it? We don't have to take it to the brothers if you're so worried. Or, if we do, we don't have to say it was from Oma. We can be mysterious — say we would rather not divulge our source. Anyway, I don't believe they will ask — all they want is the story, not the source.'

Mathilde thought about this. It would probably not do any harm to finish the story. It had been fun. All the same, she thought the brothers would be interested in the source. They were scholars, librarians and sticklers for detail. And of the two, she suspected Jacob Grimm would be the bigger stickler.

They were sitting as they had before, two seats drawn up before the escritoire in their bedroom.

'So what should happen now?' asked Helga.

'Clearly the princess must run away from the frog,' said Mathilde. 'The idea of the frog being her friend is so unbearable.'

'I know — she is so overjoyed to have her golden ball back she feels it matters not in the least who retrieved it,' said Helga, 'nor any promise she made.'

'That's good. So what would she do?'

'Run back to the palace.'

'No,' said Mathilde. 'She would *dance joyfully* back to the palace.'
She dipped her quill into the inkpot.

> And then she danced joyfully back to the palace
> as quickly as she could, leaving the frog to croak
> despondently on the wall of the well.

'Despondently is good.'
 'We needed something from the frog's point of view,' said Mathilde.
'Now what?'
 'The frog follows her to the palace.'
 'To try to make her agree to his list of wishes.'
 'Exactly.'

> Slip slap slip slap the frog jumped up the steps of the
> palace to the front door. Now he reached up, knocked,
> and shouted: 'Princess! Princess! Open up! Remember
> your promise!'
> Hearing the commotion, the princess ran down the
> white marble stairs and opened the door.
> She was about to slam the door in the frog's face
> when her better nature took over.
> 'What do you want, frog?' she asked.
> 'I would like to sit on your table and share your
> breakfast,' the frog said. 'Just as you promised.'

'This is good,' Helga said. 'The mention of her better nature — that's
very subtle.'
 'Yes,' agreed Mathilde. 'The point is to reveal her natural compassion
in spite of the revulsion she must feel.'
 'I like *natural compassion* too,' said Helga. 'You must use that.'

> With almost all of her being the beautiful princess
> wanted to close the door on the frog and his ridiculous
> request, but she remembered her promise and her
> natural compassion overrode that impulse. She
> opened the door wider and welcomed the creature in.
> 'You may come up the stairs with me, frog, and share

my breakfast. But then I'm afraid you must go back to the well.'

The beautiful princess led the frog up the white marble stairs and into the palace dining room.

Her father the king looked down in astonishment as he saw the ugly green frog slip slap slip slap into the room after his favourite daughter.

'What, my dear, is this?' he asked. 'Why is this frog following you?'

The princess told her father how she had lost her golden ball down the well and how she had been so distressed that she promised she would grant the frog anything he asked if he retrieved it for her.

'And?' asked the king.

'The frog wished to be my friend and share my breakfast,' said the princess.

'It is good that you are keeping your promise, my daughter,' said the king fondly.

Whereupon the frog leapt up onto the table and stationed himself beside the beautiful princess's plate.

'But before,' said Helga, 'we talked about the frog going to the princess's bedroom and sleeping on her bed. You haven't changed your mind about that, have you?'

Mathilde laid down her quill. 'I'm not sure,' she said. 'I think we need to talk about that.'

David's Story

The term ground on but the holidays were not far away. July would bring the long summer break: several weeks of freedom. David planned to return to New Zealand. The heat in Europe in high summer was increasingly unbearable and a bracing New Zealand winter was something to look forward to. There was a certain poignancy in his decision. He had half hoped he might persuade Cara to join him, but clearly that wasn't going to happen.

He had never got around to broaching the subject, perhaps a little wary of her inevitable teasing.

What? Home to meet the family?

Just a check to see if I pass muster?

I assume they'll want to look at my teeth. Better make an appointment with the orthodontist . . .

Now that there was no possibility of Cara joining him, he felt he could bear the ribbing, would even enjoy it.

He would stay in Christchurch with his older brother, Peter, and his wife Jan. Their two kids were at the age he liked them, no longer ankle-biters and not yet surly adolescents. He got on with all of them.

Staying with Peter and Jan was a far more agreeable prospect than returning to the parental home. His father, always distant, was growing more so with increasing deafness, and his mother had never come to grips with the fact that he was an adult who no longer needed her care and constant worry. She would also give him grief about living in Europe not 'settling down' with a wife and a brood of kids. Not to mention what she would have to say — *ad nauseam* — about the beard.

He couldn't imagine how Cara would have coped with them, but he felt sure she would have liked Pete and Jan.

Stop it, David, he rebuked himself.

Not happening.

Miranda, too, was anticipating the summer break. She would spend a week or two or three with her friend Bunny in London. Bunny, with whom she went to school, was still one of her best pals. She had survived two marriages and now, with considerable independent wealth, lived a life of serious frivolity. Miranda and Bunny would dine extremely well, do concerts and theatre and, no doubt, party. When all this had sated them, they would go walking — somewhere beautiful, pleasantly rugged, but not too demanding. Probably not the Lake District — far too many people. Perhaps Scotland, the Cotswolds, or even Dorset.

She would of course leave the girls behind with Michael. There was no question of his joining her, praise god and pass the ammunition. There was some long-overdue maintenance work needed on the chateau, something to do with pipes, and Michael wanted to supervise the contractors. In fact Michael knew less about contracting and pipes than she did about particle physics; he probably wanted to make sure they didn't steal the lead off the roof.

'What do you think of the Cotswolds?' she asked him, putting aside the handful of travel brochures she had picked up in an agency in Arras.

'I don't think of them very much at all,' he said, not bothering to set aside his *Spectator*. 'Why?'

'Bunny and I might do a walking tour.'

'Really?' He did put down his paper. 'I can't quite visualise Bunny Bulow without high heels.'

'Try not to be sarcastic, Michael. It doesn't go with your smoking jacket.'

Michael looked at her with surprise.

'I'm not wearing a smoking jacket.'

'Exactly,' said Miranda mysteriously. 'Be serious for once. What do you think?'

'I *was* being serious. I don't know much about the Cotswolds apart from having driven through them about a hundred times. Probably quite a nice place for a walking tour — not too strenuous. There, will that do?'

Miranda sensed the rebuff and bristled.

'The world is full of nice places for walking tours,' she said. 'Why is it that you and I never seem to take advantage of them? Or a bike tour for that matter?'

'What are you talking about? I've never once heard you evince a passion for walking or biking.'

'Answer the question.'

'I would have thought the answer was obvious. We have a huge responsibility here at Huntingdon, all the more so since Oliver passed on the mantle. We've had two daughters to raise and as far as I can recall you've always preferred our holidays to be in cities — large cities with shops and galleries and restaurants and more shops. Is that not so?'

Miranda was silent.

'And speaking personally, I've always preferred, when travelling from A to B, to do so in the comfort of a car, a railway carriage or a plane, rather than doing so on foot or dressed in lycra pushing pedals.'

If Michael hoped that this rejoinder would silence his wife he was mistaken.

'So you dislike walking?'

'I do,' said Michael. 'To my mind, a walking tour is merely a way of getting from pub to pub with the added disadvantage of getting wet and sweaty, and feet covered in blisters.'

'I suppose that's why you play so much golf?'

'I hardly ever play golf. Don't exaggerate.'

'I never exaggerate.'

'Stop playing red flag,' said Michael mildly, picking up the *Spectator* once more.

Miranda concentrated grumpily on her grapefruit, sending thin jets of eye-smarting juice into the air.

'Anyway,' she said, eventually returning to the fray, 'I trust you won't spend too much time on the golf course while I'm away. Remember, you're looking after the girls. It's their holiday too, you know.'

Once again, Michael put his paper aside. By now he was quite irritated.

Their two daughters, Amanda, who was thirteen, and Julia, who was eleven, had arrived quite late in their marriage after Miranda had come to realise with some alarm that her biological clock was ticking ever more loudly. Needing to do something about it, she had done something about it.

Michael had taken easily to parenthood as it had scarcely made a difference to his daily life and its various imperatives. Miranda had found it a struggle, being unprepared for motherhood and not having a lot of support. Her own mother had died when Miranda was a teenager; her father, a little like Michael, was a workaholic whose only real interest was Huntingdon; and she had few close friends except for those, like Bunny, she had made at school or at Cambridge, none of whom lived anywhere near.

She had done her best, helped by the fact that both daughters were placid and amiable babies and continued to be biddable and uncomplicated as they grew up. Miranda, who had never particularly liked children, was every so often surprised to find that she was rather fond of her own. Recently, however, Amanda was occasionally displaying signs that adolescence was upon her, with outbreaks of petulance and even, occasionally, rage.

This latter was causing Miranda some concern. It was why she was experiencing a *soupçon* of guilt at leaving the girls with Michael.

'What do you mean "It's their holiday too"?' asked Michael evenly.

Miranda was taken aback at the aggression in his tone.

'I just want you to make sure the girls have a nice time while I'm away.'

'While you're away,' Michael repeated with heavy irony. 'On holiday.'

'It's not too much to ask,' said Miranda.

'Did it not occur to you that the girls might have a very nice time on a trip to London? You know? Bright lights, big city, the London Eye? And then a leisurely stroll through the Cotswolds or the Chilterns or whatever?'

'They've been on the London Eye,' said Miranda, somewhat lamely, and knowing it was lame even as she said it.

'And did it not also occur to you that I am actually *working* most of the so-called holidays. I have a business to run, contractors to organise, the whole shebang. I can assure you I will not have the time to do a bloody Donald Trump and swan around the golf courses of northern France.'

'Bunny doesn't have the room,' said Miranda.

It was capitulation and she knew it.

She stabbed even more savagely at her grapefruit and was rewarded by sudden, searing sting in her right eye.

'You haven't told us,' said Jan Cunningham, as she ladled salad onto David's plate, 'about your trip down the Rhine. God, I'd love to do that. They're always advertising it on TV.'

'Sounds beautiful,' said Peter. 'One day, darling.'

It was, for David, an uncomfortable moment. He had forgotten mentioning in one of his infrequent emails to his brother about the river cruise he was planning for the spring break.

'Sad story,' he said, after a pause. 'At the very last minute the person I was going with had some pretty bad news from home, so we had to call the whole trip off.'

Jan glanced at him. 'That *was* sad,' she said. 'I hope the news wasn't too serious?'

'Family stuff,' said David. The faces around the table were expectant so he felt it incumbent to add something. 'I understand her father had a severe stroke,' he said.

Peter laughed. 'You don't sound too sure.'

Jan gave him a quick warning look, sensing David's discomfort.

'Why didn't you just carry on and do the cruise by yourself? I'd be tempted,' Peter said.

David shook his head. 'Didn't seem appropriate at the time.'

'Pity,' said Peter. 'Sounds a great trip.'

'It sure does,' said Jan, 'but it's so much easier for you, isn't it?' She turned to him, smiling. 'It's just down the road for you, whereas for us . . .'

The conversation shifted to other things: the comings and goings and travails of various relatives and mutual friends. David, to his surprise, found himself strangely uninterested and detached. It didn't particularly matter to him that Amy had lost her job, that Jack and Moira had moved to the winterless north, that Uncle Bill had suspected bowel cancer, or that Ella's brother had finally come out. It was a measure, he supposed, of how far he had moved on. Moved *away*.

He visited his parents and found them smaller somehow; he found it was even more difficult to talk to them. They had no real knowledge of the world he lived in and could not access it. He saw their eyes glaze over when he tried to help them understand, so he stopped trying and retreated to banalities and small talk. It was disconcerting — like talking to strangers at a bus stop. He showed them photos on his phone, thinking these might interest them, but the photos were so small that even he found them reduced, insignificant: an art gallery with postage stamps on the wall.

Only the photos and short videos of war memorials and war graves provoked some interest, in his mother at least. She repeated the names of the places like a long-remembered catechism: Ypres, Passchendaele, the Somme, Vimy Ridge. His father was uninterested.

Neither of them mentioned his beard.

'And Michael?' asked Bunny Bulow. 'How is dear old Michael?'
'You know,' said Miranda, 'same old, same old . . . Just as busy as ever. I honestly believe he's worse than Daddy. He's let the school become his whole life.'

'At least you haven't,' said Bunny.

'God no,' laughed Miranda. 'There's more to life than timetables, sick bays and whiteboards.'

'And the girls? Did you consider bringing them?'

Miranda paused. 'I did, but you know . . . I think they preferred to stay at home. It will give them a chance for some quality time with Michael.'

Bunny knew. She laughed. 'Quite so,' she said, 'and it will give you a chance for some quality time with dear old Bunny.'

'**D**o you have a girlfriend, Uncle David?'
'Liza!'

At twelve, Miles was old enough to be mortified by his younger sister's directness.

Earlier that morning David had borrowed Jan's car to take the kids to the beach as the day was sunny. The three now sat on the hot sand on the Sumner foreshore not far from Cave Rock.

David was feeling a little *distrait*. He had forgotten how attractive this beach was, with its rock walls and Norfolk pines, and he was visited by memories of childhood visits. At the same time, although several years had passed since the devastating series of earthquakes in Christchurch, he was perturbed by how much evidence remained of their destruction — ruined buildings, roadworks and lines of shipping containers stacked as buttresses against falling debris from the towering cliffs all about. Moreover, he couldn't help obsessing about how lovely it would have been, were it summer, to have had Cara lying on the sand beside him, in sunglasses and bikini, asking him to rub some more sunscreen onto her back.

These last thoughts were the ones interrupted by Eliza's question and he was momentarily nonplussed.

'Take no notice of her, Uncle David. She can't help being cheeky!'

'Was not!' said Eliza. 'I only asked!'

Recovering himself, David said, 'No, that's fine. It's a perfectly reasonable question.'

'Well?' said Eliza.

'Well what?'

'Do you have a girlfriend?'

'I have had,' smiled David. 'In fact I had a girlfriend quite recently. I was just thinking of her.'

'What were you thinking?' asked Eliza, pressing home.

'Well,' said David, 'I was actually thinking how lovely this beach is and how much she would have enjoyed it.'

'Where is she now?' asked Miles, feeling emboldened now.

David shrugged. 'Not really sure . . . I haven't heard from her for a while.'

'Did she run away?' asked Eliza. 'Like Aunty Heidi?'

'Liza!' warned Miles again.

Oh god, thought David. These are sweet kids but they don't take prisoners. He stared out over the sea beyond the breakers. There was a small ship on the horizon —heading towards Lyttelton, he supposed. He turned back to his niece and nephew.

'I reckon you guys would love France, where I live now. How about I try to talk your parents into bringing you over sometime? I know your mum is really keen to go on a river cruise, and the town where I live, Arras, is a pretty neat place. What do you reckon?'

They looked at him, eyes shining, girlfriends and Aunty Heidi forgotten.

'Cool!' said Miles.

Michael was in his office when Agnès Delon knocked and put her head around the door.

'Headmaster, I've just had a call from a gentleman who would like to make an appointment to see you.'

'Oh? Did he give a name?'

'He said his name was Martin Bernstein.'

Cara's
Manuscript

— KASSEL —

'I saw Dortchen Wild in town this morning,' said Wilhelm.

'Oh?' replied Jacob. 'And how is she?'

'She appears very well. She rebuked me for walking too quickly — quite the reproving martinet. I should have told her she was not old enough to rebuke me!'

'Dortchen is wise beyond her years,' said Jacob, smiling. 'I'm sure she was fully justified.'

'Be that as it may,' said Wilhelm, 'she did tell me something very interesting.'

'Oh?'

'It relates to the charming Fräulein Heller, the one who has set her cap at you.'

'Don't start that again, brother,' said Jacob stiffly.

'You know it's true!' said Wilhelm.

'I have never given the foolish girl any encouragement.'

'I quite agree,' said Wilhelm, 'and your lack of encouragement was very apparent on her last visit. I was proud of you.'

'You're patronising me now.'

'You should know that to some young women, discouragement is merely a signal that they must redouble their efforts.'

Jacob looked at his brother with a weary smile. 'And I, brother, remain quite mystified as to how you have become such an expert on the ways of young women.'

'Oh, I don't claim expertise,' said Wilhelm, 'but one cannot deny the evidence of one's eyes. Anyway, don't you want to know what Dortchen told me?'

'Of course I do,' said Jacob.

'Fräulein Heller and her sister are in mourning, as we know.'

'Yes, a death in the family.'

'Remember I asked them when they were here about their grandmother?'

Jacob nodded.

'And Fräulein Heller ignored the question and instead began to tell us of this new story about a princess and a frog.'

'Of course I remember. The story sounds intriguing.'

'What Fräulein Heller rather artfully avoided telling us was that it is her grandmother who has died. It is for their dead oma that she and her sister are in mourning.'

'Is this true? How does Dortchen know?' asked Jacob, surprised.

'It seems Herr Wild knows their father.'

'I see,' Jacob mused. 'This means . . .'

Wilhelm nodded. 'I know: she was such a promising source of tales. But recall how we were led astray? And were relieved that the death was apparently not the grandmother?'

'I do, I do.'

'But it *was* the grandmother.'

'That is a pity.'

'It is. But why did Fräulein Heller not want us to know?'

Jacob shrugged. 'I have no idea. It's a mystery.'

'Not really, brother,' said Wilhelm. 'Think about it . . .'

'But why should the frog not go into the princess's bedroom?' demanded Helga.

'Because . . . because — can't you see? — it is unseemly.'

'How? Why?'

'Don't pretend to be so naïve, Helga. You know exactly what I mean.'

'But earlier in the story we have announced that the frog wishes to visit her bedroom,' said Helga.

'We can change that,' said Mathilde.

'I don't see why we need to do that.'

'We need to do that,' said Mathilde, 'because Herr Grimm is a very proper gentleman. He could well be offended by the idea.'

'He would only be offended if he himself were capable of offensive ideas. A very proper gentleman, as you put it, would not put any unseemly construction on this. We are talking about a frog prince, not some philandering Bluebeard.'

'Helga!'

'But do you see what I mean? The frog just wants to be with her — at breakfast, while she naps, and presumably when she plays with her golden ball.'

'Perhaps.'

Helga did have a point, Mathilde conceded to herself. Was she being too cautious? Were they to deliver the story to the brothers — they were *not* going to deliver the story to the brothers — but if they *were* to deliver the story to the brothers, what would a perfectly innocent reader make of a frog's perfectly innocent desire to be a friend to the princess?

Was she being the unseemly one?

And yet . . . and yet . . .

She did at heart desire her lovely seemly man to see *her* as desirable, to see her as . . . and to nudge him in that direction might mean taking a small risk. She needed him to access the secret message even if it were not made explicit. For it could not be made explicit. That *would* be unseemly.

It was such a conundrum it made her head spin.

And Oma? What would Oma think?

And then she saw her seemly man once more and felt his tender hand in hers, and Oma's opinion no longer mattered.

It was only a frog.

It was only a story.

'All right,' she whispered to Helga, 'perhaps we could let the frog into the bedroom.'

David's
Story

— ARRAS —

Michael looked at Agnès Delon in surprise.
'Bernstein?'

'Yes, I . . .'

'Related to Cara?'

'I believe he is her father, headmaster.'

'He said so?'

'He did, headmaster. The first time he rang.'

'Has he rung before?'

'Oh yes, he rang two or three days ago. He wanted to speak to his daughter.'

'And?'

'Of course I told him his daughter no longer taught at the school, that she had not been here all term. He seemed very surprised.'

'Agnès, why have you not told me this before?'

Agnès stiffened and gave him a slightly defensive look. 'I did not consider it important, headmaster. Is it?'

Yes it is, thought Michael, but he said, 'It probably doesn't matter now, but we have been puzzling over Madame Bernstein's sudden departure, as you know, so . . . Perhaps Mr Bernstein — what did you say his first name was?'

'Martin.'

'Perhaps Martin Bernstein might shed some light on the business.'

'So should he come in?'

'Oh, yes. Please make an appointment.'

Martin Bernstein did not look a great deal like his daughter. Short where she was tall, thickset to the point of squatness where she was slender, and iron grey where she was dark haired. Of course, apart from the height, Cara may grow into all of these things. A definite point of similarity, though, was the directness.

'You have a nice setup here,' he said as he sank into one of the visitor's chairs.

Michael suspected he wasn't referring just to the landscape and the architecture.

'It is a rather nice place to work. Can I offer you a sherry?'

'Why not?'

Michael only occasionally offered his visitors a drink. It was a custom Oliver Huntingdon had established and Michael found useful to maintain from time to time. He kept a decanter of a rather good Amontillado in a sideboard in his office.

He considered that this was such an occasion. It was the holidays and times were rather more leisured. Moreover, he wished to put his visitor at ease, not because he anticipated the visit becoming prickly, but more in the hope of eliciting information about his elusive daughter. How had he described her to Cunningham? A woman of mystery. Besides, some titbits about Cara would be a useful gift to Miranda, in exchange for the silk tie she would inevitably bring him back from London.

He raised his glass.

'Your very good health.'

'And yours.'

'So, how can I help?' asked Michael.

'I've asked to see you to find out if you can tell me where Cara is. I was surprised to learn from your receptionist that she's no longer on the staff here.'

Michael winced inwardly on Agnès's behalf. 'Receptionist' would have stung. Then, professionalism to the fore, he asked, 'You are of course . . . ?'

'Cara's father. Sorry, I should have made that clear. You need ID?'

Michael waved away the suggestion. 'No, of course not, Mr Bernstein. But, you know . . .'

'Call me Martin.'

'I'm afraid I can't tell you much. Your daughter has not been with us for the past term. She disappeared immediately before the beginning of the spring term just past.'

'Disappeared? What do you mean?'

'Just that. She didn't resign or anything. She just failed to show up at the beginning of the term. She sent us no message, didn't answer emails or return our calls. To this day she simply hasn't been in touch.'

'Good lord.'

'We kept the position open for some time but eventually had to accept that she did not intend returning and I was compelled to appoint someone else to her job. We were sorry to lose her,' he added, to ease the pill a little. 'Cara was an excellent teacher.'

'Right up until she stopped?'

Michael nodded.

'But she might have . . .'

Michael anticipated what Martin Bernstein was about to say. 'No,' he said. 'We're sure her leaving was premeditated. Nothing suggests an accident or anything worse.'

He told Cara's father as much as he knew. About Cara's clearing out her classroom and locker, her leaving David Cunningham and checking out of the hotel in Bonn, her abruptly terminating the lease on her apartment in Arras.

Martin Bernstein listened sombrely.

'All very strange,' he murmured.

'My wife,' added Michael, 'was particularly concerned. She even arranged — quite unofficially, let me be clear — to have the police check things out. They weren't able to tell us a great deal except that they don't believe your daughter has come to any harm.'

'That's something, I guess.'

'They also said they don't believe Cara has left the EU.'

'And that's all they said?'

Michael nodded. 'I'm afraid so.'

He opened his desk drawer and took out a small, leather-bound business-card file. He flicked through and found Véronique Robert's card, which he passed to Martin Bernstein.

'This is the officer who looked into it. Again, I stress it was an unofficial investigation. In my view, though, she did a quite thorough job. She talked to a number of the staff here, especially those who knew Cara well. All the same, you might like to talk to her. She may be more forthcoming to a family member.'

'Thank you,' said Martin Bernstein, taking the card.

'Is there anything you could tell me that might shed any light?' Michael asked cautiously. 'I mean about Cara herself.'

'What can I tell you? I suppose I should say that we haven't always seen eye to eye. If I were honest, I'd have to say we're too alike. Headstrong, you know. We've had some pretty serious rows over the years. Cara's mother and I often wondered, you know . . . We often wondered whether if we'd stayed together . . . I mean, you try your best, don't you? You have kids?'

Michael nodded. 'Two daughters.'

'How old?'

Michael told him, and Bernstein sighed and said, 'Be warned. One day they'll stab you in the back. They're probably sharpening the knives right now.'

Michael laughed. 'Oh dear!'

He left his desk to pour his visitor another sherry. Martin Bernstein held out his glass, his brow darkening.

'I'm not joking. Let me tell you, Berkeley was such a bad idea.'

Michael was puzzled.

'You know — college. University. Gave her some crazy ideas. You couldn't talk to her anymore — not unless you wanted an argument. When she left home, finally there was peace.'

'Well, I suppose—'

'The main problem was Gus, of course.'

'Gus?'

'Augusta. My wife. She and Cara . . . you know how it is.'

Michael, who didn't know how it was, raised an eyebrow.

'Cara always blamed Gus. And when Miriam — Cara's mother — died, Cara blamed me. I'd left Miriam for Gus beforehand, you know how it is.'

'I see,' said Michael, who was beginning to.

'And Gus, of course, didn't like how I kept up Cara's allowance, especially when she started earning. Said I was wasting my money — that my daughter was an ingrate.'

'So you haven't seen your daughter lately?' Michael asked delicately.

'To tell you the honest truth, not for years.'

'I'm sorry to hear that.'

'She hardly ever calls. About every other year. She keeps in better with Callie.'

'Callie?'

'Her sister. But she's in Boulder, so we don't see a lot of her either.' He lapsed into a brooding silence before saying, 'You know — what the hell should I call you?'

'Michael. Call me Michael.'

'You know, Michael, those years when the kids were young and we lived in Paris — they were the happiest in my life.'

'In Paris?'

'I was with the State Department. Very lowly of course, but figured I would be important one day!'

'I didn't know that — I mean, I didn't realise Cara had lived in France as a child.'

'No, she never gives much away.'

There was another pause as Bernstein studied his drink.

Cautiously still, Michael said, 'So now you're back in France and you were hoping to . . .'

'That's it. Looking for Cara.'

'I presume she's not expecting you.'

'Oh no. She won't know I'm here. Callie told me about this place. I guess Cara must have told her at some point, so I figured I'd drop in.'

'Just like that?'

'More or less. Gus and I . . . well, we've come to the end of the line. So it came to me — there's a roadblock out of the way so . . . But she's gone, you say. I can't say I've had much benefit from my investment.'

'Your investment?'

'The allowance. I should at least have visiting rights!' For the first time Martin Bernstein allowed himself a smile. 'My whole reason for coming was to catch up with Cara. As I said, we're pretty much alike: headstrong, impulsive.' He went to stand.

'I'm really sorry we're not able to help you,' said Michael, extending his hand. 'I do hope you find her. I rather fear it's a bit of a needle in a haystack.'

'I guess so,' said Martin Bernstein. 'Tell you what, though. Could I have the names of some of those friends of hers? You know, the guy she was in Germany with just before she vanished? Might be something there.'

'Of course, but none of them seem to know any more than I do. We're all quite bamboozled. Oh, and David Cunningham is in New Zealand right now on holiday. He'll be back next week. Actually, most of the staff are off for the summer — even my wife,' he added deprecatingly. 'But we'll give you their email addresses.'

'Thanks very much,' said Bernstein. He took Véronique Robert's card out of his pocket and studied it. 'Meanwhile, I think I'll check out this lead.'

'Good idea,' said Michael, ushering him to the door. 'Please leave your details with Agnès and she'll send you that information shortly.'

'And the walking tour?' asked Michael. 'You survived it, then?'

Miranda felt gratified. The past few days had been a trifle strained, as she had expected them to be. She knew Michael didn't appreciate that there had been no option but to spend the extra two weeks in London. Bunny had set up so many engagements and immovable feasts that it had been difficult making an appropriate time for their walk — the whole thing had been a logistical nightmare. In the end they had been compelled to buy a package and had no choice at all over the timing.

'Oh, it was so lovely! So enjoyable and peaceful being away from crowds for a few days. You know, you tend to forget living up here just how many people there are in London these days.'

This was not entirely honest. The walk had been hell. Crowded. Two days of rain and then four days of searing sunshine that had both wilted and burnt her. She'd had to buy expensive new walking boots and these rewarded her with blisters that popped painfully and remained as widening circles of increasing agony. It was the blisters that brought home to her that she had never really had any real understanding of the word 'mile'. Eleven miles on a brochure sounded a lark. In reality, the eleven miles were endless. The select country hotels and charming inns the brochure promised were neither select nor especially charming, and she discovered quite early on that thatched cottages and stone churches palled very quickly when your face was red and sweaty and your feet felt as if they had been dipped in lava.

It didn't help that Bunny made this discovery a day or so earlier and kept acidly reminding Miranda that this had been one of her stupidest ideas, pointing out more than once that for the cost of the tour they could have had several amazing meals at thoroughly decent London restaurants.

One of the reasons she needed to extend her stay was to recuperate physically and visually. Her face had been bright red and her nose peeling when they returned to the bliss of Bunny's apartment.

'So do you think the girls would have enjoyed it?' asked Michael.

'Oh no,' said Miranda hurriedly. 'A little too demanding just yet. Perhaps in a year or two.'

Michael guessed from Miranda's brittle brightness that the walk had been probably a little less than lovely. He hoped so anyway.

He had been very annoyed by her delayed return, which was most inconvenient. The only real sign of contrition had been Miranda's presenting him with two ties rather than the expected one.

'Bunny chose them. She has exquisite taste.'

That may have been true, but Bunny's taste was not Michael's taste; her 'exquisite' was his 'flamboyant'.

Now, things less taut, he remembered he had not told her about the visit from Martin Bernstein.

'Michael! You bad bear! Why didn't you tell me!'

Michael shrugged. 'I'm telling you now.'

'What was he like?'

Miranda was suddenly energised. All her fascination with *l'affaire Bernstein* came tumbling back.

'Oh, I don't know. He's in his sixties, I guess. Shortish, solid. He came over as quite bitter.'

'Bitter?'

'Yes. He seemed to bring a cloud into the room with him.'

'Why so, do you think?'

'Unhappiness probably. It appears as though his latest marriage is breaking up or has broken up.'

'With Cara's mother?'

'Oh no, she's no longer alive. This would be Cara's stepmother. You know, straight out of Grimm. She and Cara didn't — don't — get on.'

'Any ugly stepsisters?'

'I don't know about that. There is a real sister, apparently, back in the States. It's through her that Bernstein heard that Cara was here.'

'Not through Cara?'

'Oh no. That's the thing — they haven't kept in touch. In fact he said he hasn't seen her for several years.'

'Interesting. So why is he looking for Cara now?'

'He didn't really say in so many words. I imagine he might be reassessing things now that wife number two is leaving him.'

'Oh, I see.'

'He banged on about his so-called investment in Cara, and his lack of return on it. Apparently he's been paying Cara an allowance for years.'

'That does sound awfully transactional.'

'It does. I can't say I warmed to the man.'

'So, no signs of a massive stroke?'

Michael smiled. 'Not even a tiny one.'

'So what's he doing now?'

'He's going to see that police officer — what's her name?'

'Véronique Robert.'

'That's the one. I gave him her card. Oh, and he wants to talk to Cunningham and some of the others.'

'So he has no idea where she might be?'

'No more than us.'

Miranda frowned. 'What a pity. One might have hoped he had something useful to share.'

Michael gave a wry smile.

'Oh, but he did. He told us we need to watch our backs.'

'Whatever for?'

'Because one day our sweet girls will plunge knives into them!'

Cara's
Manuscript

The frog followed the beautiful princess slip slap slip slap up the stairs to her bedroom.

The princess pulled back the bedclothes and climbed into her bed for a nap. Before she could protest, the frog jumped up onto the counterpane.

'What now?' asked Helga.

The quill had paused in Mathilde's hand. This was the most delicate part. A false move here and everything that had been so carefully constructed would be for naught.

'It's difficult,' she sighed.

'She must kiss him,' insisted Helga.

'Must she?' asked Mathilde. 'Would that not be too . . .' She could not think of the right word.

'She must. That is her test.'

'But it's so repulsive.'

'That is the point.'

Mathilde looked at Helga pleadingly. 'Could the frog not jump at *her* and kiss her?'

'But where would the test be in that case?'

Mathilde did not reply. She could see Helga's logic but she could not overcome her qualms. She still felt manipulated into bringing the frog into the princess's bedroom in the first place, but the bigger part of the problem was Jacob Grimm, who seemed so correct, so proper. He was bound to find the episode improper, distasteful. She sank her brow into her hands.

'Why is it so difficult?' asked Helga.

Mathilde sighed. Why was it so hard for Helga to understand? This point in the story was the fulcrum, the tipping point, the point where the whole endeavour could either founder or lead to wondrous things — to happily ever after.

It was the kissing. It was such a physical thing, such an intimate thing. The kissing may both appal and repel Jacob Grimm, and he would transfer that repulsion to the princess, and through that declension to repulsion at the one whom the princess was representing: Mathilde Heller, the one who venerated him, who truly loved him.

'It is the kissing,' she said turning to Helga in misery. 'This kissing is the problem.'

There was a pause as Helga tried to work out how to respond. Eventually she said, 'Mathilde, this is hard to say, but I do feel that it is your imagination that is unseemly, to use your word. A kiss is not unseemly. We kiss. We kiss Mutti and Papa. We kissed Oma and she kissed us. A kiss can be as chaste as a newborn. You know that, surely?'

Mathilde nodded. She knew that. She also knew, though, that in the scheme of the story they were devising, this kiss was not that kind of kiss. It was a kiss of potential passion. It was the frog's huge mouth, the frog's wetness, the frog's slap slip slap slip.

'She cannot kiss the frog,' said Mathilde finally. 'I cannot let her do this.'

Helga was frustrated. 'I do think, sister, that you are over-reacting. You're being far too precious.'

Mathilde did not respond.

Then Helga's eyes suddenly lit up. 'But we are both being silly — fixated.'

'What do you mean?'

'I mean, what *is* the kiss? Surely in our story it is merely a gesture of affection. It is a sign that the princess has overcome her revulsion. What if the gesture of affection were not a kiss but a caress, a pat on the head, even a tender smile?'

It was as if an unbearable load had been lifted from Mathilde's back.

She hugged her clever sister. 'Of course,' she laughed. 'We have been such sillies agonising over a duck egg.'

'You mean a frog egg?' laughed Helga. 'Pick up your quill. Let's work this through right now.'

His position at the Royal Library had been a godsend to Jacob Grimm. Since their mother had died less than a year earlier, he was now effectively the sole parent — father and mother rolled into one — and financially responsible for four brothers and a sister. Aunt Zimmer had helped, of course, but Jacob's now relatively generous salary had eased their circumstances a great deal.

All the same, it was a difficult and precarious situation for a young man not yet twenty-five, even a twenty-five-year-old going on sixty. He wore his responsibility heavily, along with his scholarship, and the two left little room for anything else.

He was grateful for the help and support of Wilhelm, little more than a year younger. However, Wilhelm's health was not good and he was only occasionally able to contribute financially; quite often, in fact, he was invalided and his medical costs were an added drain. While he was now earning a little money at the library, Wilhelm's position was essentially honorary.

Such issues in no way undermined the close relationship between Jacob and Wilhelm. Academically they had followed the same trajectory; their passions, dreams and ambitions were well-nigh identical. They shared the same room, the same study, the same books. They would share the same house, with occasional interruptions, until separated by death.

Their disagreements were rare and minor.

Jacob was a purist. He wanted their ancient folk stories to be told as they were received — in the manner and voice of the *Volk*. Wilhelm, for his part, felt that in transcribing the stories they should be polished, made more accessible if necessary. Rather than raw historical data for other scholars and experts in the field, he saw that the stories could have a wider audience — especially children. On this point there was some agreement. As a purist, Jacob was uncomfortable with the earthiness, the lewdness of some of the stories and was not unhappy to see such elements expurgated.

Some instinct had allowed Mathilde Heller to perceive this. She was determined to follow that instinct in the face of Helga's protests.

The princess stretched out on her bed, the frog beside her. She began to feel a little guilty that she had run away from him, had denied her promise.

The frog had kindly offered to retrieve her golden ball. It could not have been easy for the little creature to lift the heavy object and bring it up from the bottom of the deep, dark well.

The frog's request for a favour in return had been perfectly reasonable, given that her offer that he could ask anything of her was an invitation to greed.

The frog had not been greedy, had not been excessive.

All he had asked was to be her friend.

This was, now that she considered it, more than generous. He could have asked for diamonds, rubies and pearls.

To sit beside her at table, to sit on her counterpane while she napped. Such little things.

At that point the beautiful princess felt a brief moment of gratitude towards the frog. Then, before she closed her eyes, that gratitude prompted her to reach out and, with the very tip of her finger, touch the frog tenderly on the top of his head.

David's
Story

— ARRAS —

Michael heard no more from Martin Bernstein. The grapevine, though, did reveal to David Cunningham that he had visited the school.

It was not a very long grapevine.

Shortly after the summer term began, David was lunching one Saturday with Angus in Arras when the big man said, 'Oh, something that might interest you.'

'What's that?' asked David.

'During the holidays Cara Bernstein's father visited the school.'

'You're joking! How do you know?'

'The usual: Miranda. She was a little peeved she missed him herself. He spoke to Michael.'

'Where was Miranda?'

'Went off to London for the holidays.'

'That makes sense,' said David. 'She probably needed a break after working for two whole weeks.'

Angus grinned.

'So, Cara's father — did you learn much?'

'Only everything that Miranda knows.'

'Not much then.'

'Not really. He came over from the States to see Cara — no idea she'd done a bunk. Apparently they haven't seen each other for years. He found out she was at Huntingdon through Cara's sister. They must keep in touch.'

'No massive stroke?'

'Doesn't seem so. Unless there was a miraculous recovery. According to Miranda, he's a bitter old father who wants to bury the hatchet.'

'Wait a minute,' said David, with a slight feeling of excitement. 'Cara's sister? She never mentioned a sister.'

'Never mentioned her to me either,' said Angus.

'Did Michael get this sister's address?'

Angus shrugged. 'No idea. I doubt it. According to Miranda, he didn't get anything much really. The old guy knew even less than we do.'

'Which is basically zilch, *nada*, nothing,' said David.

'That pretty much sums it up,' agreed Angus.

Some days later David was watching a school tennis match when Michael, on one of his irregular tours around the school, dropped down on the bench beside him.

'So how was New Zealand?' he asked.

David responded with as much information as politeness demanded, focusing mainly on the weather, guessing that Michael would find that far more interesting than his family.

'You yourself?' said David. 'Were you able to get away?'

Michael laughed. 'How nice that would have been! No, too much work here. There was some maintenance and the usual. Miranda took a few days away to go walking with a friend.'

David managed a neutral tone. 'That must have been pleasant.'

'She enjoyed it.'

Michael was wearing a white Panama hat, a white shirt, but no jacket. It was a hot day. Perhaps his relative informality, perhaps the anonymity of his dark glasses, encouraged David to say, 'I hear Cara Bernstein's father visited the school in the holidays.'

The dark glasses turned to him. 'You did? My goodness, word gets around quickly.'

He paused, and David could not be certain whether he would continue.

'Yes, he did. He was surprised to discover she no longer worked here. We had quite a chat, in fact.'

'He didn't know—'

'Less than we do,' said Michael. 'It's actually been on my mind to tell you about it, given your ...' — he paused — 'interest in the matter. But as everything was so inconclusive it didn't seem that important in the end. In fact,' he added, 'had you been here at school, rather than gadding about in the Antipodes, he probably would have spoken to you. He was quite keen to talk to Cara's friends. He didn't email you? I gave him your address — I thought you wouldn't mind in the circumstances.'

'No, nothing,' said David. 'I understand he mentioned Cara's sister.'

Again, the dark glasses turned to him. 'You *are* well informed. Yes, he did as a matter of fact. I'm sorry, I've forgotten her name.'

'You didn't by any chance get her address?' asked David.

'No, I didn't, I'm afraid,' said Michael, standing up. 'Actually, it didn't even occur to me to ask.'

Cara's Manuscript

— KASSEL —

No sooner had the beautiful princess tenderly touched the head of the frog than he turned into a most handsome prince, whose beautiful, kind eyes were filled with tears.

He stood alongside her bed looking down upon her and said, 'Thank you a thousand times, lovely princess, for rescuing me from that deep, dark well. Only you could have performed such a deed. You must know I was cursed by a wicked witch whose evil spell changed me into the ugly, wet frog you found there. The witch condemned me to remain in the well until rescued by a princess of unsurpassed beauty. I humbly beg you to consider becoming my bride and coming with me to rule in my kingdom.'

This proposal so gladdened the beautiful princess's heart, so filled her with delight, that she accepted in an instant.

David's
Story

The next break, the autumn holiday in October, saw Peter and Jan Cunningham, with their children Miles and Eliza, visit Europe. The highlight was to be the river cruise down the Rhine that Jan had so long dreamed of. David had come to like the children more and more over his visit to New Zealand. So much so that before he left he began plotting with Jan to persuade Peter to consider the trip.

David discovered that rather than coming to regret his enthusiasm for this visit, it became an object of increasing satisfaction, a satisfaction that deepened when the family came to squeeze in with him in the Arras apartment at the end of their trip.

On holiday now himself, David was free to show the family around.

Jan was still so enchanted with their cruise when they arrived in Arras, the children so abuzz, and Peter so warm that David felt utterly vindicated, despite a deep pang of regret that the trip he and Cara had planned had turned to dust.

'So it was worth it?' David asked.

It was their first evening and David had taken them to a restaurant for an early dinner.

'Absolutely,' said Peter.

'It was lovely,' said Jan, 'and whoever would've thought we'd get to do it before you!'

The children chorused their agreement as they bent to their food.

'Expensive, though,' said Peter.

'Everything's expensive, but you can afford it.' David winked at his brother.

That was probably true. Although he often pleaded poverty, Peter was now the senior partner in the law firm their father had started over forty years before.

The cruise had started in Amsterdam, and carried on through Cologne, Bonn and the Rhine Gorge to eventually end in Basel. Their first couple of days with David, most of the conversation focused on the trip — the sights, the food, their peculiar fellow travellers and the various cultural oddities, which led to often-comic misunderstandings. There was a lot of laughter.

Somehow they all managed to get along in the small apartment, which, despite the tiny spare bedroom David used as a study, was really only designed for one person. David slept in the study, Jan and Peter in his double bed, and the children in the living room: Eliza on the settee and Miles on a borrowed mattress on the floor.

The forced physical intimacy and the mutual warmth of the shared experience seemed to lead to a closer bonding. David found a name for it: *family*. He realised he liked it very much. He also realised he had missed it, and had been missing it for years.

It was this emotional intimacy that allowed him to open up more than he had for a considerable time. When Jan asked, quite innocently, one evening, 'Whatever happened, David, to that friend whose father had a stroke or something? You know, the time you had to abandon your cruise?'

'Ah,' said David. 'Quite a long tale.'

'Thereby hangs a tale! It was a woman, wasn't it? I assume it was a woman.'

David nodded. 'I worked with her. Her name was Cara.'

And he told them the whole story.

'So you never heard from her again?' asked Jan.

David shook his head.

'Extraordinary.' She looked at him quizzically. 'Are you still carrying a torch for her?'

David laughed. 'Good god, no. I'm completely over it.'

'Do you have another girlfriend?'

David shook his head.

'Have you had another girlfriend at all since this Cara disappeared?'

'Not really.'

'That means no,' said Peter.

'It sounds to me,' said Jan decisively, 'like you're definitely still carrying a torch for her, David Cunningham!'

'No, no, no,' said David, able to smile now. 'Cara and I weren't an item for that long in the scheme of things. It was hardly Abelard and Heloise.'

'Hmm,' said Jan. 'You know what they say about absence and the heart.'

'Bullshit,' said David amiably.

'So tell me,' said Peter the next morning when Jan had taken the kids for a walk, 'since we've been on the subject of partners, you ever hear from Heidi?'

'Never,' said David. 'You?'

'Not much chance of my hearing from her if she hasn't been in touch with you.'

'When she said she wanted a clean break,' said David, 'she meant it was to be antibiotic, antibacterial and super-germicidal.'

He could laugh now, but when Heidi left him he had been devastated; so distraught he was not sure whether his life would ever return to an even keel. The healing had taken a long time and things had only really come right after he threw everything aside and started a new life in France

They had been married three years. Happily, he had thought. Blissfully at first. But the sky changed colour and Heidi left him. She did have the grace to tell him to his face, but not a lot of grace. She gave him twelve hours' notice.

There had been no other man — or woman. Either might in many ways have made things easier. No, by way of explanation Heidi had only offered the simple but painful *I've stopped loving you. Don't ask me why.*

Of course he did ask her why, but there was no reply.

There had been no children. He used to get silently angry when people said *Just as well you didn't have kids*, as if by not having kids he had escaped some kind of domestic Alcatraz.

He did sometimes wonder whether kids might have been the glue that would have caused Heidi to stick with him. But it was only an idle wonder. He was safely over Heidi — Cara had helped there — and he felt no longing for her return.

'I don't think she's ever been in touch with the folks either,' said Peter. 'The old man would be disappointed. He was quite sweet on Heidi.'

'Mum wasn't,' said David.

'That's right,' said Peter, remembering. 'No girl good enough for our little David!'

He took them to see his favourite sites in the region until Jan whispered in gentle protest, 'David, these places are haunting and moving, but I fear they're getting a bit boring for the children.'

A little chastened, David shifted his focus from battlefields, war graves and memorials and took them to the Carrière Wellington, which, because of the *son et lumière*, was much more successful.

He had been saving another attraction as something of a highlight to end their visit. He announced it the day before they were due to leave.

'Who likes climbing?'

'Where?'

'A surprise.'

'*Where*?!'

'A place called Place des Héros.'

'What does that mean?'

'More or less how it sounds: Heroes' Square.'

'Don't tease them, David,' said Jan.

'Okay,' said David. 'Heroes' Square is a large square in the centre of the city. It's all cobblestoned and it's surrounded by rather lovely terraced buildings.'

'What are terraced buildings?' asked Miles.

'All built in a row,' explained David, 'and looking very ancient. At the end of Heroes' Square is the Hôtel de Ville, which sounds like a hotel but really it's what we'd call the town hall.'

'We're going to the town hall?' asked Miles dubiously.

'Ah, but this is no ordinary town hall. Parts of it are like a museum and there's some pretty neat stuff to see: giants, underground chambers and even a belfry.'

'What's a belfry?'

'It's a great tower with a huge clock, and there's a viewing platform right up near the top. It's very high and pretty scary.'

'Yes!' Miles shouted.

'How high?' asked Eliza.

'Seventy-five metres,' said David. 'A lot higher than the spire of the Christchurch Cathedral.'

'David, it pains me to remind you that the cathedral tower came down in the earthquakes. Remember? The kids won't recall ever seeing it.'

'God, yes. I forgot. Anyway, the belfry tower is higher than most of the buildings in Christchurch. How's that?'

'Cool!' said Miles.

'Would you like to go?'

There was a chorus of *Yes!*

'That's quite a climb,' said Peter. 'It's not going to be too much for them, is it?'

'Don't worry, Pete,' David reassured him. 'There's a lift most of the way up.'

No sooner had they got out of the lift than Miles and Eliza took off running up the circular staircase, each determined to beat the other to the top.

'So you said it was scary?' Jan asked David anxiously.

'It's safe enough. I mean, you couldn't jump off or anything. Not very good for people with vertigo, though.'

'One of us should be with them,' said Jan. The children had disappeared from sight.

Peter nodded. 'Off you go, Davey boy. You're the youngest.'

'Not necessarily the fittest, though,' replied David. Then, after looking at their faces, he said, 'Oh, all right. Last one to the top's a loser.'

The spiral staircase was constructed of what appeared to be very elderly iron. The stairs were steep and the risers awkwardly organised, but David was determined to catch up with Miles and Eliza. He could hear the clatter of their feet up ahead, their laughter at their race. How were they not puffed? Already the backs of his legs ached as he stretched and leapt. He tried to take two steps at a time but the steps were too far apart, the circle too tight, and his leaps were cramped and awkward. Still, some lizard-brain will to win possessed him, an impulse he hardly recognised, hard and urgent. He sucked in air — he needed to suck in air — and he experienced a sharp stitch. He wanted to stop, to rest, to take stock, but the urge to not let the children shame him compelled him upwards, onwards, even as he felt himself stumble and gasp.

Miles and Eliza reached the platform just ahead of him and, seemingly quite unaffected by the gruelling race, were running around the platform, shouting about what they could see and how high they were.

David was done in. His stitch had risen into his chest like a crippling indigestion. He leaned against a wall for support as he tried to force his lungs to take in more air.

It seemed an age before Jan and Peter arrived.

'How steep was that?' laughed Jan. Then all thought of the climb faded as she gazed out over the parapet.

'Wow!' she said. 'Great!'

'Pretty amazing,' agreed Peter, lifting his phone to take a picture.

Miles and Eliza had completed a circuit of the platform and scampered back to their parents. Seeing Peter with his phone, Eliza shouted, 'Selfie, Dad, selfie!'

'Good idea,' said Jan. 'We can all be in it.'

She looked around for David and was suddenly alarmed to see him slumped against the wall. 'David!'

At the fear in her voice, Peter turned to look, then ran to his brother.

'Are you okay?' he asked, knowing he wasn't.

David peered up at him. Beads of sweat popped on his brow and his face was the colour of putty.

'I don't think I am, Pete,' he whispered. 'I think I need help.'

After the angiogram the cardiologist, who had excellent English, said, 'We may be able to get away with an angioplasty, but to be honest, I think it's likely to be a bypass.'

Angioplasty? Bypass? David lay blinking in a hospital bed.

'A very common procedure, quite safe and relatively non-invasive. We insert a balloon into the affected artery and inflate it to distend the artery. Usually we insert a stent at this point. Do you understand?'

David nodded. 'An uncle had a couple of stents a few years ago.'

Uncle Jim. He never looked back.

'As I said, they're quite common and usually most effective.'

'There's a "but" in your voice.'

The cardiologist said, 'Yes. Monsieur Cunningham, you have had a heart attack. A relatively mild one, admittedly — that is why we are able to have this conversation. However, it does suggest to me that the arterial damage may be too much for stents. You may need a bypass, perhaps even more than one.'

David tried to get his head around what the surgeon was saying. A bypass sounded serious. More than one bypass, positively drastic. Wasn't it the sort of thing old men had? He was not yet in his forties.

'Don't be alarmed, monsieur. A bypass is today a most common and, in nearly all cases, quite safe procedure, unless there are other health factors involved. In your case I see none of those.'

'When—?'

'As soon as can be arranged, monsieur. The sooner the better.'

'It's that urgent?'

'It doesn't pay to waste time after an episode like this. I see you are worried — please don't be. The operation is very straightforward these days and recovery time is quite fast. You will have a few days of post-operative monitoring, and if that all goes according to plan you should be able to go home a few days after that.'

David felt a welling relief.

'Of course you will not be able to race up spiral staircases for some time. We usually recommend several weeks of very light activity only. After that, you should be able to resume your normal life, all going well.'

'All going well,' said David. He was able to smile at the surgeon. He liked the man, who had been both honest and comforting. David, who had felt his life changed unalterably, had now been given to believe that normal service could be resumed.

Cara's
Manuscript

— KASSEL —

'Fräulein Heller wishes to call upon us again,' said Jacob, passing the letter to Wilhelm.

'Is this request couched in the same cloyingly affectionate tone as the last?' Wilhelm asked, scanning it. 'Oh my word, yes it is. *My dear Herr Grimm!* Why doesn't she just say *My dearest Herr Grimm* and have done with it?'

'You are overreacting as usual, brother,' said Jacob. 'She is just leaning over backwards to be polite.'

'Read between the lines, Jacob. Isn't that your forte? *My* dear Herr Grimm. When did she become *yours*? She is not leaning backwards, she's leaning forwards — towards you!'

'Poppycock!'

'She must be dissuaded. You were very good last time with your lack of encouragement but it seems not to have had the desired effect. Quite the opposite in fact, which is what you will recall I feared.'

'What would you have me do? I would like to obtain that story.'

'As would I. Very much.'

'Well?'

'It's simple. Write to her with an appointment. She will come with the story—'

'And no doubt with the talkative sister.'

Wilhelm smiled. 'Undoubtedly. She will come with the story and with the sister but, alas, circumstances will have urgently called you away on the king's business and I will have to receive the story on your behalf.'

'Wilhelm, such a stratagem involves deceit.'

'Many stratagems do,' smiled Wilhelm. 'But this is a very mild deceit. A white lie only. And a harmless means to an important end.'

Jacob was clearly unconvinced.

'All right, what about this — let me reply on your behalf. I will not mention anything about you, but will arrange the appointment for a time when you are working in the Royal Library.'

Jacob considered the idea carefully. 'I suppose so,' he conceded. 'It is still a subterfuge, but the deceit is more minor.'

'Oh, man of unerring rectitude!' Wilhelm smiled. 'And to ensure that all proceedings are quite proper and beyond reproach I will arrange for Lotte and Dortchen to be in attendance.'

'As you like,' said Jacob, 'although I have no fears for you.'

'Thank you. Your high opinion is most important to me.'

'Sometimes, Wilhelm,' said Jacob, smiling himself now, 'you can be very silly.'

'I have had a reply!' said Mathilde.

'What does he say?'

'I'm a little confused,' replied Mathilde. 'I wrote to Herr Jacob, but Herr Wilhelm has replied.'

Helga, seeing her sister's troubled face, sought to make light of the situation.

'I wouldn't worry about that,' she said. 'Everybody knows how close the two are. Dortchen says they are almost a single person, albeit with two heads, four arms and four legs!'

'Dortchen Wild?' asked Mathilde.

Helga nodded.

'When were you talking to Dortchen Wild?'

'I forgot to tell you,' said Helga. 'Mutti and I met her on the Kaiserplatz two days ago.'

'And?'

'She greeted me and I introduced her to Mutti. She was very friendly and we spoke of the brothers. Mutti was interested because she knew we had taken them the stories from Oma. She was relieved when Dortchen spoke so highly of them. Apparently, Papa knows Herr Wild. He's an apothecary.'

'What did Fräulein Wild say of the brothers?' demanded Mathilde. 'Helga, you are naughty. You should have told me this before.'

Helga shrugged. 'I did not think—'

'But tell me!'

'Dortchen said that the brothers were very serious scholars, sober and pious. She said they were older than their years, especially Jacob, who has had to bring up the entire family on his own since their mother died.'

'And Mutti?'

'Mutti was very impressed. She liked Fräulein Wild, too. Dortchen was very polite and respectful. She expressed her condolences very delicately.'

'Mutti didn't . . .'

Helga nodded sadly. 'Yes, in thanking her she did say how very sad it was to lose a mother.'

'But she was speaking of the brothers' mother?'

'No, she was speaking of Oma.'

'So Dortchen knows.'

'Yes,' Helga said in a small voice.

'So the brothers will know—'

'Mathilde, it was not a thing we could hide forever!'

Mathilde appeared troubled. 'Perhaps we should not have been so misleading.'

'We did not lie.'

'No, but we did not tell the truth.'

Helga was silent, and then, remembering, added, 'Anyway, Dortchen laid great stress on how close the brothers are. Did you know that there's only a year between them? She said she's never known two men so close. As I said, almost as if they were one.'

'So?'

'So it's not a calamity that you sent the letter to one brother and the other brother replied,' said Helga, not really believing this. 'Not a great calamity at all.'

'Yet another note from the indefatigable Fräulein Heller?' asked Wilhelm, recognising the handwriting.

'Yes, she and her sister will come on Saturday at the time you suggested,' said Jacob. 'They will deliver the story.'

'Isn't it telling, brother, that although I wrote to her, it was you to whom she addressed the reply?'

'There may be something in that, I grant you,' said Jacob.

'I wonder if this will be the last one,' said Wilhelm.

'The last what?'

'Last story. Dortchen met the younger sister and the mother in town the other day and heard that it *was* the grandmother who had passed away.'

Jacob shrugged. 'Ah well, it may be the last then.'

He sounded somewhat relieved.

'Tell me, Jacob,' Wilhelm asked pointedly, 'would you be sorry if there were to be no further visits from the Fräuleins Heller, particularly the older one?'

'I should be sorry that a promising source of stories has dried up,' said Jacob. 'Why do you ask?' He began reading another letter, then handed it to his brother.

'Who is it from?'

'See for yourself. Clemens Brentano.'

'What does he want? Is he crying out for more stories?'

'On the contrary, he says he needs more time to consider the project and his work may not go ahead. He says he did not fully understand how much work there was going to be, how time-consuming.'

Wilhelm frowned at his brother.

'*His* work?'

'I know—'

'So far it has all been *our* work!'

'Not entirely, Wilhelm. Be fair.'

'Well, mostly ours. And, I might add, mostly unsung.'

'But we agreed to that. Hitherto it hasn't mattered that Brentano will take the credit. Our only interest has been in gathering and preserving the stories.'

Wilhelm looked at him glumly.

'You know, Wilhelm,' said Jacob, thinking. 'Perhaps it doesn't matter if Clemens Brentano pulls out.'

'What do you mean?'

'Well, we've done the work — we are continuing to do the work. Why do we not publish the stories under our own names?'

Wilhelm smiled. 'That, dear brother, is an excellent idea. Why do we not?'

David's Story

David's heart attack had thrown Jan and Peter into a quandary. Their trip was at an end but they couldn't leave David to fend for himself. In the end, Jan took the children back with her on their scheduled flight while Peter stayed on to see David through the operation and immediate recovery.

The cardiologist's prognosis proved accurate. David did need a double bypass and, as the surgeon also predicted, the operation went smoothly.

'Just as well you're young,' Peter said. 'You'll recover in no time.'

'Fucking Pollyanna,' grumbled David. 'Young people aren't supposed to have heart attacks.'

'Young people can do anything these days,' Peter said.

'Yeah, so they say. Anyway, thanks for staying on. Have I thanked you properly yet?'

'Only on about ten occasions. It's nothing. Don't stress about it.'

'No,' said David. 'Got to cut back on stress. Heard from the folks?'

Peter nodded. 'A number of times. The old man's sanguine — thinks it's great they caught it when they did and you'll get a new warrant of fitness and be good forever. Mum's absolutely freaked, of course. She's convinced the French medical system is pre-Revolutionary and that they perform operations with knives and forks. She wants you to come back home immediately to prepare for the next, probably fatal, heart attack.'

David laughed. 'Good old Mum. Pessimism as high art. So she wants me to get out of here and put my faith in the Barrington Medical Centre?'

'That's about the size of it.'

Peter had been so good, David reflected. It couldn't have been easy to delay his return home, especially with the demands of the firm, but he hadn't hesitated. And he had been useful, both practically and emotionally. While school wasn't an issue, with the holidays just started, Peter had been in touch with Michael Bastion and a few other friends and colleagues, including Angus and Arlene. He had also sorted out David's insurance and organised some home help for the first days' convalescence.

More than this, though, Peter had been a calm, steady presence, visiting regularly and bringing anything he needed. Once again, David felt the strong sense of family he had experienced in the first few days when they were all crowded into his apartment. It was a long-unfamiliar feeling but he embraced it now, relaxing into its warmth and comfort.

There were other visitors. Michael Bastion came bearing gifts: chocolates and a big bag of English magazines and recent colour supplements — *Spectators*, *Economists*, *LRBs* and a single copy of *The Tatler*, which David presumed was Miranda's contribution.

'Can't get enough decent reading matter in these places,' Michael said. 'Throw them out when you've finished, or pass them on.'

David was grateful. The largesse was generous and unexpected.

They talked about his attack and its aftermath.

'Sounds to me as if you're a lucky fellow,' observed Michael, 'although the top of the Hôtel de Ville isn't the place I'd choose to have a heart attack.'

'If I were you,' said David, 'I'd choose not to have a heart attack at all. Not my favourite experience.'

'How did they get you down?' asked Michael. 'Must have been tricky.'

'It was. The trickiest part was getting down the staircase. A couple of burly medics did the business, half carrying me, half dragging. My brother and his family were with me but had no idea how to get help.

Luckily there were a few locals about. It was no time before I heard the cavalry galloping up the stairs. Once I was in the ambulance, they fed me aspirin and hooked me up to something electrical. If I hadn't been so out to it, it would have been quite exciting.'

'An excitement I could do without,' said Michael. 'So what now?'

David told him all he knew about the convalescent period. Michael, headmaster again, said, 'Looks like you won't be back at Huntingdon for at least a couple of months, maybe more, after term begins. Nothing to worry about. We'll find a substitute.'

'Thanks, Michael.'

'Might even set Miranda loose on your kids. She rather enjoyed it that time Cara Bernstein let us down.'

David gave him a wan smile. Worse things could happen than Miranda Bastion covering his classes for a few weeks. However, right at that moment he was too tired and uncomfortable to imagine what they could be.

Angus Paton dropped in one morning.

'I thought you'd be away on holiday somewhere,' David said, surprised to see him.

'I will be soon.'

'Anywhere special?'

'Going to stay with a friend in Cornwall. Nothing exciting.'

'Looks like I'm going to spend my time in Arras.'

'That *will* be exciting.'

'Hell, yeah. They're letting me out next week sometime but I'm supposed to rest up for a few more weeks, and then gradually work up to be a human being again.'

'In your case, old flower, that may be too much to hope.'

'Thanks.'

'What's it like, having a heart attack?'

'Pretty bloody awful. I overdid it chasing my brother's kids up to the top of the Hôtel de Ville. By the time I got to the top I had lost all my wind and was utterly pooped. I thought what I felt was crushing indigestion, but—'

'It wasn't,' said Angus.

'It wasn't.'

'I thought you would have been able to run up a flight of stairs.'

'So did I. I had no idea this sort of thing happened to fit young things like me. Only to unfit old codgers like you.'

Angus didn't respond beyond a faint smile. He seemed to be pondering something. 'I often wonder what it must feel like. You know, having a heart attack.'

'Why, are you planning one?'

'Hell no. No, but my father had one.'

'Is he okay?'

'He died.'

'Oh, I'm sorry to hear that.'

'Yeah, it was a bit of shock. But years ago. It was when I was at art school in Leeds.'

'We're much better off now. From what the cardiologist said it's hardly more serious than a bad flu these days.'

'Still prefer having a bad flu.'

'Me too, if I'm honest. I did ask why it happened. It's a worry.'

'I suppose you got the classic Gallic shrug.'

'A little better than that. The guy suggested family history or something congenital. But there's not much heart trouble in the family, and I've no knowledge of anything congenital. No hole in the heart.'

'They didn't find anything?'

David shook his head. 'Just a broken heart . . .'

Angus smiled. 'You're a lucky man, Cunningham.'

As Angus was leaving, David said, 'Enjoy Cornwall. I've never been there. What's it like?'

'Like everywhere: good bits and bad bits.'

'Well, enjoy. This friend?'

'She'll help me enjoy it. Keep out of trouble!'

Other visitors were unexpected. David suspected that Michael had probably organised a roster of available staff to drop in to see him. Most of these visits only served to demonstrate how little in common he had with the bulk of his colleagues. Once he had recounted the circumstances of the attack and subsequent events, conversation tended to dry up. All the same, he did manage to accumulate an extensive fruit and confectionery collection.

Occasionally someone surprised him and he regretted some earlier rush to judgment that had blinded him to their qualities. One such was Michael's first assistant, Kate Garner. She was obviously competent: one doesn't get to be a first assistant at a place like Huntingdon without having something to recommend. However, David had long written her off as a functionary, somebody pallid appointed mainly to highlight what little colour Michael had. She was young for such a role, too, despite not being an obvious status-seeker.

He could not remember ever exchanging more than polite pleasantries with her before, and was unprepared to find her sympathetic, perceptive and unexpectedly witty.

'I suppose,' Kate Garner said, 'you're revaluating a lot of things?'

'I suppose I am,' said David. 'I've been thinking about family a lot. My brother and his family have been staying with me. They've been fantastic. Especially Pete. He stayed on to help out.'

'Nothing like a near-death experience to focus the mind,' said Kate.

'You sound as if you're talking from experience.'

'Not really. Perhaps I should have said "life-changing". I have had a few of those.'

'Me too.'

Almost as he said it, though, David was wondering whether it were true. Had he had many of those moments when the sky turns green? When everything changes? When nothing will ever be the same? Most of the big events and changes in his life had been the usual transitions, which he had navigated relatively smoothly: schools, university; the deaths of grandparents and other elderly family and friends; jobs satisfactory and unsatisfactory; ditto love affairs; leaving New Zealand and living overseas. Heidi's departure had hit him, of course, but time had refashioned even that into something like a youthful misadventure.

In recent times, the closest candidates for life-changing experiences had been Cara's disappearance and now this medical chapter. When he was back in New Zealand he had laughed at Jan's suggestion that he was still carrying a torch for Cara, but he had been bluffing Jan and fooling himself. He had got over Heidi, but he was still a long way from getting over Cara.

And the heart attack? It loomed very large at the moment but he imagined it would fade and the adjustments would be minor: some medication, some changes in diet.

'So,' said Kate, breaking into his thoughts, 'if this *has* been one of those, what changes do you have in mind?'

'Actually, I was just thinking about that. I mean, it's been very dramatic, and painful, but I'm not sure it will be life-changing.'

'You can't mean that, surely?'

'In the short term it will, of course. I'll be under house arrest and I'll have to watch what I eat and there'll be pills and things, but later on? I'm not so sure.'

Kate stared at him, smiling, 'My word, Mr Cunningham, I had no idea you were so — what's the word? — *stoic*? *Phlegmatic*?'

'Perhaps I'm just resistant to change.'

'So you have no intention of throwing over everything, becoming what you always wanted to be, shaving your head, becoming vegan, learning to fly, joining the Cirque du Soleil?'

''Fraid not. I think I'm a kind of emotional Luddite.'

'You so disappoint me!'

'Sorry,' said David. 'So is this whole conversation just a plot to get me to resign from Huntingdon?'

'Oh god,' laughed Kate. 'Am I so transparent?'

'Caught you out!'

'No, seriously,' she said, 'I'm so pleased you're doing well. It must have been awful. And I won't say hurry back, for that might not be good advice. But, joking aside, do come back to us as soon as you're up to it.'

'I'll try not to!'

She laughed. It was such a pleasant laugh and he remembered it after she had gone, all at once feeling foolish he had been so blind to her before. Kate wasn't colourless at all. Getting to know her better would be one of the things to look forward to when he did get back to Huntingdon.

The cardiologist approved David's going home after ten days. Peter stayed on for a week or so longer to make sure he would be able to manage reasonably. Kate Garner and Arlene Abramson dropped in at the apartment from time to time to help with shopping in the earlier days of his recovery. Gradually, bed rest gave way to a quiet, sedentary time, and eventually this progressed to rather more activity: walking and then being driven — Kate and Arlene again, and occasionally Angus — to places where he could walk greater distances.

David remained cautious and did not try to rush things, and slowly, palpably, he became aware that his life was returning to normal.

Cara's
Manuscript

Mathilde and Helga Heller were both apprehensive on the Saturday morning of their next appointment with the Grimm brothers. Mathilde was in a state: flustered, forgetful and in an agony of anticipation. She read and reread their story and every so often found something she had to change, and because she was in a terror of presenting it before Jacob — she was now entirely discounting Wilhelm — if something was less than perfect she felt the need to rewrite the entire thing. It was driving Helga to distraction.

Helga was very nervous on her sister's behalf.

'Why are you changing that?' she demanded.

'It didn't ring true,' said Mathilde grimly. 'She would not dance gaily.'

'Why not?' asked Helga. 'She has her ball back — she would be delighted.'

'But gay and delighted are not the same,' Mathilde insisted.

'You're splitting hairs.'

'The point is,' said Mathilde stubbornly, 'the princess would be neither gay nor delighted. She really just wants to escape from her obligation and rush back to the castle. *Gay* does not ring true.'

'So, you're going to bang a coin on the counter to test every word?' asked Helga. 'We have to leave soon. It is not a short walk.'

'Leave me to finish, then,' said Mathilde.

They arrived right on time. In her reticule Mathilde had stowed two rolled copies of the story they now called 'The Frog Prince'. One would be her reading copy; the other, tied with a velvet ribbon, she would present to Jacob Grimm.

Throughout the whole writing process, which had begun in such high spirits, she had seesawed between excitement and doubt. In the latter stages the story had at times loomed as something hugely ugly and deceitful that she was about to visit on the brothers, something that painted her as ugly and deceitful as well. If it hadn't been for Helga's prodding and pushing she may well have abandoned the entire enterprise.

She trembled now as those feelings came rushing back. She was defiled. She knew it and the brothers would see it too. Were it not for Helga's hand at her elbow, she would have turned and fled down the beautiful tree-lined Bellevuestrasse, all the way back to honesty and self-respect.

Mathilde smiled nervously and passed the script she had been reading to Helga who, as she took it, looked at her sister with a mix of compassion and curiosity.

Mathilde, ordinarily an animated reader with a natural ability to dramatise and bring a story to life, had read in a flat and faltering way, her voice often trembling but for the most part rapid and expressionless, as if her only intent were to finish as quickly as possible.

For that reason alone, Helga was pleased that Jacob Grimm, the intended audience, was not there to witness the farrago that had been Mathilde's rendition. She wondered why he was not present. It may be true, as they had been told, that urgent business at the Royal Library had detained him, but she had understood earlier from both

Lotte and Dortchen that there was hardly any work to be done at the library except that which Jacob decided to do — and that was almost entirely his own scholarly research. If this were true, it seemed Jacob had chosen to stay away.

Poor Mathilde. She was blind but she was no fool. She must have sensed this herself. Oh, the irony. It was possibly her agitation at his not being here that had caused her to read so disastrously.

Despite this, Dortchen, Lotte and Wilhelm applauded politely at the story's conclusion.

'What do you think, Dorothea?' asked Wilhelm, using Dortchen's more formal name.

'It is a perfect tale,' said Dortchen, smiling at Mathilde, 'and all the better for being one of a kind. I have not come across this one before.'

'Quite so,' agreed Wilhelm. 'It is a valuable addition. We are very grateful to you, Fräulein Heller, for bringing it to us. Herr Brentano will be grateful as well.'

Mathilde and Helga exchanged a small, relieved smile.

'You will leave me your copy?' asked Wilhelm, reaching for the paper Helga still held.

'Not that one, Herr Wilhelm,' said Mathilde. 'I have transcribed a good copy for you and Herr Jacob.'

She opened her bag and withdrew the roll tied with the black velvet ribbon.

'Thank you,' murmured Wilhelm. Perhaps it was the mourning garb, perhaps it was the black ribbon that prompted him to add, 'And let me again express our condolences and our appreciation to your late grandmother for sharing these stories, and to you for bringing them to us.'

Again the sisters exchanged glances. There was a finality in Wilhelm Grimm's words, suggesting that both this meeting and their series of meetings were at an end. Any uncertainty was soon dispelled as he stood up, and Lotte and Dortchen also. All were smiling, but it was clear that this time there was to be no coffee and cake.

Wilhelm, the rolled story in his left hand, shook Mathilde's and Helga's hands in turn, made his farewells and left the room.

David's
Story

A fortnight after David's return to his apartment he received an email:

> *Sorry to hear you've been unwell. Get better soon.*
> *Cara*

Cara's
Manuscript

As soon as Lotte had closed the door on the Heller sisters, Wilhelm returned to the living room, his earlier departure from it having been purely theatrical. He flourished the story at Dortchen and Lotte and said, 'So now we can share what we really think of this tale of the frog and the princess. What would you say, Dortchen?'

'I would like to read it from the text.'

'She did not read well,' said Lotte.

'She certainly did not,' said Dortchen. 'She seemed unaccountably nervous, and as a result her reading did the story little credit. However, I would not alter my opinion. It is a perfect tale. So strange, though, that none of us has heard before.'

'I suspect that,' said Wilhelm, 'is because it is a perfect confection.'

'What do you mean?'

'I don't think this is a folk tale at all. Nor do I not believe that Fräulein Heller heard this story at the lap of her oma. In fact it would not surprise me if she wrote it herself.'

Lotte and Dortchen looked at him in astonishment.

'But why would she do that?' asked Dortchen.

'It would probably explain her nervousness,' mused Wilhelm.

'But why?'

'Can't you see?' said Wilhelm. 'This is very cleverly crafted but is not really a story at all. It is a stalking horse.'

'Brother,' said Lotte, 'I am completely confused. What are you talking about?'

'I could be wrong,' said Wilhelm. 'In fact, I hope I am. But so much about this tale simply does not ring true.'

'It rang true to me,' said Lotte. 'I felt it was quite charming.'

'Too charming,' said Wilhelm.

'I agree with Lotte,' said Dortchen.

'What do you mean by a stalking horse?' asked Lotte.

Wilhelm summoned his thoughts. 'What does the story comprise?'

'A princess,' replied Lotte, 'who rescues a prince who had been bewitched into a frog by a wicked witch. She treats him tenderly and this tenderness restores him to his true self, and the princess is rewarded by marriage to the prince.'

'She does have to be persuaded to treat the prince tenderly, though,' added Dortchen. 'It is not easy for her to treat the frog as she should.'

'Just so,' said Wilhelm. 'Now, the two of you may not have observed this, but Fräulein Heller has quite clearly developed an infatuation for Jacob. She writes notes to him, couched in the most inappropriately affectionate terms. When she visits she treats him to moon eyes and fluttering lashes. Some of the visits are clearly contrived, with little purpose.'

Dortchen and Lotte looked startled.

'Jacob, of course,' Wilhelm went on, 'is quite oblivious to these attentions, which means Fräulein Heller has to try even harder. Then suddenly she loses her source of stories when her oma dies.'

'I am sure that Fräulein Heller admires Jacob,' said Lotte, 'just as she does you. I am sure there is nothing untoward there.'

'Consider the story as you described it to me just now,' said Wilhelm. 'Now replace the princess with Fräulein Heller and replace the frog with my brother Jacob, and what do you get?'

'Confusion?' said Lotte.

Dortchen regarded Wilhelm thoughtfully. 'I'm beginning to see what you mean,' she said. 'But isn't it all rather too subtle? And do you really think she would have done this so deliberately?'

Wilhelm nodded. 'I do. Jacob as a frog represents someone who needs to change, or be changed, into the prince he rightly is. The thing is, he can't do this by himself. He needs the help of a beautiful, tender maiden who can transform him through love — or at least affection. It's my belief that Fräulein Heller is suggesting that she is that maiden.'

'Clever,' said Dortchen.

'Too clever, I feel,' said Lotte. 'I don't want to believe you, Wilhelm.'

'You said it was too subtle, Dortchen,' said Wilhelm, 'but doesn't it need to be? If it were overt, Jacob would immediately see it for what it is and dismiss it out of hand. But if it's sufficiently subtle, the seed will be sown. In time it will germinate and gradually grow.'

Lotte was alarmed. 'To think that Fräulein Heller is capable of such subterfuge! What is to be done?'

'We have to show Jacob the story,' said Dortchen. 'He is expecting it — looking forward to it.'

'There is only one thing to be done,' said Wilhelm. 'But we cannot do it here, as Jacob may return unexpectedly. Dortchen, we must away to your summerhouse. Will that be all right?'

'Of course,' said Dortchen. 'But why?'

Mathilde hurried away from Bellevuestrasse so quickly Helga found it difficult to keep up.

'Why so fast, sister?' she puffed. 'You're practically running!'

Mathilde glanced over her shoulder. 'I'm sorry,' she said, slowing down a little.

'Mathilde, you are agitated. What is the matter?'

Mathilde stopped in her tracks and turned to her sister. 'You must know, Helga. It's because of what I have done. It's because of what *we* have done. I am feeling ashamed.'

'But why? All we have done is deliver the story we promised.'

'You are being disingenuous. You know very well that the story is a lie, a complete fabrication.'

Helga sighed. 'We have been through this a thousand times. *All* stories are fabrications.'

'Helga!'

'What?'

Mathilde did not reply, could not reply. She found her chest heavy and her eyes began to smart with the need to weep.

Helga reached out and drew her closer.

'You are being too sensitive,' she whispered. 'All will be well. In fact, all may be better than well, especially if Jacob—'

'Don't,' protested Mathilde. 'You know I can never go to that house again. I could not look either brother in the eye. Or their sister. Or Fräulein Wild.'

'That's nonsense and you know it,' said Helga.

'So where was he?' demanded Mathilde. 'He was so cold last time. He did not answer my letter. He knew I was coming this morning and yet he stayed away.'

'You must not put the worst possible complexion on it, Mathilde. There could be all manner of reasons.'

'I see only one reason. He wishes to avoid me.'

'But why? Has it occurred to you that this might be because he is so attracted to you he finds it impossible to be in your presence? Have you considered that?'

Mathilde had not considered that, but did so now. It was possible, she supposed, but very unlikely. Jacob Grimm was a serious man with serious responsibilities and a scholar's drive. He would not welcome distractions, and the discovery that a young woman in his orbit was threatening his equilibrium was the more likely cause of his absence.

It was a seductive idea and she wanted to believe Helga's theory. But when she recalled his stand-offishness at their last meeting her sense of rejection came tumbling back.

She shook her head.

'No, Helga, he feels nothing for me. I sense it. I know it. Yours is a pleasant theory, and I wish it were true, but I am nothing to Jacob Grimm and he has gone to some pains to let me know this.'

'You are letting grief go to your head.'

'No, I am letting reality go to my head.'

'What shall we do?'

'We should go home.'

'And the princess and the frog?'

'We must let them live their own lives.'

In her dream Mathilde was lost in the forest. It was a forest she had been in before; a forest Oma had warned her of. Once she had been unafraid because there were dells and dingles reached by shafts of sunlight. Wildflowers grew there and she had gathered them. Now they could not be found. Instead of flowers there were only things that grew in the dark and gloom: toadstools, puffballs, stinkhorns.

She found herself on pathways that led nowhere, instead becoming narrower and narrower until they were completely overgrown and she had to retrace her steps and start again. The next path in turn grew narrower and narrower.

Previously when in the forest, Mathilde had felt the presence of Oma, unseen but very much there, somewhere nearby in a deeper grove, watching her with kindly eyes, stretching out a gentle hand she could all but touch.

Previously when in the forest, Mathilde had felt the presence of her prince, unseen but close by, and she felt protected At the slightest hint of danger — a witch, an evil wizard, a wolf, a giant woodchopper — he would be at her side, rapier drawn, ready to fight for her safety. And after the battle she knew he would take her in his arms and lead her to his castle, its towers and turrets shining in the sunlight, its bright pennants fluttering in a breeze.

But now in this forest, a completely different yet strangely identical forest, Mathilde had never felt so alone. She was frustrated by its endless, fruitless pathways, and the only presences she sensed were dark and malign.

No Oma. No prince.

She was defenceless and afraid.

She was surprised, then, to turn onto yet another dark pathway to find it leading to a pool of black water. The water shone like pitch and hid its depths with deception and guile. Things may have been living beneath its surface, but they were black as well.

The path followed the circle of the pool and the trees above leaned over the water like guilty thoughts, like dangerous yearnings.

'Where is the forest, Oma?' she had once asked.

'It is where we live,' her grandmother had replied.

And all at once there he was, lying stretched out and apparently asleep on a patch of grass between the path and the water.

Her dear boy. He was so lovely.

He was wearing a doublet of green and his tights were sage. A velvet cap had fallen to one side and his chestnut hair splayed about his head.

With a joyful cry of recognition, Mathilde hurried towards him and dropped to her knees beside his head. Tenderly she brushed the curls away from his brow and gazed down at his face. His eyes, his lovely eyes, were closed and his dark lashes highlighted his pallor. He was breathing slowly and easily, his lips, his lovely lips, opening and closing, quivering slightly with each breath.

Unable to do anything other, Mathilde lowered her own lips to his and closed her eyes.

Their lips touched.

His were surprising cold and clammy, and Mathilde opened her eyes in surprise.

He had gone!

Where was he? Her lovely boy? Her prince?

And then she half-stood in horror.

A large green frog crouched there, opened its cavernous mouth and croaked.

The frog sprang high into the air above the water and plunged head first into the pool's black depths. All Mathilde could see was ring after ring of ever-widening black circles.

David's Story

David stared at the screen, reading and rereading the message. Cara.

How long had it been? Complete radio silence for nearly a year, and now, out of the blue, this.

He could hear her voice. A surge of feeling — a blend of shock, giddy hope, resentment and anger — swirled through him. Pretty clearly he had been kidding himself that he was over her. He was not over her. A dozen or so words from her and everything he had felt came tumbling back.

She had heard. She knew.

All he could think of writing in response was:

Where are you?

He pressed send.

For some moments, mind racing, he stared at the screen, half expecting an immediate response, then rebuked himself. Why would that happen? It might be another year.

How did she know?

All at once he realised she must be in contact with somebody he knew. But who?

He worked through the possibilities in his mind and none seemed likely. Whoever it was had been very discreet. He felt another flare of anger, a sense of betrayal. Was it someone who had maintained contact with Cara right from when she disappeared, or someone who had re-established contact relatively recently? It had to be someone he knew, who knew of his relationship with her, and yet they had not had the decency to tell him.

Why not?

He read the message again, desperately trying to unpack it, but there was very little there.

No *love*.

Why would there have been? Cara was many things but she was not a hypocrite.

There did seem to be affection there, though. *Sorry. Get better soon.*

It may have been residual, but it definitely was affection — or caring at least.

It could have come from anywhere. That was the trouble with email — the time of arrival might have given a hint of the time zone but nothing more.

Could she not have given him something more? Or perhaps this message was the first in a series, so that eventually he might receive an explanation . . . How long would he have to wait?

He now regretted being so hasty and abrupt in his response.

He had a year's worth of things to say to Cara, and instead he had just blurted out three words. There was perhaps implicit in Cara's note a hint that she would welcome some news about him, about his health since the operation. Her informant had no doubt told her some things, but unless her informant was a close friend of his — and he couldn't even go there — she or he would not have had a lot to tell beyond the medical facts.

Perhaps his perfunctory reply would make no difference. His previous attempts at communication had been ignored; this one probably would be too. However, there was a *hint* here that Cara was listening. He would write at greater length. He would fill her in with everything that had happened. He would tell her again of his fears for her, his ongoing concern about what might have prompted her sudden departure.

There would be no recriminations. He was past that.

B ut who could her informant be?

Over and over again, David sifted through the staff list. Cara had many friends but few intimates. She was amiable but private. Just as she was covert about her own background and feelings, she was incurious about the background and feelings of others. She disliked gossip, and whenever talk veered that way she would deflect it. At first David used to think this was a measure of her professionalism, but he came to realise that it was deeper than that, as if coming from the core of her being.

The more he looked at the names, the more unlikely it seemed that one of Huntingdon's teachers could have been Cara's confidant. Any of the likely suspects — Angus, Arlene, Kate — surely would have mentioned it to him. They were all as mystified as he was about Cara's vanishing. As far as he knew, the only people Cara knew in Arras or the wider region were those who worked at the school. And even if she did have unknown friends in the district, they would have to have known him as well, or at least enough about him to have heard about the heart attack. Possible, but unlikely. He could think no mutual acquaintance not directly connected with Huntingdon.

Maybe it was one of the students? Steffi Fox? But she had left school now and would have no knowledge of his illness, surely.

He was going around in circles, and continued to do so for days.

Cara did not responded to his initial email, nor to his second, longer (rather rambling) message. He had found it very difficult to write as he struggled to strike the right note. It was hard to be natural in such an unnatural situation; to be loving where there had been no expression of love for so long. The approach demanded neither formality nor informality; neither anger nor calm; neither recrimination nor forgiveness.

And it appeared that all the agonising had been for naught.

Finally, David decided he needed help. He considered contacting Michael Bastion but thought better of it. If Michael knew anything, David was sure he would have shared it, and besides, he would pass everything David told him on to Miranda, in which case all of Arras would find out in due course.

He decided the best person to talk to would be Kate Garner. After her visiting him in hospital and a couple of subsequent home visits he now saw her as smart, observant and discreet. He had no idea whether Cara saw her the same way, but if Cara had any other special friend on the staff, the sort of friend she might have continued corresponding with, then Kate may well know.

He called her. After the initial pleasantries he said, 'Kate, I've had an email from Cara.'

'Really?'

'Yes, it was a bit of a surprise. It's the first time she's made contact with me since she disappeared. It was only one line, however.'

'What did she say?'

'She'd heard I'd been sick and just wanted to wish me well.'

'Nothing else?'

'Not a skerrick.'

'So we're no further ahead.'

'Well, I'm not sure about that.'

'I mean, it was kind of Cara to get in touch, but what else does it tell us?'

'That's why I've called. It suggests that someone here must be in contact with her.'

'Someone? Who?'

'That's exactly the point. I've no idea who it might be. I wondered if you might.'

'David, it's not me if that's what you're asking.'

'No, not entirely. But it did occur to me that you might know of someone on the staff who could be a likely candidate. I've been over and over all the possibilities and can't think of anyone, but I'm certain it has to be someone connected with the school.'

'Why do you say that?'

'Because it has to be someone who knows both of us reasonably well: Cara and me. I can't think of anyone beyond the confines of the school who fits that bill.'

'I see.'

'I hope I'm not asking anything that makes you feel uncomfortable, Kate. I'm not wanting you to be unprofessional or anything.'

'David, no, not at all. You needn't worry on that score. But I can't think of anyone either. In fact, the only person I know of who became a particular friend of Cara's was you.'

'What about Angus?'

It was a stab in the dark. Angus's name sprang unheralded from somewhere in his subconscious, but once released it seemed, all at once, almost plausible. David had been disconcerted when he discovered that Cara had posed for Angus. He suspected intimacy but Angus had denied it and David eventually believed him. Is this why he had shuffled Angus out of the equation?

The suggestion evidently surprised Kate. 'Angus? I wouldn't have thought so. Why him?'

David could only mumble, 'Not sure. Something Arlene said.'

'I was going to suggest Arlene but thought better of it. Arlene and Cara are rather chalk and cheese, aren't they? With Cara the chalk and Arlene the cheese, of course!' Kate laughed. 'In any event, Arlene's still on holiday. So is Angus, if it comes to that.'

'Oh, well,' said David. 'Sorry to trouble you with this. Just clutching at straws basically.'

'I'm distressed that you consider me a mere straw, Mr Cunningham!' Kate laughed again. 'Do you want me to quiz Michael?'

'No,' David said hurriedly. 'No, I'm sure Michael would have said something to me. We've talked about Cara quite a lot. Besides, there's—'

'Miranda? Yes, I understand. Say no more. In any event I can assure you that Michael has never mentioned to me that he's been in touch with Cara, and I very much doubt she will have reached out to him.'

'I'm sure you're right,' said David.

'I'm pleased the convalescence proceeds apace,' said Kate, concluding the conversation. 'Keep in touch, won't you?'

After he hung up, David found he could not stop thinking about Angus Paton. They had had that brief time of mutual animosity, followed by a developing friendship. He would have thought that all suspicion, all resentment had long since faded.

In the post-Cara phase of their friendship, her name, as if by some unspoken agreement, had hardly been mentioned. Would Angus have told him if he was communicating with Cara? David was no longer so sure. One peculiarity he had trouble getting his head around was the odd fact that Cara was quite relaxed about their relationship being more or less public, whereas her connection with Angus had been completely clandestine. Until Arlene spilled the beans, he had had no idea there had been anything between them. Cara had never referred to it. Even now, Kate Garner was apparently surprised at the suggestion.

Given that history of secrecy, it was quite possible that Cara and Angus had maintained their connection — or perhaps re-established it after her disappearance. The secrecy, he realised, would almost certainly have been at Cara's insistence. Angus was naturally gregarious and open. He liked to shock sensibilities and challenge convention. He was not the type who would tiptoe around unless his partner demanded it.

It had to be Angus.

As Angus began to take centre stage in his suspicions, David recalled their last conversation before Angus took off on his holiday. Where was he going? Devon or Cornwall?

He remembered the man's nudge-nudge expression when he let slip that the old friend he was staying with was a woman.

Cara's
Manuscript

The summerhouse in the garden of Rudolf Wild's property was charming. It was an octagonal structure set among cherry and peach trees, asparagus patches and strawberry beds, and it doubled as a greenhouse. In the summer months when the Grimm brothers visited the Wild family they would often retreat there, the brothers and Lotte enjoying the company of the seven-strong Wild clan of children: brother Rudolf and the six sisters. The older sisters, Rose, Dortchen and Mimi, were especial friends. Jacob and Wilhelm swapped one milieu for another — the male-dominated Grimm world for the female-dominated Wild world — and they relished their visits. Six years on from first meeting the Wilds, the Grimm brothers visited them regularly, even Jacob enjoying the light relief of the banter and teasing.

Now, in the summerhouse, and relatively safe from any possible interruption by Jacob, Wilhelm did not waste time before explaining his plan for Mathilde's story.

He, Lotte and Dortchen sat on wicker chairs around a small table. Wilhelm had spread the story before him. 'It seems obvious to me what we must do,' he said. 'We must turn the songbird into a crow.'

'More riddles, brother?' said Lotte.

'Not really,' said Wilhelm. 'We agree, don't we, that Fräulein Heller's story is a thinly disguised allegory casting herself as the princess and my brother Jacob as the frog?'

'So naughty of her,' murmured Lotte.

'In the allegory the princess, despite her repugnance at the frog and resistance to his presumptions, is essentially tender-hearted and disposed to goodness. It is this essential goodness that sees her redeem the frog and transform him into the prince he really is.'

'Agreed,' said Dortchen. 'So?'

'So we must change the nature of the princess. We must turn her into a shallow, callow creature, cruel rather than tender-hearted, and vindictive rather than kind.'

'Ah,' said Dortchen, 'a crow, not a songbird.'

'Exactly,' said Wilhelm, smiling.

'Is this not a cruel thing to do?' asked Lotte, a little troubled.

'It is cruel only to be kind,' said Wilhelm. 'Jacob is not and never will be interested in Fräulein Heller or any other romantic attachment. Therefore her continued ministrations, unless nipped in the bud, will prove only a pestilence and a distraction. Jacob has more important things to do than continually swat away Mathilde Heller.'

'You make her sound like a fly, Wilhelm,' said Dortchen. 'Flies, crows — too many horrid metaphors.'

Lotte was not convinced. 'If, as you say, Jacob could never be interested in Mathilde, why do we need to do this? Surely her efforts are doomed to fail anyway?'

'I agree with Lotte,' said Dortchen. 'We are being cruel without being kind.'

'Don't you see, Dortchen,' said Wilhelm, 'it is not for Jacob's sake we must change this story, but for Mathilde Heller's. It is necessary that she be disabused. If we do not, she will keep nurturing the doomed hope that she will find a way to Jacob's heart. I have told Jacob to turn a cold face to her and he has done so, and what is the result? Mathilde comes back for more. It's almost as though whenever she hears *no* she hears *yes*.'

'I understand that,' said Dortchen, 'but how will changing her story change her feelings?'

Wilhelm shrugged.

'I think,' said Lotte, 'that you are not as convinced of *Jacob's* feelings as you claim.'

Dortchen glanced at Lotte, who smiled knowingly. Dortchen turned back to Wilhelm. 'Lotte is quite right,' she said. 'At your house not long ago you told us the story was a stalking horse. It can only be a stalking horse if there is a chance of it being successful. You also said that Jacob was quite impervious to Mathilde Heller's initiatives. Confess, Wilhelm — you *are* worried that the tale will break through Jacob's defences. You cannot pretend otherwise.'

'If you are *not* worried,' added Lotte, 'there is no need to rewrite the story.'

Wilhelm considered his response.

'Perhaps,' he said at last, 'I am not completely confident about Jacob's resistance to these blandishments. But I know my brother better than anybody; his welfare and happiness are my greatest concern. I value this even more highly than my own. I *know* this connection would not be good for Jacob. It would be a brake on his scholarship and would plunge all of us into great difficulties. You, Lotte, better than anybody, know what a struggle and hardship it has been since our dear mother's death. Jacob has had to support five of us. To my eternal shame, I am only able to offer a pittance of help myself.'

'Don't be so harsh on yourself, Wilhelm,' said Lotte. 'Your ill-health is not of your choosing.'

'You say your greatest concern is for Jacob's happiness, Wilhelm,' said Dortchen. 'Would it not be in his best interests to have love in his life? The love and support of a thoroughly respectable young woman like Mathilde Heller? What do *you* say, Lotte?'

Lotte thought for some time before replying. 'Nobody knows Jacob better than Wilhelm,' she said at last. 'You know that, Dortchen. And I must say I do agree that Jacob is only concerned with his work and his family. There is no woman on earth he would allow to take precedence over that.'

Dortchen shrugged. 'Knowing Jacob as I do, I suppose I would not argue with that. But, getting back to the story, Wilhelm, what are you saying about it?'

'I believe I am saying,' said Wilhelm, 'that the tale, as it is, suggests a story of romance and possibility, a story of how one denied romance can be redeemed by it, by the tenderness of a young woman. I am convinced that Fräulein Heller has conceived it this way. I do agree that it is a remote possibility, but I would rather obviate that remote risk before exposing Jacob to it.'

'I suppose you're right,' said Lotte hesitantly.

'Cruel to be kind,' said Dortchen.

'Right,' said Wilhelm, clearly relieved. 'Now, Dortchen, could you find us some paper, some pens and some ink?'

'Of course,' said Dortchen, standing up.

'And Lotte, would you be our secretary?'

'I wonder why Herr Jacob is avoiding you, Mathilde,' said Helga. The two were alone, taking coffee in the drawing room at home. Since the debacle at the Grimm house Mathilde had been quiet and withdrawn, quite resistant to Helga's attempts to comfort her with optimistic constructions of what had happened and what might still happen.

For all of Mathilde's lack of response, Helga remained undeterred.

'It is not something I want to think about, Helga. Please,' said Mathilde.

'But we must talk about it, for it was so puzzling,' said Helga.

'I don't see why it was puzzling at all. Herr Jacob is avoiding me because he dislikes me.'

'The puzzle is *why* he dislikes you, if he really does, and I'm not at all persuaded that is true.'

Mathilde shook her head. 'I have no idea, Helga, but it does appear to be the case.'

'But you are sweet and attractive and you have excellent manners. You come from a most respectable family, you are God-fearing, you have no bad habits or vices. On top of all of this, you have been going out of your way to assist the brothers in their search for stories.'

'I tried to be helpful,' said Mathilde, 'and at first they were pleased to have that help. I believe Wilhelm still is.'

'Is he so pleased, in fact?' asked Helga pointedly.

'What do you mean?'

'I am coming to believe that Wilhelm has been quite devious.'

'How can you say that, Helga? I thought you liked Wilhelm.'

'I'm not so sure I do anymore,' said Helga.

Mathilde looked at her sister. 'Whyever not? What has he done?'

Helga thought for a moment. 'Consider this,' she said. 'We visit the brothers. Is the older one in charge? Jacob, the head of the household? No, it is Wilhelm who does all the talking, while his older brother scarcely says a word. You write a letter to Jacob. Who answers? Wilhelm. We take the story of the frog prince to Jacob. Who is there to receive us? Wilhelm. Who is not there at all? Jacob. Who takes the story from us? Wilhelm. Who was the story really written for? Jacob.'

'That is all true, but—'

'It's obvious to me that Wilhelm has taken charge, and I believe he has done so to shield his brother from you.'

'But why?' Mathilde was almost in tears now.

'That is what we must find out.'

'I don't follow.'

'I mean, is he doing this at Jacob's behest, or is he doing it of his own volition?'

'Does it really make any difference at this point?'

'It makes all the difference,' said Helga. 'If Jacob has asked Wilhelm to take these actions, you have every reason to feel aggrieved and sad. However, if this is something Wilhelm has embarked on independently there may be still hope.'

'There is no hope,' said Mathilde, shaking her head.

'I agree that there is no hope if Wilhelm continues to be a wall between you and Jacob. But if we could somehow get around the wall—'

'And how do we do that?' asked Mathilde, persisting in spite of herself.

'We must contrive to talk to Jacob when Wilhelm is not there to shield him,' said Helga.

David's
Story

David's suspicion grew. What had Angus said? An old friend? No, just a friend. Going to stay with a friend in Cornwall.

That suggested that the friend *lived* in Cornwall, although it was possibly a shared holiday destination. And the friend was definitely female. There was definitely an element of nudge-nudge wink-wink in Angus's parting shot.

Cara?

It was possible. If Angus had been her informant, it made sense that it should be Cara. Was Cara living in Cornwall? Had she and Angus arranged a holiday there together?

Should he challenge Angus?

Part of him wanted to. Send a text. An email. Ring him and demand to be told the name of the woman he was fucking in St Ives or wherever.

Perhaps not the latter, he decided.

All the same, a note to Angus was a good idea. Not a challenging one: he could write telling him how well he was recuperating, and just say he hoped the Cornwall holiday was going well.

Should he mention the email from Cara?

Probably not quite yet. Set up a to-and-fro and see whether Angus comes clean.

The bastard.

A ngus did not come clean.

The identity of the friend in Cornwall was not revealed.

David had written a brief, chatty email focused on his increasing ease in getting around, with a few comments on various enormities in the international news. Angus replied with an even briefer note consisting mainly of a diatribe about Trump and the horrors of Brexit.

The idea was to and fro, so David responded.

More Trump. More Brexit. A mention of Kate Garner and how he felt he now knew her a little better. In signing off he added:

> I trust you and your friend are having a ball. Where
> exactly are you?
>
> Best, D.

Angus did not respond immediately, but after couple of days he responded briefly:

> A ball is being had by all. Near Bodmin Moor. You'd
> hate it — not a war grave in sight.
>
> Cheers. A

David waited a casual two days before responding, telling Angus he had never been to Bodmin Moor but had googled it and it sounded peaceful and not really the place he imagined for a ball. He added:

> Best and best to your friend.

After a protracted pause he received a reply:

> A ball can be had anywhere as long as you have the
> right equipment.

Cheers. And my friend sends her love.

David stared at the screen. Was this something? Or was it Angus merely winding him up?

David couldn't help himself. He replied immediately:

> By the way, I had a note from Cara Bernstein. It was quite brief — only wanting to know how I was after the operation and wishing me well. She didn't say where she was.
>
> Best, D

There was an immediate response.

> So this is what all this BFF bullshit has been all about. Rest assured, old sunshine, that Cara B is not with me & frankly glad she's not. Just ask next time.
>
> A

So that was that.

Reviewing the email chain, David felt the rebuke was probably justified. He had been pussyfooting about like a jealous teenager. Would it have mattered, anyway, if Cara had been with Angus Paton? Wherever she was now, whoever she was with, whatever life she had did not include him.

That was the trouble with convalescence — you spent too much time alone with yourself, allowing wild imaginings to take over. Now he felt petty. A little like DH Lawrence in 'Snake', a poem he liked to teach, he felt he had something to expiate. He felt he had thrown a stick at Angus — not that Angus was a lord of the universe, of course. Heaven forbid.

And the idea made him smile. Trouble was, he didn't dare test Angus's forbearance by writing yet again with some sort of bumbling apology-cum-explanation. He would have to wait until Angus came back to Arras and he could buy him a beer.

What he could do was write yet again to Cara. There was even something comforting, liberating, in the fact that she was unlikely to reply. It allowed him to be more honest, more open than he usually was. It was like sending uncensored messages out into the ether — it hardly mattered what he said or how he said it.

This realisation made it so much easier to write. His earlier agonising about tone and pitch evaporated and he relaxed, became fluent.

From then on, he emailed Cara every few days. He found it easier to imagine that she had simply gone on a long holiday and he was filling her in on all that was happening back home. He bared his soul but not his resentments, as he could not know whether they were justified until he knew the full story, which only she could tell. He asked her about the book she had written or been writing, and expressed the wistful hope that he might be able to read it one day.

He teased her gently, recalling how they used to laugh together and spin out absurdities.

Cara did not respond to any of his overtures.

Undaunted, he continued to write. He told her about Pete and Jan's visit and how he had enjoyed his niece and nephew, despite their inadvertently being responsible for his heart attack. He talked of his developing friendship with Angus, without elaborating on its shaky beginning or mentioning the drawings. After pondering for some time, he even decided to admit to his gaucherie in thinking Angus might have been holidaying with her in Cornwall.

Perhaps it was this admission that finally moved Cara. Her reply was brief and cryptic:

Talk to Arlene.

Cara's
Manuscript

L otte sat, quill in hand, looking at a fresh sheet of paper.
  'Where do I start?'

'What we must do is paint the princess in a different light. We must turn her from an essentially kindly and sweet creature into a darker figure entirely — a selfish, even cruel person.'

'But wait a little,' said Dortchen. 'If she were like that, why would she keep any of her promises to the frog? She would laugh at them.'

'More to the point, why on earth would the prince want to marry her?' asked Lotte.

Wilhelm frowned. 'It is a problem.' Then his face lightened. 'I see it. She must be *made* to keep her promises. Her father, the king, must be a man of rectitude and honour. He will insist she honours her word.'

'That might work,' said Dortchen. 'It would mean, too, that she would resent both her father and the frog!'

'Yes. Double resentment and double meanness. Excellent!'

'You haven't answered my question, though,' said Lotte. 'If she is so nasty and mean, why does the prince wish to marry her?'

'Because he is a man of honour and had given his word to the wicked witch that he would marry his rescuer,' said Dortchen.

'Or perhaps he is just completely shallow and cannot see beneath her beauty,' said Lotte.

'This is the point,' said Wilhelm, smiling. 'This is the question the reader must be confronted with. Why *would* he marry such a harridan? The reader must answer: *you* might marry such a wretched woman, but *I* certainly wouldn't! The question must remain even if it means making the prince a little stupid.'

'Honourably stupid?' said Dortchen.

'Remember,' explained, Wilhelm, 'that the most important reader of this story is our brother Jacob. He is the one who must withdraw in revulsion at the selfishness of the princess.'

'Let me be your friend,' croaked the frog.

In her delight at having her golden ball returned, the beautiful princess had quite forgotten the frog, had quite forgotten the one who had returned the ball to her.

She now turned once again to the creature still squatting on the brick wall of the well.

How ugly, he was, how squat and ugly! How slippery and green, how repulsively green! How could such a creature ever be her friend? How could such a creature ever *expect* to be her friend?

'I could come visit you at your palace,' croaked the frog. 'I could share your breakfast. I could play with you in your garden.'

The princess laughed at the frog's audacity.

'You hideous fool,' she cried. 'How can you imagine you could be a friend of mine?'

'But your promise!' the frog protested.

'More fool you to believe it!' laughed the princess.

'That should do it nicely,' said Wilhelm. 'The princess comes across as untrustworthy and deliciously ignoble.'

'Not too much, though?' asked Lotte anxiously. 'You're not overdoing it, brother, are you?'

Wilhelm shook his head. 'The message must be hammered home,' he said.

'I'm with Lotte, Wilhelm,' said Dortchen. 'You are hammering it home with a very blunt instrument, I feel.'

'Nonsense,' said Wilhelm. 'What next?'

'The frog wants to share the princess's bed,' said Lotte, reading from the original. 'This must be delicately done.'

'There must be nothing offensive, I quite agree,' said Wilhelm. 'Let's see . . .'

> 'You promised you would grant my any wish,' croaked the frog. 'I would go to bed with you and sleep on your coverlet.'
>
> The beautiful princess found this suggestion so repellent she shouted, 'Disgusting!' And she turned her back on the frog and danced back down the path to the palace.

'This is better,' said Wilhelm. 'But now we must bring in the king.'

> Slip slap slip slap the frog hopped up the steps of the palace. Now he reached up, knocked, and shouted: 'Princess! Princess! Open up! Remember your promise!'
>
> Hearing the commotion, the princess ran down the white marble stairs and opened the door.
>
> There sat the frog, who said, 'Princess, remember your promise. I would like to sit with you as you eat your breakfast.'
>
> With a cry of fury, the princess slammed the door in the frog's face.
>
> However, her father the king had also heard the commotion and followed the princess down the stairs.
>
> 'Why did you slam the door like that?' he asked.
>
> 'Because it was a hideous frog who insisted I keep a silly promise simply because he returned to me my golden ball!'

'A promise?' asked the king. 'Tell me, daughter,
about this promise.'

So the princess told the king about how the frog
had rescued her ball and how she had promised him
anything for doing so. And her father was very angry
at her.

'A promise is a sacred thing, and ten times as sacred
when made by a princess, you wicked girl,' he cried.
'Open the door and invite this poor creature to sit with
you at your breakfast.'

The princess did as she was told because she did
not dare do otherwise. But she did give the frog a
venomous glance before he followed her slip slap
slip slap as she flounced up the marble staircase.

'Excellent!' beamed Wilhelm. 'Farewell, sweet-tempered, kind-hearted
princess; welcome spoiled brat!'

'Oh dear,' murmured Lotte, 'I dislike her intensely already.'

'Poor Mathilde,' said Dortchen.

Lotte picked up a new sheet of paper and looked up enquiringly at
her brother. 'How are you going to transform the scene in the bedroom,
Wilhelm?' she asked. 'This is the part where the princess's tender instincts
come to the fore and she strokes the frog on his head.'

'We cannot have that,' said Wilhelm. 'There can be no tender instincts!'

The frog followed the beautiful princess slip slap slip
slap up the stairs to her bedroom.

The princess pulled back the bedclothes and climbed
into her bed for her nap.

Before she could protest, the frog jumped up onto
the counterpane.

'Horrible creature,' the princess snapped. 'Why do
you insist on being where you are not wanted?'

'Are you going to take your nap, dear princess?' the
frog asked.

'I am not your dear princess, you insolent creature!'
she snapped once more. 'And I am certainly not going to
nap as long as you are crouched on my counterpane!'

With that, the princess seized the frog by the leg, drew back her arm and with all of her might flung the little creature against the wall.

'Perfect.' Wilhelm Grimm smiled.

David's
Story

*T*alk to Arlene.

David's mind was racing. Why had Cara suggested he talk to Arlene Abramson? As far as he knew Cara had always regarded the self-styled counsellor with the same slightly amused tolerance as the rest of the staff at Huntingdon.

He himself had recently come to a more nuanced view of Arlene, as he had of Kate Garner, but he had no reason to suspect that Cara felt the same. Then again, what did he know?

Very little, apparently.

He called Arlene and got her voicemail message. He sent her a text and an email but there was no immediate response.

He called Kate.

'Arlene? No, she isn't back from holiday yet. Just a moment, I'll check the schedule she gave me.'

David waited for a few moments.

'She's in London visiting friends. Actually, she may be in transit — due back in a couple of days. Is it urgent?'

'Possibly, but probably not,' said David. 'I've had another message from Cara. It kind of hints that Arlene could be our Deep Throat.'

'Arlene? That does surprise me!'

'Me too,' said David. 'Thanks for your help.'

It did surprise him. If Arlene had been the confidante, she had certainly deceived him. He recalled her visit to his rooms in the chateau, when she appeared as bewildered as everybody else by Cara's disappearance. She even had a few theories — what were they? That's right, she said there was probably some physical reason such as amnesia, catatonia or some such bullshit. He had, though, been gratified that she had not doubted him at all, or at least that's what she said. She had pooh-poohed the rumours of fights or worse. Now that he considered the matter, Arlene had been quite defensive of Cara, had spoken highly of her.

Of course the real purpose of her visit, he remembered now, was to tell him as gently as possible that Cara and Angus had been an item. He had been unhappy to hear this at the time, but now he realised it had been useful to know, to be forewarned.

Except that Angus's chalk drawings had still rocked him.

Perhaps at the time of her visit Arlene was not in contact with Cara, he thought, giving her the benefit of the doubt. Perhaps if there were contact, it had come later.

But if that were the case, why hadn't she come to see him when the contact happened? She knew the whole Cara thing was driving him nuts. It didn't make sense.

And if she *had* been in contact with Cara before she came to see him soon after Cara vanished, what was her game?

What had Kate said? Arlene was due back in a few days. Not long to wait. After all, he had waited this long already.

Weird that she wasn't answering her phone or email, though.

Perhaps she had caught the Cara disease.

Cara's
Manuscript

No sooner had the frog smashed into the wall than he turned into a most handsome prince with beautiful, kind eyes.

He stood alongside her bed smiling. 'Thank you, thank you, beautiful princess, for rescuing me from that deep, dark well. Only you, with your outstanding beauty, could have performed such a deed. For I was cursed by a wicked witch whose evil spell changed me into the wet, green frog you found there.

'The witch condemned me to remain in the well until rescued by a princess of unsurpassed beauty, a beautiful princess I am bound to marry. I beg you to become my bride and come with me to help rule my kingdom.'

The handsome prince's proposal so surprised the beautiful princess, she immediately forgot her previous repulsion and accepted upon the instant.

'It's finished now?' asked Lotte, pleased to be able to lay down her quill.

'The prince comes out of it quite well,' said Dortchen with heavy irony.

'The princess does not,' said Lotte.

'She does get the prince, Lotte.' Dortchen smiled.

'She does not come out of it well in terms of character. She does in terms of material things, as you say, but thoroughly undeservedly. We have made the story ring false.' Lotte glanced up at Wilhelm. 'So, brother,' she continued with a touch of bitterness, 'can we leave the story there? Have you made the princess sufficiently horrible?'

'Oh, I believe so,' said Wilhelm.

'Did you mean to make the prince so unbelievably stupid?' asked Dortchen. 'I *cannot* see why he would offer his hand to that insufferable woman.'

'We've been through that,' said Wilhelm easily. 'The point is that he is a man of honour. He had pledged to marry the woman who rescues him. Besides, making him stupid makes it hardly likely brother Jacob will identify with him.'

'So, a victim of rather bad luck,' observed Lotte. She blew on the last page to dry the ink and handed it to Wilhelm. 'Here we are, all ready for Jacob.'

'I'm not so sure,' said Wilhelm, after scanning through the pages. 'There's something missing yet. I can't quite put my finger on it.'

Lotte and Dortchen exchanged a somewhat exasperated glance.

All at once Wilhelm lifted a finger into the air.

'It has come to you?' asked Lotte.

'Something small, yet significant,' Wilhelm glanced at them. 'Fräulein Heller called her story "The Frog Prince". I suggest we rename it "The Frog King".'

'Why?'

'Think,' said Wilhelm. 'A prince is young, invariably romantic, but waiting in the wings. A king, on the other hand, is usually older, already powerful and in command of the wealth of his kingdom. A princess motivated by material things would almost certainly prefer a king to a prince. Making Fräulein Heller's prince into a king will subtly underscore the mercenary nature of her attraction.'

'All right. Now are we done?' asked Lotte.

Wilhelm shook his head. 'Not yet. There's something else.'

'What?' asked Dortchen. 'Do we not already have the classic ending: marriage and happy ever after?'

Lotte smiled. 'I don't think happy ever after can be guaranteed given the bride the prince — the king — has ended up with.'

'I feel that for Jacob's sake the story needs something more,' said Wilhelm.

'Surely any hidden message Mathilde Heller had introduced has been expunged by now?'

'More than expunged, Dortchen,' said Lotte. 'Exploded, I would have thought: night into day, black into white.'

'Or the other way around,' smiled Dortchen.

'I feel we've been rather mean,' said Lotte. 'I quite like Mathilde and she will be very upset when she learns what we have done. It is quite a liberty to refashion somebody's story so drastically.'

Wilhelm, his brow creased in thought, was not listening. 'Would you excuse me, ladies? I would like to go for a little walk. I sense an idea coming and I would like to pursue it.'

'Very well,' said Dortchen. 'We two shall have some more chocolate to drink.'

Within half an hour Wilhelm had returned. With a satisfied clap of his hands, he said, 'I have it!'

'Do tell,' said Dortchen.

'Better,' said Wilhelm, 'I will dictate! Quill, Lotte, and ink and paper!'

> Next morning there arrived a coach drawn by eight white horses. The coachman was the king's loyal servant, Faithful Heinrich.
>
> When the wicked witch had turned his beloved master into a frog, the distraught Heinrich had ordered three iron bands to be fitted around his chest to prevent his heart from breaking.
>
> He assisted the king and the princess into the carriage and took up his post on the driver's platform. His beloved master had been saved and Heinrich's joy knew no bounds.
>
> They had not been long on their journey before the king heard a resounding crack.
>
> Fearing a coach wheel had broken he turned about

and said, 'Heinrich — the coach? Is something wrong?'

'It is nothing, my lord, but the snapping of an iron band binding my heart!'

Twice more the king heard the cracking sound, twice more he imagined the coach was breaking, but twice more Heinrich reassured him that the sound was only that of another iron band snapping.

This was a measure of Faithful Heinrich's happiness at the knowledge that his master was finally safe and happy.

'Well?' demanded Wilhelm, as Lotte lay her quill aside.

'I'm not sure, Wilhelm,' said Dortchen frowning. 'This addition seems to have nothing to do with the story of the frog and the princess—'

'On the contrary, Dortchen,' said Wilhelm. 'It has everything to do with the frog and the princess, at least in the spirit of the story as told by Fräulein Heller. So much so that I propose we subtitle the story "Iron Heinrich".'

'But that is perverse,' said Lotte. 'I agree with Dortchen. This Heinrich is an afterthought, not a centrepiece. He has nothing to do with the story.'

'I am resolute,' said Wilhelm.

'Like Faithful Heinrich?' asked Dortchen.

'In a way, I suppose,' said Wilhelm. 'Look, I heard what you said about the mismatch at the end, and it's true that a folk tale should end with a perfect match, not a mismatch. What do we have here? A marriage between a king — made foolish by the plot — and a shallow, perfidious and tiny-minded princess who has only beauty to redeem her.'

'But you made her that way,' said Lotte. 'Mathilde's princess was much more worthy.'

Wilhelm ignored this. 'I saw that what the story needed was another character, a character who represented the qualities the princess lacked — devotion, fidelity and loyalty.'

'Faithful Heinrich,' Dortchen said.

'I see what you've done,' said Lotte. 'I was forgetting our number-one reader.'

'Quite so,' said Dortchen. 'Jacob will rightly despise the princess but can only admire the qualities of Iron Heinrich.'

'Poor Mathilde,' said Lotte.

'But am I right?' demanded Wilhelm.

'Given your purpose,' said Dortchen pointedly, 'you are, though you have made one small error.'

'What's that?' asked Wilhelm.

'You called the faithful one Iron Heinrich, when I imagine you should have called him Iron Wilhelm.'

After supper that evening, when the brothers, pipes at the ready, eased into their chairs in the parlour, Wilhelm handed Jacob the story they had worked on through the afternoon.

'Here we are, brother,' he said. 'This is the story the indefatigable Fräulein Heller has long promised us.'

Jacob took the script from him and glanced through it. 'But this appears to be written in Lotte's hand.'

'It is,' said Wilhelm easily. 'We took the liberty of editing the tale in order to smooth out some infelicities, that sort of thing. Read it — I think it would be a useful enough addition to our collection. It is sad that, given the grandmother's death, this is likely to be the last offering from the Heller sisters.'

'Unless they find some other source,' said Jacob. 'They seem keen enough to go off hunting on their own account.'

Indeed they do, Wilhelm thought to himself.

'Read it. I'll be interested to hear what you think.'

David's Story

Three days later David received a response from Arlene Abramson:

> David, sorry about the radio silence. I go into purdah
> on holiday. Back on deck now and understand you'd
> like to talk. Let me know.
>
> Kind regards, Arlene

He rang her immediately.

'There's so much to explain, David, and you are owed such a lot of explanation. Far too much to go into over the phone. Can we do lunch?'

'Yes, but—'

'I'm not trying to fob you off. I hope you'll understand when we talk.'

'Of course. Where do you suggest?'

Arlene named a place and they agreed to meet the following day.

It seemed to David that Arlene was being unnecessarily mysterious but there was little he could do about it. He had three simple questions, although the second two probably didn't have simple answers. Where was Cara? Why had she disappeared? And why had she, with Arlene's apparent connivance, kept him in the dark for so long?

So many other questions came crowding in, he wondered whether a single lunch would be long enough.

He found Arlene waiting for him when he arrived at the restaurant, a vegetarian crêpe place that already, as far as David was concerned, had two strikes against it.

'I'm so glad you're feeling better,' Arlene said, standing up to embrace him.

'It's been slow,' he said, 'but I'm improving all the time. Michael's given me an extra couple of months' leave to fully recuperate.'

'Make sure you take it,' said Arlene. 'No risks, please.'

A waiter came to take their orders and Arlene, taking charge, made suggestions, which David accepted gratefully.

'I like this place,' she said. 'I come here often.'

David was beginning to wonder how long the shadow-boxing would last when Arlene, running her hand through her close-cropped hair, said, 'I'm glad Cara did get in touch with you.'

'It was a bit of a surprise. But how did you know?'

'I've been encouraging her to do so for some time,' said Arlene.

'So you have been in contact with her?'

'Yes.'

'For how long?'

'David, let's not get into that right now. Suffice it to say, I have. I've been keeping her up to date from time to time. The heart attack news rather shocked her out of her complacency.'

'Complacency?'

'Perhaps not the right word . . . I should have said procrastination. She had been meaning to get in touch with you, you know. It's just that she kept putting it off.'

David looked at her incredulously. 'Putting it off? Arlene, it's been nearly a year!'

'I know . . . I know . . .'

'And how come you know? How is it that you've been having conversations with Cara while I've been left in the dark all this time?'

He didn't say *you of all people*, but it was implicit in his tone.

'There's a reason for that.'

'I'd like to hear it.'

'You will, and much more besides. Let me order a bottle of wine.'

The lunch was delivered, the wine was poured, the pleasantries over; it was time for the second beginning.

'So?' asked David.

'Why haven't I let you know this before?'

'I don't really know anything yet,' said David. 'But yes, that'll do for a start.'

'It was not my decision, it was Cara's. She came to see me in my role as counsellor, and asked me to keep everything in absolute confidence.'

David was astonished. *In her role as counsellor* . . . He almost laughed out loud at the idea of Cara Bernstein consulting Arlene about some problem or other. Somehow he had landed in a strange new world.

'This meant I was quite unable to tell you anything until I had Cara's permission.'

'Even after she left?'

Arlene nodded seriously. 'Absolutely. All I could do was drop hints. That's why I asked to see you not long after Cara left you in Germany.'

'I must have been rather obtuse,' said David. 'I don't remember any hints. All I remember your telling me is that she'd once had a thing with Angus Paton.'

'That was part of it,' said Arlene. 'Don't be cross, David. I *couldn't* tell you. I did suggest to you I thought the problem was physical, rather than a fight or an argument, and I did tell you I believed you when others were not so sure. I hoped that would help reassure you but I couldn't go further. I could see how confused you were, and how you were suffering, but my hands were tied.'

David re-ran their earlier discussion in his mind.

'Actually,' Arlene continued, 'I shouldn't have said as much as I did. I found myself trying to run on a slippery barrel. It was unfair to you and could have been a betrayal of Cara's confidence.'

David remembered. Amnesia . . . catatonia . . . That had been weird shit.

'So Cara had clearly seen you before we went off on holiday.'

Arlene nodded. 'Just before.'

'And afterwards? She contacted you after she'd sloped off?'

Arlene nodded again, taking a sip of wine.

'And you've been in contact ever since?'

'Yes, we have. In fact I saw her in London just a few days ago.'

David shook his head in disbelief. 'Arlene, I have to say, priestly vows or the sanctity of the confessional or whatever, this all feels pretty shabby.'

Arlene did not respond.

'Almost as shabby as what Cara did in the first place — running off like that without a word and leaving me agonising for *a year*!'

'I can understand why you feel that way,' said Arlene drily, 'but Cara didn't feel she needed your permission to leave. In any event, it's not part of my brief to judge Cara; I'm only here to tell you what happened, and why she did what she did.'

'Well, we're not getting very far on the *why*. So tell me — why did she just disappear like that?'

'A number of reasons,' said Arlene, 'but the main one was, as I clumsily hinted, physical. Cara was pregnant.'

There was a long silence as David tried to digest this startling information. Finally he said, 'I don't understand.'

'What don't you understand?'

'If she was pregnant, why that would be a reason to drop everything and run? Especially from me! For god's sake, I'm the father!'

Arlene shook her head. 'It may seem strange to you, but according to Cara she had a host of reasons, involving you, the school, her family. She just all at once didn't want to deal with any of it. She says she needed to get away somewhere quiet and safe and focus on what was really important.'

'And what was that?' asked David, hurt. 'Clearly I was not important. Jesus!'

'You were,' said Arlene, trying to comfort him. 'You were one of the most important things. You made her happy. She liked you very much.'

'So what was more important?'

'The baby, of course.'

'You said Cara liked me very much. You didn't say love.'

'I'm only telling you what Cara told me. But you should know that when she left the school at the beginning of the holiday to sail down the Rhine with you, she had no intention of returning to Huntingdon. She had packed up everything. It was nothing to do with you — she had left open the question of when and how to tell you. She was worried that you would want to throw everything away and go with her.'

'She didn't want that?'

'It was complicated. What happened that last afternoon was pivotal. You were so happy there, Cara said, wandering among the graves. She always found your passion for graves rather amusing. She realised that if she told you at that point, especially when you'd brought out the ring, everything would be thrown like confetti up into the air.'

'Confetti?' said David, with an edge of bitterness. 'A little irony there, Arlene.'

'There had been a slight chance she was mistaken about the pregnancy — a missed period is not definitive proof — but she'd bought a kit and—'

'I'll have to give her this,' said David, even more bitterly, 'she's wasted in teaching. Could have been an Academy Award-winning actor.'

Arlene ignored this. 'Once it was confirmed she was forced to re-evaluate everything, and sooner or later she knew she had to tell you. She didn't plan to ruin your holiday together.'

'How thoughtful.'

'So she decided to leave you while you were in a happy place. After the cruise.'

'But she didn't wait for the cruise. She chickened out!'

'The ring, David—'

'But she didn't seem in the least put out by the ring! There was no big drama. Anyway, cutting and running would hardly have left me happy at whatever stage. She must have known that. A baby? Nothing would have made me happier!'

'Are you sure about that?'

'Absolutely!'

'Cara wasn't.'

'Cara wasn't what? Sure I'd be happy, or sure she'd be happy?'

'She knew things would be utterly different, but she wasn't sure in what way and didn't want to take the risk. And I'm sorry to have to tell you this, David, but she knew she didn't want to marry you.'

David slumped. He had a sudden flashback to that final afternoon on the slopes of Venusberg. Context changes, she had said. He thought she'd been talking about trees.

'So did she have the baby, or . . . ?'

Arlene nodded. 'She did briefly consider an abortion but decided to keep the baby. It's a little girl. A cute wee thing. She's called Emily.'

'Who does she look like?'

Arlene glanced at him. 'Like Emily, mainly,' she said.

'And they're in London?'

Arlene nodded. 'Near Wimbledon. Cara has done a little supply teaching — she's not after a permanent job.'

'Living on her own?'

'Does that matter?'

Arlene's answer may not have been meant as a rebuke but David felt it as such.

'I guess not. Just curious. I would have thought . . .'

There was a pause as they turned their attention to their food. Though the conversation was uncomfortable and disconcerting, the crêpes were surprisingly good.

'Are any other Huntingdon people in touch with Cara?'

Arlene shook her head. 'Not as far as I know. Steffi Fox might have been, perhaps. That was Cara's problem — she felt she had no one to turn to. Apart from you, they were essentially colleagues. She was estranged from most of her family. Her mother had died; her father had always been remote — he had left Cara's mother earlier and remarried, and she had only occasional contact with a sister back in the States. There was her brother, but he was also on the outer with the rest of the family. Presumably you knew about all that.'

David smiled bleakly. 'None of it. Cara never talked about her family. You know, I'm a little pissed off that Cara felt she couldn't turn to me.'

Arlene shrugged. 'As I said, I'm not one to judge.'

'But you *are* one to judge, aren't you, Arlene? Isn't that what this conversation has actually been about?'

'I don't quite follow you, David.'

'No? Aren't you here as Cara's emissary, a go-between?'

'Well, in a way—'

'I think in every way,' said David angrily. 'A year on, I hear from Cara for the very first time — a few words and nothing else except an indication that I should talk to you. She's had my baby, for god's sake! And I assume that just as you're bringing me Cara's view of things, you're going to go back to her with mine.'

'In a sense, I suppose.'

'Tell me this isn't true: you'll go back to Cara, and if David passes muster in your report, Cara may deign to talk to David again?'

'It's not really like that.'

'Isn't it? What is it like, then?'

'I'm sorry, David. I *am* finding this very difficult.'

'Well I'm not finding it easy either!'

'David, I see little point in recriminations. The fact is, Cara has made contact with you again. For reasons of her own — which I know you find very hard to understand — she found it difficult to make contact with you before this. I know you've been hurt. The point is, she *has* now made contact and we should move on from here. I do confess that she's used — is using — me to gauge your reactions. But is there any harm in that?'

'It suggests a lack of trust.'

'Perhaps, but not in you, David. A lack of trust in her own ability to read the situation.'

'So what are you going to tell her?'

'What would you like me to tell her?'

David shrugged. 'It would be good if we could at least talk again. It's been incredibly frustrating sending messages out into deep space and hearing nothing back.'

'I can tell her that.'

'Could I visit her?'

'Would you like to?'

'Of course! Very much. And naturally I'd like to see Emily.'

The waiter removed their plates and refilled their glasses.

'By the way,' David said, 'did Cara's father ever find her?'

'Her father?' Arlene was surprised.

'Yes. Did you not hear he visited Huntingdon? At the end of the first term Cara missed when she sloped off.'

'No, I didn't know that.'

'Sorry, I thought everyone did. He spoke to Michael, so Miranda was all over it of course. Angus told me.'

'Nobody told me.' Arlene sounded disappointed.

'So I assume he didn't find her.'

'If he did, Cara didn't mention it. What did he want?'

'According to Angus he wanted to make peace with Cara, so I presumed there had been bad feeling. There wasn't much more, except that he had clearly not suffered a massive stroke — or, if he had, he'd made a miraculous recovery. Oh, and he talked about a sister, but no mention of a brother. I asked Michael if he'd got the sister's address, but of course he hadn't.'

'I'm guessing he didn't find Cara,' said Arlene. 'Or, if he did, there's been no reconciliation.'

'Will there be a reconciliation with me?'

Arlene smiled at him and covered her hand with his. 'There's no need for a reconciliation. With you, David, it's a reconnection that's called for.'

David shrugged and gave her a wan smile. 'Let's hope,' he said.

David's
Story

'Arlene's told me Cara's had a baby.'

Angus looked at him and whistled under his breath. 'I guess that explains a lot.'

'Does it?'

'May I congratulate you, old son. Well done!' Angus paused. 'It is yours, of course?'

David was taken aback. 'Of course!'

'And Arlene confirmed that?'

'Arlene didn't actually say. She was pretty cagey. She could apparently only say what Cara had sanctioned, so—'

'And the baby? I mean, what is it?'

'A girl. She's called her Emily.'

Angus shook his head. 'Well, this is quite a turn-up. How old?'

'Not sure. Three or four months, I guess.'

'Calls for another drink!'

It was a few hours after David's lunch with Arlene. He had been agitated all afternoon and, feeling the need for help in processing the startling news, had rung Angus, who was now back in town. Arlene's revelations had completely disabused him of the notion that Cara was the mysterious woman friend the art teacher had been holidaying with.

Angus had responded cheerfully enough and arrived at the apartment armed with a bottle of Calvados. David, who was not fond of spirits, took a glass for conviviality's sake, but thereafter demurred. Angus was not so circumspect. By the time David had summoned up the courage to give him Arlene's news, Angus had downed a couple of glasses and was now contemplating a third.

He poured a generous slug and raised his eyebrows at David.

David shook his head. 'Doctor's orders,' he lied.

'I'd change my doctor,' said Angus. He raised his glass. 'Here's to Emily,' he said, 'and all who sail in her.'

David gave him a sharp look. 'Not funny, Angus.'

Angus waved his hand dismissively. 'So what are you going to do?'

'Go and see her of course.'

'Cara? Emily?'

'Both.'

'Cara's given you the green light?'

'Not exactly but I'm going anyway.'

'Good luck!'

'Think I'll need it?'

'Indubitably! She's a dark horse, that Cara. Or should that be a dark mare? But of course you know all about that.'

David considered all he knew of Cara and all she had withheld. He gave a rueful smile, reminded that he had learnt far more about her since her disappearance than he had in their weeks of intimacy.

They sat in companiable silence for some time, Angus sipping his drink occasionally. David presumed he was processing the information. For his part, David was considering Cara's reticence about so many things — family, feelings — and comparing it with her uninhibited manner at other times. He turned to Angus.

'One thing puzzles me,' he said.

'Only one thing?'

'Well, a raft of things, really. But this thing, anyway: how come Cara — you know, such a private person — agreed to pose for you?'

'Naked, you mean?'

'Yes.'

Angus laughed. 'Really, Davey boy, you're like the bear that wouldn't let it alone.'

'But—'

'I think you're equating private with prudish. Cara is, as you no doubt know, anything but prudish.'

'I'm just surprised at the contrast, that's all.'

Angus took another draught. Then he said, 'It was an intellectual challenge, I think. She dropped into the art room one day after classes — I can't remember the reason. I was working on a chalk drawing. Well, finishing the drawing really, from some preliminary sketches. It was a picture of a little *église* I'd found in a village somewhere south of Arras. Anyway, Cara watched me working on it for some time and seemed surprised to find I could actually draw.' He drained his glass.

'She asked if there were other pieces she could see and so I pulled out a selection. They were mainly of buildings, in the countryside hereabouts. She made appreciative noises, then asked if I ever drew people, portraits. From time to time, I said, but not often. It's hard to get people to sit still for so long in these busy times.'

'So she asked if you would draw her?'

'Not at that point, no. I said I wasn't particularly interested in people as such. I was more into architecture. Faces didn't move me but I was interested in the architecture of bodies. Bodies, as landscape, you know? Manet?'

'That *Déjeuner sur l'herbe* thing?'

'Yes, that one, but more *The Body of the Dead Christ*. You know it?'

David shook his head.

'Magnificent. Anyway, so I rabbited on a bit about Manet and form. The idea must have intrigued Cara — she has quite an aesthetic sensibility, you know. All the same, I was pretty startled when she came out with it: *What about me?*'

Just like that, thought David. He could almost hear her. Disconcertingly direct.

'Another?' Angus reached for the bottle, glancing at David, who shook his head.

'I wasn't sure whether she was serious or just playing about so I pushed the envelope. I said, *Nude?* And she just said: *Why not?* And that was that. We made an arrangement to come here — obviously we couldn't do it at school — and it all carried on from there.'

'All?'

David had a nervous lump in his throat. Angus had drunk enough to become expansive, even confessional, and David was caught between needing to know and dreading the knowledge. He looked around the living room and at the closed bedroom door. That was where the drawings were made, of course. Who had suggested the bedroom? Was it Angus, or had Cara led him in? Led him on?

'How many drawings were there?' David asked tentatively.

'You saw them. Just the three.'

'Cara didn't want to keep one?'

Angus laughed. 'Couldn't afford them! No, to tell the honest truth, she hated them.'

David recalled the drawings. Despite his initial shock at the discovery, he had considered the pictures very good. That Cara should have hated them rather surprised him.

'Why?' he asked.

'I remember her words exactly. She called bullshit on my "body as landscape" theory. She said that as far as she was concerned, the pictures were just typical examples of the male gaze.'

'The male gaze?'

'You know, the objectification thing men do. Seeing the woman merely as a sex object, the necessary gratification of lust but little else — all that sort of thing. I guess she saw the drawings as the visual equivalent of a wolf whistle.'

'That must have pissed you off.'

Angus laughed again and measured a little more brandy into his glass.

'Not at all. She'd hit the nail on the head. They were exactly that. What did dear old Monet say? I paint with my prick. Cara with her clothes off and me drawing with my prick! I was positively priapic the whole time!'

David felt anger rising.

Angus looked at him speculatively. 'You want to know, old son, don't you? You really want to know. Did we fuck? Of course not. Haven't I made that abundantly clear by now? I have to confess it was damned hard not to try.'

David realised Angus was a little drunk. His words were increasingly slurred.

'A lot of people think you did try,' David countered.

'A lot of people think the world is flat, the moon landing was staged and Donald Trump is god. How the hell would *a lot of people* know, anyway?'

'Were you in love with her?'

Angus wagged a roguish finger. 'Love? God, you have a quaint, old-fashioned view of the world, Davey boy. I was in lust, of course. Lust unrequited. Love's the wrong word. Lurve's the word and lurve didn't come into it. You're the man, Davey boy, who believes in lurve.' He poured another drink.

'What do you believe in, Angus?'

'First cut is the deepest, old boy. You know the song.'

He had lost David at this point, but Angus did not elaborate. After a few seconds he leaned towards David confidentially. 'You didn't get very far in the lurve stakes, old son. And I didn't get very far in the lust stakes. I did have some heavy weaponry though, just between you and me. Not that I stooped to it. A possible means of persuasion.' He wagged his finger again.

'Persuasion?'

Angus brought out his phone and flourished it. 'Took the precaution of taking a few pics of la Cara *in flagrante delicto.*' He giggled at his difficulty in getting around the Latin phrase.

Again, David felt anger. 'You were blackmailing her!'

'Never call it blackmail, old son,' the big man said. 'Call it persuasion. Gentle persuasion. Nobody hurt. Just the possibility of a little rewarding fun.'

'You really are a bastard, you know that, Angus?'

'Fully agree, old son. Thoroughly unprincipled. Thoroughly unprince . . . unprincipled bastard with an Instagram account.'

'A complete and utter bastard.' David could not keep the contempt out of his voice, but, if anything, it seemed to encourage Angus.

'Couldn't agree more, old son. Couldn't agree more.'

Angus stood up a little unsteadily and drained his glass. 'And at this point in the proceedings,' he said, 'I feel I must prevail upon you to allow me to use your loo. Don't bother showing me. I know the way.'

He lurched out of the room and into the bathroom, leaving both doors open so that David was forced to listen not only to Angus's audible stream but also to a just recognisable rendition of 'The First Cut is the Deepest'.

For a long time after Angus went home, David sat in a state of swirling resentment. What had Arlene said about Cara's decision not to return to the school after the holidays? Personal issues — nothing to do with him. It was now pretty obvious what those issues were about.

The realisation hardened his resolve to go to London, and as soon as possible. He would force Cara's address out of Arlene. He went to the bedroom to find his laptop.

When he returned to the living room he saw Angus's mobile on the coffee table. Angus had clearly forgotten it when he shambled out of the flat. With a grim little smile, David slipped the phone into his jacket pocket and opened his laptop.

Cara's
Manuscript

To get to the Royal Library on Bellevuestrasse, Mathilde and Helga had to pass the Grimm house. They instinctively hurried by, even though there was little chance of their being noticed from the house.

The library was not open to the public and the sisters had to wait a considerable time before the door was opened.

'*Oui?*'

An elderly retainer stood there, eyeing them suspiciously.

'We would like to speak with Herr Jacob Grimm, the librarian,' said Mathilde. 'Is he here, please?'

'Do you have an appointment?'

The man could speak German, but badly and with a heavy French accent.

'No, but it is a matter of business.'

'Royal business?'

'Private business.'

'At present Herr Grimm is engaged with a gentleman. Also on private business,' the man said drily. 'Something to do with their stories.'

'Our business is with stories, too,' said Helga quickly.

The man seemed to be thinking as he studied them. Then he shrugged, and as he turned he said, 'Follow me.'

He led them through halls and passages and upstairs before opening a door into a large and airy, book-lined room. Leaning over a manuscript-scattered table at the far end stood two men. One was Jacob Grimm, the other was a strangely dressed man with thick curls and a harried expression. Neither of them had ever seen the stranger before. They would have remembered if they had, given his orange coat and apple-green trousers.

Jacob Grimm looked at them with great surprise. Soon recovering, he nodded formally and greeted them.

'Fräulein Heller, this is opportune.'

The sisters exchanged glances.

'Fräuleins, allow me to introduce Herr Brentano. I may have mentioned him. It is for Herr Brentano that we have been gathering our folk tales. Clemens, these young ladies are Fräulein Mathilde Heller and her sister . . .'

Jacob had clearly forgotten Helga's name.

'My sister Helga,' said Mathilde, quickly coming to his rescue.

'Ladies, I am delighted to make your acquaintance,' said Clemens Brentano.

'Yes, Clemens,' said Jacob, 'these young ladies have provided us with several tales, including the remarkable one we have just been discussing.'

Brentano turned to the sisters, beaming. 'Really? Then this is, as you say, Jacob, most opportune.'

'The remarkable one?' asked Mathilde.

'Oh yes!' exclaimed Brentano. 'As a writer myself, I have a fine ear for what distinguishes the remarkable from the mundane. My good friend Jacob, here — own up to it, man! — is fond of dust. Dusty old tales and spotted manuscripts, the more moth-eaten and mildewed the better. He's happiest among the tales that have the single redeeming quality of antiquity.'

Jacob coughed. 'You are being a little unfair, Clemens. It is authenticity I cherish, for it is there we can discover all manner—'

'Authenticity is usually denoted in Jacob's mind by boring predictability — happy ever after. What nonsense!'

The sisters glanced at each other, unsure where this debate was leading and what it had to do with them or their story.

Brentano turned back to them. 'What distinguishes your story, my dear young ladies, is that it has that quality I so admire, which is so rare in most fusty folk tales: unpredictability. It is a paradox, is it not, that these so-called folk stories are supposed to be fanciful and yet they rarely contain genuine fancy? Unpredictability, that's the thing. Consider one of my favourite lines from Novalis: *In a work of art, chaos must shimmer through the veil of order*. In your story, dear ladies, chaos *shimmers!*'

Brentano was becoming increasingly expressive, gesturing wildly as he spoke. Helga smiled, enjoying his performance. He's a conductor, she thought, and we are an orchestra. Mathilde was less sure. She was trying to relate his wild words to the story they had left with Wilhelm. Chaos? She was sure he must be talking about the same story, but that story *did* have a happy ending. It was not in the least chaotic — was it?

'In my opinion,' Brentano carried on, clearly not expecting a response, 'what makes this tale so special is the matter of character. The characters in most of the tales we have gathered, Jacob, you must agree, have no subtlety, none whatsoever. They could move from one tale to another and no one would notice. Princesses — all the same. Princes, witches, woodchoppers, tailors and stepmothers — all evil, by the way, the stepmothers. Stock characters with no nuance and no surprise. None change unless by enchantment or when they are restored.'

'Like the frog?' asked Helga, unsure of what Brentano was saying.

He turned to her. 'Yes, the frog. What a good example! A king before enchantment and a king after, quite unaltered except that now he is saddled with that odious woman, obliged because of the plot to make her his queen and no doubt condemned to a life of misery.'

'But . . .' began Mathilde, confused. 'But the princess is not odious. She is tender and lovely.'

'She is hardly lovely: she only "rescues" the king by attempting to smash him to pieces against a wall!'

By now, Mathilde was thoroughly alarmed. She looked at Clemens Brentano, unable to decide whether he was completely confused or perhaps a trifle mad.

'This is what makes this frog king story so wonderful,' Brentano continued, addressing Jacob. 'It turns everything on its head and makes a mockery of stock characters and situations. The princess is beautiful, but she is selfish, facile and thoroughly unlikeable. And yet in spite of this she gets to marry the king! The king is a poor fool trapped by a foolish prophecy that he must marry the one who rescues him. Now he is doomed to a life of regret and recrimination. Just wonderful.'

He turned back to Mathilde and Helga, still beaming. 'Jacob tells me, ladies, that your grandmother, who told you this astonishing story, has passed away. My very sincere condolences and, I am bound to add, my deep regrets that the source of such a tale is with us no more. It would have been so good to have had more of its ilk.'

Mathilde could cope no longer. The version of their story trumpeted by the exuberant Clemens Brentano was a bizarre travesty.

'Herr Grimm, would you mind showing me your copy of the story I left with Wilhelm?'

Her voice was shaking, but her tone had ice in it.

Jacob, slightly bewildered, said, 'Of course', and handed her the script. Helga hurried to read over her shoulder.

Mathilde was immediately puzzled. 'This is not my handwriting.'

'Indeed not,' said Jacob. 'It is written in the hand of my sister Charlotte.'

'But why?'

'My brother Wilhelm,' began Jacob, somewhat embarrassed. 'Wilhelm said there were a number of minor infelicities in the original draft and that he had taken the liberty of correcting them.'

As he was explaining this, the Heller sisters were quickly scanning the document.

'It was a liberty indeed,' said Helga angrily. 'He has altered the original story considerably.'

'Then it must have been for the better,' said Clemens Brentano cheerfully, 'for to me, the story is quite delicious, quite perfect.'

'Wilhelm often takes the trouble to smooth out a story to make it more readable,' said Jacob, speaking to Brentano especially. 'I wish he wouldn't. We have several times argued about the issue. But given what you said earlier about my passion for dust, I'm in no doubt that you will agree with his point of view.'

'In this case, certainly,' said Brentano. 'The story is a treasure. It will take pride of place in the collection! Remember what the great Novalis said, if I may take the liberty of quoting him again: *All poetry is translation.*'

'But no, this cannot be!' cried Helga.

'Fräulein, is something wrong?' asked Brentano.

'No, Herr Brentano, nothing is wrong,' Mathilde said quickly. She looked pointedly at her sister. 'Helga, nothing is wrong.'

Then Mathilde turned back to the poet and the scholar. 'Gentlemen, my sister and I must leave. I am sorry we interrupted your meeting. Please excuse us and accept our farewells.'

'Of course, of course,' said Jacob, so quickly that Mathilde looked up at him.

He quickly averted his eyes.

There had not even been the pretence of a plea for them to prolong their visit. She continued to look at Jacob, who, she noticed, appeared quite diminished compared to the passionate Brentano. His pretty face piqued, his goosy neck suddenly scrawny. She couldn't bear it and turned away.

Clemens Brentano announced that he too would take his leave, and offered to escort Mathilde and Helga part of their way home if they would do him the courtesy of allowing it.

'I must away to my sister, Bettina,' he said to Jacob. 'Next time she will accompany me, for she is keen to see you and Wilhelm again. For some unaccountable reason she is very fond of you both.'

'It must be hard for you to understand Bettina's being so fond of dust, I imagine,' said Jacob wryly, taking Brentano's hand. 'But come to our house, not this place. Wilhelm and Lotte will be there.'

He did not offer his farewells to the sisters.

Once upon the street and their direction determined, Brentano stationed himself between the sisters and took each by the elbow. Then he led them forward, continuing the monologue he had barely left off back at the library. His eccentric dress and loud declamation aroused the curiosity of every passer-by, and Mathilde and Helga were mortified by the attention. Eventually they managed to interrupt the flow to persuade Brentano of their pressing need to visit an aunt nearby, and thus were able to escape while still many streets away from their home.

It was not until they were leaving their aunt's house that they were able to discuss what had happened.

'I had thought better of Lotte,' said Helga.

'It would not have been Lotte,' said Mathilde.

'It was her handwriting, Jacob said.'

'It was not her doing, though,' said Mathilde. 'This would have been the work of Wilhelm. Oh, I wish we had been able to put our story in the hands of Jacob directly.'

'The story with the fusty, predictable ending?'

'Not to Herr Brentano's taste, apparently, as he may have mentioned.' Mathilde allowed herself a wan, ironic smile.

'Should we talk to Wilhelm?'

'No! He clearly saw what we were trying to do and deliberately turned our message upside down and inside out. What could we possibly say to him?'

'We could tell him that what he did was wrong!'

'But why bother?'

'Because it *was* wrong.'

Mathilde stopped walking and turned to her sister. 'Helga, don't you see that what *we* did was wrong. What we offered the brothers was not a folk tale. It was not a story Oma had told us. We misrepresented it from the start in order to send a message to Herr Grimm. And now we have received our comeuppance.'

'We have been through this so many times,' said Helga.

'I know, I know,' said Mathilde. 'And do you know why we've been through it so many times? Because we have been trying to persuade ourselves that what we were doing was *not* wrong.'

'It was not.'

'Helga, it is. You know that deep down. It's as plain as the nose on your face.'

For some time the two walked in silence.

At last Helga said, 'What should we do, then?'

'What can we do?'

'There must be something. Do we just let them get away with what they have done to our story?'

'It's our own fault. I have been foolish, and it was all for naught. You saw how Herr Grimm was. He would not take our hands. He could hardly look at us. Herr Brentano waxed enthusiastically over the story but Herr Grimm said hardly a word. He did not even thank us.'

'He hardly had a chance to get a word in with Herr Brentano going on and on.'

'I'll give you that, but there were opportunities to thank us. He did not take them.'

The conversation lapsed again.

'There is something else,' said Mathilde, catching her sister's arm as they approached their door to their house.

'When Herr Brentano accused Jacob of being dusty, Jacob did not deny it.'

Helga giggled. 'Well, he couldn't, could he? With all due respect to your feelings, Mathilde, he is not the most colourful character.'

'If that means wearing an orange jacket and green trousers, I suppose he is not!' said Mathilde. 'But do you remember what he *did* say?'

'All I can remember is Herr Brentano's voice, although I scarcely understood a word of what he said. I don't remember Jacob saying much at all.'

'You should have, sister, because it showed how much we have miscalculated in what we have done.'

'How so?'

'They were debating folk stories, remember? Herr Brentano said they were boring and full of stock characters and similar situations. That's why he liked our story.'

'You mean the story he thought was ours.'

Mathilde nodded. 'Correct. He was arguing that it was fine to recast stories to make them less *predictable*. That was his word. But Herr Grimm insisted that authenticity was the bedrock. It did not matter whether the story was boring or full of stock characters as long as it was authentic.'

'Yes, I do remember now.'

'He even said he had had differences with Wilhelm on this point. Presumably he had disagreed with — what did he call it? — Wilhelm's *smoothing out a story to make it more readable.*'

'So what is your point?'

'I'm asking you to imagine how Jacob would feel if he ever discovered how *totally inauthentic* our story really is!'

'You're right,' said Helga. 'He would never forgive us.'

'He most certainly would not.'

'But do you know what, Mathilde? That does not worry me, and it should not worry you either.'

'Why do you say that?'

'Because, despite not being able to understand more than a quarter of what Herr Brentano was saying, there was one thing I totally agree with him about.'

'And that is?'

'Herr Jacob Grimm is only fond of dust. In actual fact I am beginning to believe he is made of the stuff.'

Mathilde continued to ponder this throughout the day. Was it true? She did not think so, although she was no longer sure whether he was made of flesh and blood. He seemed altogether more brittle. She could not help but compare him with the flamboyant Clemens Brentano, whose vitality and enthusiasm were as colourful as his clothing. Clemens Brentano, who embraced unpredictability and surprise. How pallid and dry he made Jacob look — Jacob who embraced his pallor, his dryness, who saw alteration and enhancement as something to be deplored. Dusty — yes, perhaps so.

Helga was quite right, too, about Jacob's likely reaction if he discovered their story was a fraud. She would be found guilty, of course, as would Helga, and in all likelihood also Wilhelm, Lotte and Dortchen, all parties to the deception.

Wilhelm — how had he known? Had they been so transparent? He clearly saw through their story immediately. The changes he had made insisted on that. Every subtle message had been overturned, turned it into its negative.

There was something pleasantly plausible about Wilhelm, but this was beyond deceitful. He had constructed a fence around Jacob and denied her entry. He had completely sabotaged her hopes, she suspected gleefully so. Thinking back to Wilhelm's version of the story, although she had read very quickly, she saw just how clever he had been. The princess had been transformed into someone petty, vindictive and unpleasant.

Was this how Wilhelm Grimm saw her?

The only small satisfaction, and it was very small, was that Jacob would not for one second associate the very unpleasant princess with Mathilde Heller. Why would he?

And actually, did it matter?

To her surprise, she realised it did not.

Helga, romantic and spontaneous as she was, had quickly seen through both Wilhelm and Jacob Grimm. But Mathilde's infatuation — it was an infatuation, she saw now — had blinded her. In fact, it had been fanned by the very thing that should have extinguished it: Jacob's utter indifference.

She looked up, sensing that Helga, sitting in the chair opposite, was looking at her with a troubled expression.

'Oh, Mattie,' whispered Helga, 'I am so sorry.'

Mathilde found she was able to smile. 'It doesn't matter, Helga. It really doesn't. Please don't worry about it.'

David's Story

D avid pressed the doorbell and waited apprehensively. There were two doors side by side and he was not sure whether he had pressed the right button. He was about to press the other when the door opened.

He had been trying to frame his expression in anticipation of Cara opening the door, but that crumbled into irrelevance when a man stood before him.

'Yes?'

'Hello, I hope this is the right place. I'm looking for Cara Bernstein.'

'Well, it is the right place. Why do you want to see her?'

'Nothing official. I'm an old friend. From France. We worked together at Huntingdon. David. David Cunningham.'

'Okay, I'm sure you're fine. You don't really look like the CIA. Cara expecting you?'

This could be a problem. Cara wasn't expecting him.

He had briefly weighed up whether to negotiate with Cara or just jump on a plane, and he had opted for the latter. Arlene had intimated that Cara would not be averse to seeing him, and he was wary that if he sought Cara's permission she might take forever to respond or find some reason to fob him off completely. And he really wanted to see Emily.

He was on her doorstep two days after extracting the address from Arlene.

Now, however, as he followed the man up the steep stairs, he had a sinking feeling. He had asked Arlene whether Cara was living with a man and Arlene had equivocated.

He didn't really have a plan; he realised that now. His driving idea was to get to Cara and Emily as quickly as possible, and hadn't really thought further than that. He had been cheered by Arlene saying he and Cara didn't really need a reconciliation, all he needed was a reconnection. So here he was reconnecting.

Beyond that, if he were honest he was probably harbouring some vague hope that they could continue along the path that had come to an abrupt stop in Venusberg. 'Love Mountain', he remembered. It had been a bitter private joke. I went to Love Mountain and fell off.

But here was a man in the house. You didn't have to be Sherlock Holmes to know that he wasn't a visitor. Everything about him said *ownership*. The flat, certainly. Cara? Probably.

'Mustn't be much fun bringing the groceries up and down these stairs,' David said to the man's back. Instead of *groceries* he had been about to say *the baby*, but thought better of it. The man didn't bother turning around, simply grunting in response.

The stairs led directly to a small living room. Glancing over the banister near the top David could see that the room was empty, although the floor was littered with baby things: a couple of soft toys, a changing blanket and, tucked in a corner, a folded-up stroller.

Reaching the top, the man shouted, 'Cara, you have a visitor. Some guy from Huntingdon.'

He had forgotten his name already.

As David stepped into the living room, Cara Bernstein did as well from an opposite door.

She glanced at David and burst into gales of laughter. The man, standing between them, turned towards David and grinned broadly.

It was not quite the welcome David had expected. He had rehearsed various scenarios, mostly full of warmth and forgiveness, coupled with honesty and long-awaited explanation.

Uncontrollable laughter had not featured.

Cara quickly pulled herself together and said, 'David!' Still smiling broadly, she hurried towards him and hugged him in welcome. She released him and backed away again.

'I'm sorry,' she said. 'It's that ridiculous beard. I had no idea!'

David had forgotten that Cara had not seen him with it. He had been living with the beard for such a long time now it had become part of him, the part he recognised each morning in the mirror. Perhaps it had been a foolish whimsy, but he had persisted with the thing after Cara herself had suggested it that last afternoon on Venusberg. Grow an unruly beard! she suggested, and promptly vanished.

So he had — a full Charles Darwin beard, as a kind of pledge, something owing perhaps to courtly love. Cara had left him no token, no favour, girdle or glove in her sudden departure, but he had obeyed her last command: he had grown and maintained the beard.

Now she had greeted it with laughter.

'It was your idea,' he said plaintively, stung by her response.

'Was it?' she said. 'I don't remember.'

'That last day, before you left. In Bonn. *You* suggested it.'

'Did I really?' asked Cara, still smiling. 'If it *was* my idea, I have to say, David, it's well up there as one of my worst.'

'You really don't remember?'

She laughed. 'Sorry. Seeing it now, I'm not sure which of us is the crazier: me for suggesting it or you for going along with it. You look like a wild man of the mountain.'

Love Mountain?

David tugged at the beard's extremities. 'Different planets again, I suppose.'

Cara glanced at him curiously. 'If you mean what I think you mean, then probably.'

She turned to the man. 'Max, be a dear and fix up some coffee for us, would you, please? And, David, find some place to put your bag down.'

She was quite lovely. His anticipation and excitement at seeing her again had long quashed his residual resentment, and now anticipation and excitement turned in an instant into hope.

David shrugged off his backpack and took a step back to view Cara anew. She had not changed much at all. She still wore her hair long; her body was as athletic as ever. If anything, she appeared more relaxed, more assured. Motherhood apparently suited her.

'This is such a surprise,' she said.

He looked at her carefully. Had her tone been neutral?

'Not an unpleasant one, I hope,' he said.

'No, not at all.'

'Arlene said—'

'It's okay, honestly. But are *you* okay? Are you up to travel?'

'I did manage to get here,' David smiled self-deprecatingly. 'Yes, I'm pretty much on the mend. Michael's given me the term off, and my doctor says I'll be fine as long as I don't try to run upstairs or climb mountains.'

'That's good news. But all the same, sit down. Sit down.'

David made his way to the settee and eased down into it. All at once he was feeling rather tired and he realised he had been running for some time on nervous energy.

Seeing or sensing this, Cara, who had taken a seat in an adjacent easy chair, looked at him with some concern.

'Are you sure you're all right?'

'Never better.' David smiled, not altogether convincingly. 'But anyway, where's the baby? Where's little Emily?'

'Not so much a little baby anymore,' said Cara. 'She's sleeping right now. She gives me twenty minutes of precious freedom every now and again. Otherwise she's a little tiger.'

David felt a little awkward. 'What was it like?'

'What was what like?'

'Having the baby. Looking after it . . .'

'A very steep learning curve. If it hadn't been for Max, I'm not sure I would have managed. I mean, she's a real sweetie but there have been times I would happily have thrown her back.'

Max.

He didn't quite know how to ask about Max. There had been no introduction, either by accident or design — the former, he suspected — and he wasn't sure how to rectify the omission without sounding like a suspicious prat.

'I'd like to see her.'

'You will. She's due to wake any time. I'm surprised Max didn't wake her when he called out. Are you staying nearby? I'm sorry, the flat is too small for guests but you could couch-surf if it's only for a couple of nights.'

'No. Thanks. I have somewhere.'

That was a lie, but he would find somewhere. It wouldn't be appropriate to land out of the blue and expect to doss down with her. Them. Cara and Max. Cara and Max and Emily.

How strange. He had known of Emily's existence only a day or so, had not even seen her yet, but already he felt a possessiveness and a growing resentment that another man should be acting as father.

As if on cue, there was a cry. It was a slightly tinny cry, coming from a coffee table next to Cara.

'You've heard her, David. Come over here and you can see her.'

David was momentarily confused.

'Baby monitor,' she explained, handing it to him.

On the screen there was a cot and a baby under a wrap, moving from side to side and crying fitfully, her face scrunched up like a small fist.

A dusting of hair.

Emily.

'I'll just go and fetch her down,' said Cara.

'Can I—?'

'No, you stay here.'

David would have loved to follow Cara up the stairs, and wondered with a jealous pang why she had so swiftly disallowed this. Was it because of the sleeping arrangements? Had the place not been tidied? Was she worried about the effect on Emily of a strange man?

As Max came back into the living room with a tray loaded with cups and a coffee plunger, David rebuked himself. Cara had never been especially self-conscious. He was reading far too much into things because of his insecurities. There would have been no agenda beyond the most obvious — she was concerned about his health and didn't want him traipsing up and down stairs unnecessarily.

'Milk or sugar?' asked Max, glancing at him, this time with a shy smile. This all at once lit up his face and David could see the attractiveness of the man.

'Neither, thanks,' said David.

'We're a little thin in the cake department,' said Max, 'but I could rustle up some cheese and an elderly cracker or two.'

David waved the offer away with a smile. 'Nothing for me. Really. Coffee's all I need.'

'Been in London long?'

'Just got here. Came straight from St Pancras.'

Max glanced at him again and David felt the need to explain.

'Cara and I . . . we'd lost touch. I just learnt from a colleague where Cara is and thought I'd—'

'Oh, Arlene.' Max regarded David with renewed interest. 'So you must be the guy who had the heart attack?'

David nodded, then they heard Cara coming back downstairs with Emily.

David experienced another slight pang of jealousy when Cara asked Max to find the baby wipes. Cara sat down again, bouncing Emily gently on her knee for some minutes before laying the baby down gently on a blanket on the floor. David watched all this with rapt attention.

'Okay,' said Cara. 'Keep an eye on her, will you, David, for a moment? I'll just see how Max is getting on with those wipes. I need to change her.'

David felt surprisingly pleased to be given this responsibility. He kneeled on the floor beside the blanket.

'Hello, Emily,' he said.

Emily's expression was serious, but David was enchanted. She was so very pretty with her green eyes. He had no idea whether she was big or small for her age. In fact he had no real idea of her age, although he now thought six months or so.

Max returned to the room with the wipes. 'She can push herself up already and roll over. She can't move very far yet, though. Be big trouble when she can!'

'Does that mean she's pretty advanced?' said David.

'No idea. Not much of an expert on babies.'

'I'm David,' said David, smiling at Emily. 'I've come all the way from France to see you.'

Emily looked up at him.

Cara returned to the living room and poured herself a cup of coffee.

'You're right,' said David, 'she's a sweetie.'

'Most of the time.'

Emily lost interest in David and gazed at her mother instead. He remained kneeling for some time in the hope of evoking a further response, but when it became apparent that he had been forgotten he stood and returned to the couch.

Max's presence, David felt, was most constraining. He had so much to ask Cara, but it was all a bit difficult with someone else in the room. And he didn't feel he could talk about what was happening at Huntingdon because that would exclude Max.

Cara, too, appeared unwilling to initiate conversation, so David tried to fill in the gaps with small-talk about life in London or Emily and her development. As he knew next to nothing about babies, his attempts were clumsy and flat-footed.

He did mention the visit of Cara's father to Huntingdon. He noted that Max seemed interested in this news as well.

Cara was surprised. 'I didn't know he'd gone to Huntingdon. When was this?'

'The vacation after you left. I only heard about it when I came back from New Zealand.'

'Callie must have told him where you were,' said Max.

'Callie?' asked David.

'My sister,' said Cara, 'back in the States. Do you know what he wanted?'

David shrugged. 'No, he talked to Michael, who mentioned it to me in passing. He didn't give any details.'

He was a little annoyed that Max was so familiar with Cara's family when he, David, had never even known Cara had a sister, let alone her name.

'Probably something to do with Gus,' said Max. 'According to Carrie, that's been running hot and cold for months now. Anyway, duty calls.' Max got to his feet.

'Are you off somewhere?' asked Cara.

'The office. I promised Denny I'd work on the new portfolio.'

'Back for dinner?'

Max shook his head. 'No, my sweet, you'll have to cook for yourself tonight. See you.'

He leaned over Cara, pecking her on the cheek. Then he turned to David and shook his hand. 'Ciao, David. Might see you again if you're in London for a few days?'

'Not sure yet,' said David. 'Possibly.'

'You're quite a hit,' observed Cara.

Emily, newly changed, was sitting once more on Cara's knee. She was gazing at David and from time to time making chuckling, babbling noises and smiling.

'She has quite a vocabulary,' said David.

'A bright little thing,' said Cara. 'More coffee?'

With Max's departure, David felt considerably more relaxed. Cara was also more relaxed now that Emily was changed and nursed. But then she had been fairly laid-back since his arrival, not at all discountenanced by David's unannounced intrusion into her new domestic arrangements.

'Thanks.'

As Cara filled his cup, David felt emboldened to ask, 'Max . . .'

'Yes?'

'I mean, you and he . . .'

'It's working out well,' said Cara. 'He's been all I could have asked for, really. I didn't have too many options when I left Huntingdon. I knew what I needed to get away from, but where I needed to get *to* wasn't so clear. Max stepped up to the plate, dear boy. It was supposed to be a stopgap measure, but look: I'm still here. It does help that Max adores Emily, of course.'

David was stuck back at the point when Cara spoke of knowing what she needed to get away from, which clearly included him. Max was clearly an old friend — another piece of Cara's past she had chosen not to reveal when they were together.

'You've known Max a long time?'

Cara looked taken aback. Then she burst out laughing once more.

'Oh, David, why can't you just say what you think?'

'What do you mean?' asked David, faltering in the face of the laughter.

'You imagine Max and I are lovers or something, don't you? Go on, own up! That's what you assumed!'

David reddened a little at the onslaught.

'I guess so. What was I to think? It seems all very cosy—'

'It is *cosy*. Couldn't you come up with a more pussyfooting word?'

'Sorry—'

'David, you klutz! Max is my *brother*.'

David smiled with relief. Perhaps he was a klutz, perhaps he was a pussyfooter, but all at once he felt as though a heavy slab had been lifted from his chest. 'Oh, that's all right then,' he said.

'Is it?'

'You know.'

'I'm not sure I do know, but I imagine you do.'

He decided to take up Cara's challenge to say what he was thinking. 'Is there another man in your life?'

Cara laughed again. 'Oh, for god's sake, David, what is this, the third degree?'

'Is there?' For better or for worse, David stood his ground.

'Clearly you've never had to raise a baby on your own. You don't get to hang out in singles bars that often, you know.'

David was privately delighted.

'However, the answer to your question is no.'

'You never replied to my question about the book you wrote. Arlene told me. About the frog prince.'

'No,' said Cara.

'Was there a reason?'

She smiled at him. 'I'm sorry, David. You sent me so many questions. I do have a child to look after, you know.'

'So tell me now.'

'What?'

'Are you fobbing me off again?' David smiled this time, to let Cara know he wasn't being aggressive.

'No, I'm not fobbing you off. It's just not especially interesting.'

'Why not?'

'It wasn't written for you. It was written for teenage girls.'

'Like Steffi Fox?'

Cara looked at him sharply. 'You have been digging about.'

'Call it homework.'

'Spadework, I'd call it — digging stuff up.'

'Well, I wasn't getting any answers out of you.'

'Fair enough. If you must know, I did write a book manuscript and it was kind of about the Grimm brothers' story about the frog prince. You know it?'

David nodded. 'The one about the princess and the frog who turns into a handsome king.'

'That's what everybody thinks. In the original story, though, the princess is actually a complete bitch, not to put too fine a point on it. Most people think she kisses the frog, but in reality she flings it against a wall, hoping to dispatch it!'

'Really? That's quite a twist.'

'I know. And when the frog hits the wall it turns into a handsome king who then marries the bitch princess.'

'How bizarre is that? It must have been love . . .'

'Possibly, but you must agree that it's a pretty weird storyline. I tried to imagine a way in which that weirdness may have come about.'

'I'd love to read it.'

'Perhaps one day.'

'When it's published?'

'Oh, I don't think it'll ever be published.'

'You showed Steffi.'

'Because, as I said, Steffi's in the target audience. She was helpful. One of the characters in the book falls for one of the Grimm brothers, quite inappropriately, and she had some suggestions about that.'

'Just like me falling for you?'

'Don't be such a solipsist, David Cunningham. I'd written most of it before you came on the scene.'

Just as David felt he had been justifiably rebuked, Cara added, 'Although there is a sense in which you played a part.'

'How so?'

'You didn't know Steffi Fox had a crush on you?'

All at once he had an image of a small fish being consumed by a bigger fish being consumed by a bigger fish . . .

'No. I didn't know that.'

Cara smiled. 'That doesn't surprise me, but she did. She was really smitten for a while. It was probably her telling me about it that prompted that aspect of my story.'

'So how does your story end?'

'Stories don't end.'

'Very cute.'

'It's not meant to be. It's what I believe.'

'I remember your telling me that context changes.'

'Of course . . . and scales fall from eyes and all that sort of thing. Often abruptly and for quite unfathomable reasons.'

'Like heart attacks?'

'Heart attacks and deaths and babies.'

'Was I the frog or the king?' David demanded suddenly.

Cara glanced at him mischievously. 'Still all about you, is it? Perhaps you were the princess.'

'Am I the princess?'

'The frog and the king are the same, David. They have to be. You could choose to be either, I suppose, if you really want to be in the story.'

Confused and exasperated, David blurted, 'What has any of this got to do with why you ran away when we were in Bonn?'

Cara rocked Emily, calming her. 'If, some day, you read my manuscript,' she said, turning to him, 'the final chapter is some sort of explanation of that. Probably as good as I can do.'

'Would you like to go to the park, Tiger?' Cara asked Emily.

Emily, now back on the floor, looked up at her mother and laughed.

'I take it that's a yes,' said David.

Cara went to fetch the stroller from the corner.

'Can you please take this downstairs for us, David? I'll fetch Emily's things.'

Shortly afterwards, they were walking down the narrow street of terraced houses. David was pushing the stroller and feeling stupidly proud to be doing so. He felt especially happy when they passed another pedestrian, and positively gleeful when anyone paused to smile or say a few nonsense words to the pretty little baby in the stroller, the pretty little baby with the wide eyes.

He would always remember the swans. How they sailed elegantly on the lake at Wimbledon Park like great, white-feathered boats. Only when they stepped ashore did the swans become ungainly and heavy-bodied.

They sat together on a park bench, keeping a watchful eye on Emily asleep in the stroller. Cara had pulled the hood down to protect the baby's face from the watery sun.

'How long will you stay?' Cara asked.

'Not sure,' said David. 'I'll play it by ear.'

'Don't overdo it.'

'I'll be careful.'

He glanced again at Emily sleeping peacefully.

'Is she always this tranquil?'

Cara laughed. 'When she's asleep. She can be pretty feisty at times. Why do you think I call her Tiger?'

'Not a bad quality to have,' said David. 'I wish I had it at times.'

'You have other qualities. I'm not so sure I'd like you to have feistiness as well.'

In his vanity, David was tempted to ask her what those qualities were, but thought better of it. It was nice to know she felt there were aspects of him to admire. In any event, he smiled to himself, it appeared he wasn't feisty enough to ask what they were. Or to reach for her hand, although he was sorely tempted.

But even without her hand in his, it was quite lovely to be sitting with Cara on a warm summer day amid the sound of laughing, shouting children and the white noise of distant London traffic. How much the world could change in a couple of days.

'Are you very familiar with London?' asked Cara. 'I can't remember.'

'Pretty much. I worked here for a couple of years shortly after university. That's a Kiwi rite of passage.'

'Ah yes. I do remember you talking about it,' said Cara.

'Arlene said you're getting a bit of work.'

'Here and there. Supply teaching — English mainly. Not so much call for French. It's pretty dire most of time. I wouldn't recommend it.'

David couldn't tell whether she was making a general statement or whether there was a subtle hint of dissuasion there. He glanced at her but her expression was neutral.

'Relief teaching's never much cop,' he said.

Cara stood up. Emily was stirring.

David watched fondly as Cara rocked the stroller gently for a few moments, which seemed to have the effect of waking Emily completely. She gave a few plaintive cries. Cara leaned over the stroller and lifted Emily up and out.

'Is she very heavy?' David asked as they joined him on the bench.

'Getting heavier all the time. Aren't you, Tiger? Do you want to hold her? Emily, will you let David hold you?'

Cara passed Emily over and David took her into his arms. She didn't cry, and it felt very good. He was surprised at how heavy Emily was. He bent to touch the top of her head with his lips and her hair tickled his nose. He liked that.

'Let's walk around the lake,' Cara suggested.

'Good oh.'

They set off, side by side, Cara pushing the stroller, David with Emily in his arms. For some time they walked in companionable silence, David or Cara every now and again pointing out something of interest to Emily — a flurry of swans bad-temperedly flapping, a dog chasing a tennis ball, a radio-controlled launch operated by an elderly man.

Suddenly Cara stopped and grabbed David by the arm. 'Oh my god, I've been forgetting. You're supposed to be convalescing, and here I am having you lug Emily about like a sack of potatoes!' She quickly relieved him of Emily. 'Sorry!'

'It's not a problem, Cara. She's not really that heavy. I'm not quite an invalid.'

'Possibly. But I don't want another heart attack on my watch. I've done you enough harm already.'

It was the first time she had alluded to the effect on him of her leaving, and David was briefly encouraged. He could have taken the opportunity this time to reach for her hand, but she was bent down placing Emily back in the stroller and the chance was lost. Should he try to talk about it? He decided to approach the matter obliquely.

'I'm sorry for making a bit of dick of myself about Max.'

Emily safely secured, Cara stood up.

'You didn't really,' she said. 'Perfectly understandable.'

'Part of the problem,' said David, 'was not knowing anything about your family. I mean, before today I had no idea Max even existed.'

'Well,' said Cara, a little stiffly, 'there's no reason why you should.'

'Cara,' said David carefully, 'there's every reason why I should. Before you took off we were pretty good friends.'

'Say it, David: we were lovers.'

'Okay, we were lovers. So why didn't you ever tell me about Max? About your father and your sister?'

'Because I don't choose to be defined by my family.'

'You wouldn't have been defined by them — and even if you were, Max seems a pretty nice guy. What's the problem?'

'Max *is* a pretty nice guy. I've said so, haven't I? Some of the others are pretty obnoxious. My father was — is — a control freak. You wouldn't want to know them. I don't want to know them.'

'It wouldn't have hurt to let me know they existed. I mean, I've talked to you about my family.'

'That was my decision to make, and yours to respect.'

Okay. David sensed Cara's irritation and decided to let it ride.

Their earlier easiness was fading. There was a brittleness in the air. David stayed silent, hoping the good feeling would return, but the continuing silence merely exacerbated things. Cara was not going to help out by volunteering anything, and Emily contributed to the mood by starting to make complaining noises.

'She's hungry,' said Cara, stopping by a bench. 'I'll need to give her a feed.'

She unstrapped Emily from the stroller and passed her to David. 'Look after her for a moment.' He did so as Cara sat down and opened her front.

'Here we are, Tiger,' she said.

'How can I know who you are, Cara?' asked David. Emily was now back in her pram. Cara and David were sitting on the bench gazing at her.

Cara did not reply — her mind was miles away. Then after a few moments she turned to him. 'What did you say just before?'

'I said, how can I know who you are?'

Cara observed him speculatively. 'Why do you want to know that? Isn't that a kind of arrogance?'

'Arrogance?'

'Isn't knowing somebody a form of possession? If *knowing* somebody is at all possible anyway.'

'I don't see how it's arrogance. It's interest.'

'I don't see how you *can* know somebody.'

'That's silly.'

'Is it? You can only know your opinion of somebody, you can only know your feelings about somebody. When we say we know somebody we're only admitting to knowing something about ourselves.'

'The eternal mystery?'

'Of course.'

'So, do you know me?'

She looked at him. 'I know what I think of you.'

'Can I ask what that is?'

'You can ask, but I can't tell you.'

David was surprised. 'Why not?'

'It's complicated.'

He sat, unable to make sense of this. A sudden sound from Emily pulled his attention away, and he made as if to stand up and move over to check her. Cara grabbed his arm.

'Leave her.'

David gave her an aggrieved glance.

'Sorry,' she said. 'That must have sounded a little peremptory.'

He grinned. 'It goes with the territory. You are a schoolteacher.'

She laughed. 'Sometimes you are a sweet man, David Cunningham.'

All the good feelings surged back. The lake. The swans. The sunshine. Little Emily now so real. And Cara, restored to something like good spirits. All at once he remembered the red velveteen box in his pocket: the box with the ring inside it.

He took a deep breath and turned to her. 'Marry me?' he asked.

Eyes widening, she laughed again.

'What? David, you can't be serious.'

'You sound just like John McEnroe. Why not?'

'You *are* serious?'

'It seems a pretty good idea to me. We could pool our resources. I could come to London, get a job here, help with Emily—'

'I already have help with Emily.'

'She would have a live-in father instead of an uncle.'

'But marriage?'

'Why not?'

'Are you trying to make an honest woman of me, David Cunningham? How pathetically Victorian.' Cara laughed.

David was stung. 'Okay, if marriage is not your strong suit, why don't I just come over anyway?'

Cara paused. 'You are a sweet guy, David, but you don't need to do this.'

'I don't need to — I want to.'

David was hurt. Cara looked at him sympathetically and said nothing.

'Well, the offer's there,' said David. 'I'll leave it on the table.'

Conversation lapsed again as they turned to watch Emily, who had awakened once more.

'To use a poker analogy, you have to know when to fold 'em,' said Cara.

'Okay,' said David disconsolately.

'Actually I'm talking about Emily. It's time to get moving. She'll drop off again once we're on the move.'

'She has beautiful eyes,' said David. 'Where did the green come from?'

'From her father,' she said.

David felt a slight buzzing in the air.

'What do you mean?' he asked.

'I'm sorry?'

'But I thought—'

'Oh, David,' she whispered. 'I thought you knew . . .'

David stood, shocked and silent.

'You thought *you* were Emily's father?'

David could say nothing. He did not trust himself to speak.

'Oh, poor David . . . Would I have run away if you were Emily's father?'

David stared at her. He felt a little short of breath.

'Why didn't you tell me?'

'I wanted to — it was beginning to break me in two,' she said. 'But you were so happy, you had this impossibly romantic view of me, and then you proposed . . . How could I tell you I was having another man's child? By the time Arlene told you about Emily, I assumed you would have worked it out.'

David stood silent for a moment.

'Angus?'

Angus's eyes. Angus sniggering. Angus lying through his teeth.

'Does he know?'

Cara shook her head. 'I'm not ready for him to know yet,' she said. 'I'm not sure I'll ever be.'

Cara's
Manuscript

— KASSEL —

M athilde read the card carefully and passed it to Helga.
'What is it?'

'It's an invitation from Dorothea Wild.'

The sisters had been invited to an afternoon tea in Dortchen's summer-house.

It was a surprise. In the weeks since their abrupt departure from the Royal Library there had been no communication from the Grimm ménage, nor had they expected any.

She had been quite serious that afternoon when she told Helga it didn't matter any longer. In the days following she had felt quite liberated as she realised the truth of what she had said. There was, of course, the residual embarrassment of the deception she had initiated, and its even more embarrassing reversal, but she had cast aside the infatuation with Jacob Grimm. It felt like taking off a heavy coat on a hot summer's day.

'I wonder whether she's just being nice or if there's something she wants to tell us?'

'I don't know,' said Mathilde.

'Should we accept?'

'We should. Dortchen has always been friendly, and the Wilds are a most respectable family. There is no reason why we shouldn't.'

'But what if the Grimm brothers are there?'

'That would not be a problem.'

'You are strong, Mathilde,' said Helga admiringly.

'I don't think so,' said Mathilde, 'just a little older.'

The brothers were not in attendance, although their sister Lotte was. It soon became apparent that the purpose of the invitation had not been merely social: Dortchen Wild did indeed have something to tell them.

It was at once confession and explanation.

It was Lotte who broached the subject.

'I understand from my brother Jacob that you have seen the edited version of your frog prince story,' she said.

Mathilde nodded. 'Some time ago, at the Royal Library. Herr Jacob told us the handwriting was yours.'

Helga bristled. 'I would not say use the word *edited*,' she said. 'I would say it was completely rewritten.'

'It was,' said Dortchen quietly.

'Why?' asked Mathilde, knowing the answer but wanting it made explicit.

'My brother Wilhelm felt that the character of the princess needed to be . . . adjusted,' explained Lotte.

'But why?'

Lotte was about to explain but Dortchen forestalled her by raising a hand. 'Let us be honest, Lotte. We can be honest here. We are women together. This is not a time for fudging or subterfuge.' She turned to the sisters. '*May* we be honest?'

'Please do,' said Mathilde.

'And will you be honest with us?'

'As honest as needs be.'

That answer seemed to satisfy Dortchen. 'Wilhelm is an observant man. He had observed that you, Mathilde, appeared attracted to Jacob.'

Mathilde lowered her head, feeling her cheeks redden.

'When you gave Wilhelm the story, Wilhelm saw it as what he called a stalking horse.'

'What did he mean by that?' asked Helga.

'He meant, as in the old myth, that your story was an attempt to break through Jacob's defences and establish yourself by subterfuge in a good light.'

'Was it that obvious?' asked Mathilde.

'Probably not to most, but to Wilhelm, yes.'

'So he sabotaged our tale,' said Helga angrily. 'Was that not a malicious thing to do?'

'You will see it that way,' said Dortchen gently, 'and Lotte and I were both a little uncomfortable with what we were doing.'

'We were,' said Lotte.

'But we were persuaded by Wilhelm's reasoning, which was not at all malicious.'

'What was it?' asked Mathilde

'He said we must be cruel to be kind,' said Lotte.

'It was cruel,' said Helga. 'In what way was it kind? The princess was changed from a warm, tender-hearted person into a vicious, spiteful creature.'

'The princess,' explained Dortchen, 'is only a character in a story. While you and Mathilde wanted to suggest that the warm-hearted. tender creature represented Mathilde, once Wilhelm changed her, Mathilde disappeared from the story.'

'That does not explain why causing Mathilde to disappear was kind,' said Helga.

'It was kind because Mathilde, you were chasing a rainbow.'

'A rainbow?'

'Jacob could never love you.'

Helga began to protest but Dortchen raised her hand.

'Not because of who you are, Mathilde, but because of who Jacob is. Jacob Grimm could never love any woman. Jacob is passionate only about his scholarship, and the one human on earth whom he truly loves is his brother. Wilhelm knew this. Lotte and I knew this. And we were alarmed that you had persuaded yourself that Jacob might love you. There was no malice or spite involved. But no woman could ever hope to come between Jacob and Wilhelm and you needed to stop wasting your time trying.'

Mathilde nodded. 'I have come to see this.'

'Stories are lies,' said Dortchen.

'No happily ever afters?' asked Helga.

'Not even any endings,' said Dortchen. 'Just ongoings.'

'But people change,' said Helga. 'People can change — Jacob may change.'

'The frog in the story,' said Dortchen, 'no matter how often he's kissed or caressed, will always remain a frog underneath.'

'Jacob will always remain Jacob,' said Lotte.

'I am sad for you, Mathilde,' said Dortchen, 'but glad that you have come to understand.'

'Herr Brentano helped,' said Mathilde.

'Clemens Brentano?' asked Lotte. 'How?'

'He talked about dust,' said Mathilde enigmatically.

'Herr Brentano felt the prince was a trapped victim,' said Helga, 'and quite foolish.'

'My brother is not foolish,' protested Lotte.

'No,' agreed Mathilde, 'but I could see how foolish it would be for him to marry the princess. His only consolation would be his faithful man-servant.'

'Iron Heinrich?' said Lotte.

Mathilde nodded.

'Iron Heinrich was Wilhelm's idea,' explained Dortchen. 'He represents Wilhelm himself, of course.'

'Fiercely loyal,' said Mathilde.

'Indeed,' said Dortchen.

David's Story

David and Cara left Wimbledon Park and made their way back to Max's flat, Cara pushing the stroller, David walking beside her, silent with growing fury. From time to time Cara glanced apprehensively at him, taking in his grim expression and set jaw.

Eventually she stopped at an intersection but made no attempt to cross the road. Instead, she turned to David, challenging him.

'Why are you so angry? You are, aren't you?'

He flashed her a bitter look. 'You have to ask?'

Cara leaned on the handle of the stroller and sighed. 'Well, yes. Quite frankly, I do.'

'Well, quite *frankly*,' said David, mocking her expression with heavy sarcasm, 'quite *frankly*, it's all a bit much for me to take in right now. I need to process things. Fucking Angus!'

'You're angry with Angus? Does it matter so much that it was Angus?'

'Of course it bloody does! He fucking lied to my face about you! And anyway, why are you so sure it was Angus? How do you know it wasn't me?'

'You were always so very careful, David. Remember?'

'And Angus wasn't — I get it. Great.' He felt his anger rising again. 'And that means, while we were . . . you were . . .'

Cara looked away from him, up and down the road. When Emily gave a little waking whimper, Cara abruptly began to push the stroller across the intersection and continued pushing it faster and faster down the street so that David had to hurry to keep up. Then suddenly she stopped again. She was angry herself now.

'Has it occurred to you,' she demanded, 'that your reaction right now is one of the reasons I felt I had to leave you in Bonn? Has it?'

The question silenced David. There were people all around them and this didn't seem the right place.

'Cara,' he said, a little chastened, 'could we discuss this back at your place? This is a bit public.'

'Fine!' snapped Cara, and began walking again.

They continued the rest of the way without speaking.

Cara unlocked the door and lifted Emily out of the stroller. Stepping into the foyer, she made little soothing noises before glancing over her shoulder at David.

'Please bring the stroller up,' she said, immediately starting up the stairs.

For a moment or two, David disconsolately watched her climbing back before he bent to fold the stroller. By the time he made his way up to the living room Cara and Emily had both disappeared. David assumed she had taken the baby upstairs to change her and would reappear reasonably quickly, but he found himself waiting for an unconscionably long time.

Was she letting him stew? It wouldn't have surprised him. Well, two could play at that game. If Cara thought she could hide upstairs until he grew sick of waiting and left, she could think again. But then Cara was not someone who resiled from awkward situations. Perhaps he should go up and see what was going on.

Before he could act on this, he heard Cara's steps on the stairs and she re-entered the living room. Without a word she moved to the coffee table and switched on the baby monitor.

'I'll make some coffee,' she said. 'I need it.'

David felt he needed something stronger than coffee. While Cara was in the kitchen, he tried to formulate what he could say to her. It had been his suggestion they 'discuss' things in the apartment, but now he could find no clear path forward. His head was still lost in a forest of confusion, betrayal and anger.

Eventually Cara took the initiative. As soon as she laid the tray on the coffee table she said, 'When you lost it on the way back, you said something about Angus lying to you. What was that all about?'

David, unwisely, decided to take the brutal route. 'He lied about fucking you. He claimed he never had.'

Cara halted in the act of pouring coffee to look at him. 'Why on earth would he do that?'

David couldn't meet her eye. 'Because *he* thought that *I* thought that he had.'

'But why ever did you think that?'

'Because of the drawings.'

'What drawings?'

'The drawings Angus made of you,' David said miserably. 'The naked chalk drawings.'

'Angus showed you those?' Cara was astonished.

David shook his head. 'No, no . . . he didn't. I . . . found them.'

'You found them?'

'I had no idea where you'd gone and I heard a rumour that you and he — you know. So I went to the art room to talk to Angus. I thought if he knew you that well, he may have some idea why you'd disappeared.'

'Go on.'

'He wasn't there so I waited. I figured he might have gone for a coffee and wouldn't be long. I just started looking through his filing cabinet to pass the time and there they were.'

'You looked through his filing cabinet?!'

'I don't know . . .'

'I do. You were perving through his work and struck gold!'

'It wasn't like that!'

'It absolutely was. And then I suppose you accused Angus of fucking me simply because he had drawn me.'

'I didn't—'

'How pathetic. God, men! Stags and antlers! So, as you now know, Angus did fuck me. What of it? The posing thing was not my greatest career move but I figured why not? It was a new experience. I was an idiot to trust Angus, of course — he can be a plausible bastard when he puts his mind to it.'

Once again, David found himself caught between wanting to know, and really not wanting the knowledge.

'While I was in the bedroom, sans clothes, sans everything, he hit on me. I don't know why I expected otherwise. Perhaps in some dark recess of my being I wanted him to. I do know it broke every rule I'd made for myself. Still, it was not unpleasant and he promised absolute discretion.'

'Cara, I—'

'I'm not making excuses, nor am I blaming anybody. It happened.'

'But *Angus*?'

'He's nothing to me. I'm nothing to him except another notch on his belt.'

'He said you hate the pictures.'

'Of course I do. But not because of the sex. I hate them because they embody, if that's the word, the male gaze.'

'He told me.'

'You two seem to have had quite a lot to say to each other about me.'

'Not really.'

'Still, if what you say is true, I'm impressed that Angus didn't give anything away. You weren't two grubby schoolboys swapping notes.'

David let that pass, but Cara pressed home.

'Only one grubby schoolboy.'

'That's unfair,' protested David. It was time for what he hoped would be his trump card. 'You talk about grubby schoolboys . . . Did you know that Angus took photos of you? Nude photos?'

'Of course I knew, you idiot. That's what artists do. You don't really think he expected me to sit there naked for hours and hours, do you? He works from photographs.'

'But he said he might post them on Instagram.'

Cara laughed. 'Why on earth would he do that?'

David faltered. He found Cara's trust in Angus unbelievable.

'Blackmail!' he said.

'Why would Angus want to blackmail me?'

David realised he had no reply. He wanted to say sex, but that horse had bolted.

'He's winding you up, you silly man,' said Cara.

David realised she was probably right. Suddenly he was awash with the unfairness and hopelessness of it all. He had stuffed everything up.

Then he remembered he had brought Angus's phone with him, and fished it out of his jacket pocket. The ring and the phone sat together in his pocket. The ring hadn't worked out too well; he had no idea how the phone would fare. Perhaps he would score a few points.

'Here,' he handed it to her. 'It's Angus's.'

'What?'

'He left it at my flat.'

David suddenly realised he hadn't told Cara he was now living in her old flat, and at once regretted he hadn't said 'room'.

Cara, however, didn't pick up on the word.

'Why have you brought it here? Does Angus know?'

David shook his head. 'Those pics are on it. You could delete them.'

Cara seemed amazed. 'You stole his phone?'

'I didn't steal—'

'How else would you describe it?'

David didn't answer. He'd got it wrong again. He lapsed into silence once more, nodding perfunctorily when Cara passed him a mug of coffee.

'You're angry with me,' said Cara, looking at him.

David flashed. 'Yes, I'm bloody angry.'

Cara flinched at his vehemence.

'You know that fucking frog you told me about? That's what I feel like: a fucking frog flung against a fucking wall.'

'Oh, David—'

'And remember what you called that fucking princess? A complete bitch? You were so right!'

He pushed his coffee to one side, stood up, retrieved his backpack and shrugged it on. 'I can't see that there is anything more to be said. Thanks for the coffee and the walk. I'll be off.'

As the door slammed, Cara gave a rueful smile and murmured, 'Goodnight, sweet prince. And flights of angels . . .'

David's Story

Michael Bastion wiped his chin with his napkin and leaned back in his chair.

'I've had a rather unexpected email from David Cunningham,' he said.

'Oh?' said Miranda. 'Pray tell.'

'He's handed in his notice,' said Michael.

Miranda looked at him with surprise. 'That *is* unexpected. Wasn't he on the mend?'

'He is, yes, but it transpires his father's been taken ill.'

'How is that grounds for resignation? Couldn't he just go back to see him? He's still on leave.'

'Quite serious, according to Cunningham.'

'Ah well, not too much of a ripple,' said Miranda, 'seeing as we have a reliever already in place.'

'Yes, we'll keep Stephanie on. She's working out quite well.'

Miranda sipped her coffee.

'You didn't like him much, did you?' Michael asked.

'No, not much.'

'I could never understand why. He's always seemed quite inoffensive.'

'Oh, I'll give him that. Just woman's intuition, I suppose. Didn't Cara Bernstein's father take "gravely ill"? Is this one a severe stroke too?'

'Cunningham didn't say. He did say, though, that he had to leave immediately. He's not even coming in to collect his things.'

'So he gave his notice by email, and he's not coming in even though he's in Arras. I smell a rat,' said Miranda.

'No, he's not in Arras,' said Michael.

'Did he say anything else?'

'Oh, just the usual. Thanks for our kindness during his convalescence, heaps of praise for the school and all it meant to him, and profuse apologies for his manner of leaving.'

'I still smell a rat.'

'There was one other thing — very odd. He included a postscript warning me to watch out for Angus Paton.'

'Angus? Whatever do you mean?'

'He said he could not provide details but he had irrefutable proof that Angus is a predator with women and poses a risk to young female staff, even senior students. He said the school was at risk of a me-too scandal.'

Miranda snorted with laughter. 'Angus? A predator? What a hoot!'

'No idea where Cunningham got that idea.'

'It's utterly delicious,' said Miranda. 'Hasn't he been quite thick with Cunningham since the heart attack? He's coming for dinner next Wednesday. I'll press him for details. What fun!'

'What fun indeed,' smiled Michael, reaching for *The Times*. He took out a pen. 'Calls for a crossword.'

David's Story

He left the graveyard and found the wide track that led down the hill, the love mountain he had fallen off. Before the track left the trees he paused to survey Kessenich below. The main artery whose name he could never remember was his destination. There was the hotel, the one they had stayed in last time. The Astoria, an odd name for a German hotel. Perhaps it was trying to piggyback on the Waldorf Astoria. If so, it was an attempt doomed to failure. There was nothing remotely upmarket about it, although the hotel was comfortable and comfortably situated, with trolleybuses at the front door to run you into the city and the river only a short walk away.

He looked beyond the built-up area towards the Rhine. Even from this elevation it was a big river. Large ships and barges upstream and downstream serviced cities for hundreds of kilometres. It shone silver in the late afternoon sun and he could feel a slight stir of anticipation. His long-delayed cruise began the next morning.

He strode down the track to reach the cobbled back streets on the lower slopes.

Water, bridges, and water under the bridge.

He had posted Angus's phone back to him at Huntingdon. He had been in two minds over whether to include a note telling him Emily was his daughter but decided against.

It wasn't his place.

Cara and her secrets. How the hell had she been able to recruit so many people to keep them? Angus, Arlene, Steffi Fox . . .

Now he had joined their ranks: another guardian of Cara's secrets.

He paused by an odd war memorial in the middle of a small roundabout on the hilly back streets and sat down on a stone bench to check his phone. He rubbed his jaw: before he embarked in the morning he would shave off the beard. Perhaps he could exchange it for a poodle in a matching jacket.

It hadn't taken him long to regret his crazy behaviour in London. As soon as he slammed the door of the apartment and stood on the footpath, he knew.

He hadn't just slammed the door. He had locked it. Forever.

By the time he got off the Eurostar his regret had turned to mortification.

He had blown it utterly; he knew that. Nevertheless, he fired off a barrage of apologetic emails, to which of course he received no reply. She probably didn't even open them.

She did send him one email, though. It arrived the day after his return to Arras. He'd opened it eagerly, but there was no message, just an attached file.

Cara had sent him a copy of her manuscript.

He remembered her telling him there was an explanation of sorts in the final chapter. His first instinct had been to turn immediately to that chapter, but he managed to discipline himself to read the entire book from start to finish. Context is important, he told himself wryly.

When he closed the book, he felt as if he had been lost in one of those dark forests that haunted Mathilde Heller's dreams. All the same, despite parsing the characters desperately, he knew finally that he was not among them. He remembered Cara's rebuke.

It wasn't about him. It was about her.

Since his return, it had been difficult for him to think of Emily without bitterness. As he considered things now, he felt a sudden tenderness for her.

He sighed. Doors slammed. Bridges burnt. Walls splattered.

Huntingdon gone.

He would travel down the Rhine, then he would return to New Zealand.

Abruptly, he stood and carried on down the hill.

Cara's
Manuscript

In her dream she was lost among the trees, tall trees with hammered bark, dark leaves, the pathways damp, narrow and confusing.

She was not sure why she was there. The forest had not been there before. Something about finding Oma? Yes, that was it. She searched around for Oma's white linen cap. Oma had lost it on the forest floor but the cap was nowhere to be found.

This distressed her beyond measure but she did not give way to weeping. She did not have time to pause.

At every fork in the pathway she hesitated, but not for long, sensing that it didn't matter whether she turned left or right, so she followed her instinct.

At one point she thought she heard something, and stood still, straining to listen.

Somewhere at the far reaches of audibility she heard the faintest music. Woodwinds: oboes, a flute. Distant. The music was sad, plangent.

She stood listening. Unmoving.

Then she realised that voices had joined the woodwinds, low, soft voices in harmony. They were calling her. She could not work out the words, but it didn't really matter. All that mattered was that she needed to follow the sounds. Wherever they might lead. Oma's voice sounded in her head, warning her against going into the forest in the first place, but it offered such promise.

It was more straightforward now. She did not hesitate at junctions in the path; she followed the music, which gradually grew louder.

Finally, as the music swelled to a diapason of possibility, the trees gave way to a forest glade containing a dark pool of black water.

Impossibly white waterlilies dotted the surface, and the large plates of lily pads.

There was no suggestion of Oma, no lost white cap, but she knew this was the place she had been seeking.

She ventured to the edge of the water and there, sitting on a lily pad, was the frog.

The frog's chest was quivering, swelling like the music, although the world was silent now.

'You have come,' said the frog.

'You knew I would come,' she said.

'I knew you would come.'

A blue dragonfly hovered.

'You know what you must do,' said the frog.

'I know what I must do,' she said.

'When you kiss me,' said the frog, 'the transformation will be complete and we will at last be together.'

She closed her eyes and leaned towards the lily pad, leaned towards the waiting creature.

Her lips found the clamminess of the frog's head.

No sooner had her lips touched the frog than the transformation was complete.

She made a wishbone of her legs and leapt high, beyond the dragonfly. And then fell down.

Down into the cold, black water.

Historical
Background

The event that inspired *The Frog Prince* took place some time back when I bought a copy of Jack Zipes's monumental translation of the collected stories of the Brothers Grimm (*The Complete Fairy Stories of the Brothers Grimm*, translated and with an introduction by Jack Zipes, 1987, expanded edition 1992; Bantam Books, NY).

In keeping with the tradition of all collections of the tales, this one opens with the story 'The Frog King, or Iron Heinrich'. It is quite a brief tale — only four pages — and in many ways quite odd in terms of character and structure. I wrote *The Frog Prince* to offer reasons why the story came to be so strange. To this end, I invented the Heller sisters, who may have been among the many contributors of folk tales to the famous brothers.

While the Heller family and the staff of Huntingdon School are entirely fictional, some other characters are based on historical figures, most significantly the Grimm brothers themselves. At this time, around 1811, they were living in Kassel in the then kingdom of Westphalia. After several difficult years the brothers were on a better financial footing, having secured positions as court librarians in the library of the king. This region of northwest Germany had been lost to the French during the Napoleonic wars, and the emperor had installed his brother, Jérôme Bonaparte, as king. Within a year or two Jérôme would be ousted, with the defeat of Napoleon, but in the meantime the people of Kassel chafed under French rule.

Jacob and Wilhelm were in their twenties at the time this book is set. Even so, as the eldest, Jacob had responsibility for the care and wellbeing of four brothers and his sister Charlotte (Lotte). Their father had been a relatively prosperous magistrate but had died in 1796, plunging the family into poverty, made worse by the death of their mother in 1808.

Wilhelm and Jacob were only a year apart and closely bonded. They were very bright, and after great success at school attended university, where they studied law, although both abandoned it early on to study German language, culture and history. This, particularly philology and folklore, remained their field of study for the rest of their lives.

Another historical figure, Dorothea (Dortchen) Wild, was a friend of the Grimms, and in 1825 she married Wilhelm, more than a dozen years after the events of this book.

Clemens Brentano, who features in the novel, had achieved renown as a romantic poet before he met Jacob Grimm at university. He had already published to great acclaim a collection of folk songs, *Des Knaben Wunderhorn* (The Youth's Magic Horn), which was much later set to music by Gustav Mahler. Brentano conceived a project of collecting folk stories to follow this up, and enlisted the Grimms to help gather them. When Brentano, famously unreliable, lost interest in the project, the brothers took it on themselves.

Although presented here with a broad brush, the characters of Jacob, Wilhelm and Clemens Brentano are in accord with the historical record: Jacob scholarly, somewhat austere and a slave to study; Wilhelm equally scholarly but more outgoing; Clemens Brentano flamboyant in dress and manner.

Jacob Grimm (b. 1785) died in 1863. His brother Wilhelm (b. 1786) died in 1859. Wilhelm and Dorothea had four children, one dying in infancy. Jacob never married but lived with Wilhelm and Dorothea for the rest of his life.

Acknowledgements

In addition to Professor Zipes's collected stories mentioned above, I must reference his invaluable life of the brothers, *The Brothers Grimm: From Enchanted Forests to the Modern World* (Palgrave Macmillan, NY, 2002). Another biography I found very useful was *Paths through the Forest: A Biography of the Brothers Grimm* by Murray B. Peppard (Holt, Rinehart and Winston, NY, 1971). *The Brothers Grimm: Two Lives, One Legacy* by Donald R Hettinga (Clarion Books, NY, 2001) also proved an excellent source of illustrated material.

I want to thank the trustees of the Randell Cottage for offering me a residency in 2018; particularly Sarah Dennis and Sian Robyns for their friendship and ongoing help during my stay. The six months in this lovely cottage in Thorndon, Wellington, allowed me the time and space to complete the first draft of the book.

For several months over three years we stayed in the beautiful city of Bonn with our daughter Elisabeth and her husband Alejandro Gaurin-Kappaz. I must thank Lissie and Alejandro for their hospitality and for facilitating visits and walks around the city and its environs.

I'd like to thank our friends Carsten Bazant and Cécile Damlencour, who took us to Arras in northern France for several days, where we stayed with Cécile's parents, Ludovic and Annie Damlencour. Our visits in and about Arras and its hinterland provided the setting for the fictional Huntingdon International School.

Finally, a huge debt of gratitude to my publisher at Penguin Random House, Harriet Allan; to my editor at large, Rachel Scott; and to my editor at home, Joan Melvyn, all of whose sensitive readings of the various drafts and subsequent perceptive suggestions improved both text and plot beyond measure.

In addition to editing almost 20 collections, James Norcliffe has also written the following:

Poetry—

Deadpan (Otago University Press, 2019)
Dark Days in the Oxygen Café (Victoria University Press, 2016)
Shadow Play (Proverse Press, 2012)
Villon in Millerton (Auckland University Press, 2007)
Along Blueskin Road (Canterbury University Press, 2005)
Rat Tickling (Sudden Valley Press, 2003)
A Kind of Kingdom (Victoria University Press, 1998)
Letters to Dr Dee and Other Poems (Hazard Press, 1993)
The Sportsman and Other Poems (Hard Echo Press, 1986)

———————

Fiction—

Adult:
The Chinese Interpreter (Short stories: Hazard Press, 1993)

Children/YA:
Mallory, Mallory: Trick or Treat (Puffin, 2021)
Mallory, Mallory: The Revenge of the Tooth Fairy (Puffin, 2020)

Twice Upon A Time (Puffin, 2017)

The Pirates and the Night Maker (Longacre Press / Random House, 2015)

Felix and the Red Rats (Longacre / Random House, 2013)

The Enchanted Flute (Longacre Press/Random House, 2012)

Packing a Bag for Mars (Clerestory Press, 2012)

The Loblolly Boy and the Sorcerer (Longacre Press/Random House, 2011)

The Loblolly Boy (Longacre Press, 2009)

The Assassin of Gleam (Hazard Press, 2005)

The Carousel Experiment (Hazard Press, 1995)

The Emerald Encyclopedia (Hazard Press, 1994)

Penguin Bay (Hazard Press, 1993)

Under the Rotunda (Hazard Press, 1992)